SGT.

D0031812

BREAKAWAY

ALSO BY LAURA CRUM

Slickrock
Roped
Roughstock
Hoofprints
Cutter

BREAKAWAY

LAURA CRUM

THOMAS DUNNE BOOKS

St. Martin's Minotaur

New York

THOMAS DUNNE BOOKS.
An imprint of St. Martin's Press.

BREAKAWAY. Copyright © 2001 by Laura Crum. All rights reserved. Printed in the United States of America. No part of this book may be used or reproduced in any manner whatsoever without written permission except in the case of brief quotations embodied in critical articles or reviews. For information, address St. Martin's Press, 175 Fifth Avenue, New York, N.Y. 10010.

www.minotaurbooks.com

Library of Congress Cataloging-in-Publication Data

Crum, Laura.
    Breakaway: a Gail McCarthy mystery / Laura Crum.—1st ed.
      p. cm.
    ISBN 0-312-27181-6
    1. McCarthy, Gail (Fictitious character)—Fiction. 2. Women
veterinarians—Fiction. 3. Santa Cruz (Calif.)—Fiction. I. Title.

PS3553.R76 B74 2001
813'.54—dc21

                                        2001019260

First Edition: July 2001

10 9 8 7 6 5 4 3 2 1

For
Andrew Brian Snow
and
Zachariah Andrew Snow,
my family

I would like to thank those people whose expertise contributed to this book:

Ruth Cavin, my editor,

Meredith Phillips, my copyeditor,

Lieutenant Patty Sapone of the Santa Cruz Police Department,

Dr. Craig Evans, D.V.M.,

Dr. William Harmon, M.D.,

Jean Lukens, who explained her way of painting,

Marlies Cocheret, for a European point of view (and much more),

Caroline DuVernois, the best bartender in town,

and Kleine Lettunich, who, along with V. Sackville-West, Beverly Nichols, Gertrude Jekyll, Susan Irvine, Henry Mitchell, Michael Pollan, and a host of other magical garden writers, ignited my passion for old roses.

AUTHOR'S NOTE

Santa Cruz County is a real place, but Harkins Valley exists only in my imagination, as do all the characters in this book. Lest the reader think I am stretching the bounds of fiction too far, however, the central premise on which this plot is based did occur in a barn where I once kept my horses, many years ago.

BREAKAWAY

ONE

D r. McCarthy, I would like you to come check my horse."

Seven o'clock on a Saturday morning, and the voice on the other end of the line was female and unfamiliar.

"What's wrong?" I said dully, my mind still clouded with sleep.

A brief silence. Then, "She has been violated, I think. But I would like you to say what you think. Will you come?" The voice had a slight accent; I couldn't place it.

"If you need me."

My lack of enthusiasm must have sounded loud and clear because the unknown woman's tone grew stronger. "Yes, I would like you to come."

"All right. Is the horse in any kind of distress?"

"No, I don't think so."

"Then I'll be out in an hour or so," I said firmly.

Taking an address and directions, I hung up. Damn. Not ten minutes earlier, I'd been dozing, watching the fog-gray light outside my window and wondering what it would take to propel me out of bed and into the kitchen. Then had come the page from the answering service; my return call had elicited this strange conversation.

Her mare had been violated? What the hell did that mean? Maybe the neighbor's stud horse had gotten loose. In any case, it looked like I had to get up.

Getting up used not to be so difficult, I reflected wearily. At one time I had bounced out of bed with relative enthusiasm. Even this early in the morning. But today and yesterday and the six months previous, I awoke to the same steady, insidious apprehension. I didn't want to leave the bed, didn't want to face the day. Not a useful trait for a veterinarian, or anyone else who needed to earn a living.

Which I did. So, get up Gail, I admonished myself. Take a shower, make coffee. You'll feel better.

But I still lay on my side, staring out the window at a patch of foggy sky. There was no reason for this feeling. My life was going just fine. My boss had recently made me a partner in his business. Two years ago I'd purchased the house and property of my dreams. I owned two horses, a dog, a cat, and a cow. I was thirty-six years old and I'd achieved all the goals I'd set for myself when I turned eighteen. So why in hell was I so sad?

Lonny. His name jumped into my mind. Lonny Peterson, my boyfriend of several years, had decamped. Not without asking me to marry him. But the marriage proposal had included the rider that I be willing to leave my job and home and move to the Sierra Nevada Mountains with my new husband. Born and raised in Santa Cruz County, I felt this patch of rolling coastal hills on the northern edge of California's Monterey Bay was home. I was proud of what I'd achieved here in my career as a horse vet. I was staying, I told Lonny.

I'm not sure what I expected. Perhaps that he would choose to stay in order to be with me. It didn't turn out that way. Lonny had left, pursuing his own particular dream of owning a ranch in the Sierra foothills. We'd stayed in touch; we were still fond of each other. But it wasn't the same. Solitary for most of my life, I hadn't realized how much I'd come to count on Lonny's companionship in the years we were together. Suddenly "alone" didn't seem bearable. Six months ago, Lonny and I had agreed that we could date other people, but instead of feeling freer and happier, as I had expected, I found myself sinking deeper into this strange inertia.

I shifted restlessly, and the dog lying on the bed next to me, who had been curled comfortably in the curve of my body, got up, stretched, and licked my face.

"All right, Roey, all right."

The dog, a small, red, female Queensland heeler who looked very much like a little red fox, wagged her tail and licked my face again. I rolled away from her and let the momentum carry me out of bed.

First the coffee had to be made, then the dog got a biscuit and was let outside, then a shower and the obligatory minimal hair and face touch-up. I studied my closet without interest and pulled out a pair of jeans and a chambray shirt—almost a uniform as far as I was concerned.

Dressed and as ready as I was getting, I put some honey and milk in a blue willow mug and poured the strong French roast into it. The coffee steamed into the cool early morning air and I settled myself at one end of my couch and stared out the big windows.

A leaden gray sky, heavy with fog, matched my mood. Laid out before me, like some romantic landscape painting, was my neat vegetable garden, the grape stake fence adorned with climbing roses. My long border of wild perennials provided a foreground for the backdrop of rounded brushy hills. It was June, and the garden was at its peak, but the vividly balanced lavender-blue versus golden-orange color scheme that I'd orchestrated with such care looked as gray as the sky to me now.

In the corrals farther down the slope my two horses, Gunner and Plumber, stared hopefully over the railings toward the house. Plumber gave his shrill, high-pitched nicker, and Gunner echoed him. Daisy, the cow, lowed plaintively from the small riding arena where I kept her. Come feed us, they said.

I took a long swallow of coffee. What in the hell was wrong with me?

What I had, many people would give anything for. A few years ago, I would have said that owning this property, these horses, complete with the degree of financial success I'd achieved, would make me completely happy. I simply was not prepared for the intensity of the despondency I felt.

Was it all about Lonny? I wouldn't have said I was that dependent. There were other men who wanted to date me, men I was attracted to. Was it simply your classic midlife crisis?

All I knew was that, irrational as it seemed, I was beginning to feel that I couldn't go on like this. My life had lost all interest for me.

Plumber nickered again and I finished my coffee. The animals still had to be fed, the woman with the violated mare was waiting. Reluctantly I got up off the couch. Putting one foot in front of the other seemed like too much, but I didn't know how to quit.

Ten minutes later I was driving down the road toward Harkins Valley, a horsey little community not fifteen minutes from where I lived. The chilly fog of a California coastal summer lay heavily over everything; and whether it was my mood or the weather, I could see little beauty in the oak trees and meadows and redwood-filled canyons that used to delight me.

This is what they call depression, I told myself, not for the first time. You need to do something about this, Gail. You need to get help.

But not now. Now, I was pulling into a stranger's driveway and putting on my professional face. The competent, steady, reliable veterinarian, ready for anything.

Looking around, I walked in the direction of a smallish wooden barn—nothing fancy—more or less a large garage converted to a box stall, feed room, tack room setup. A woman came out of the box stall and walked to meet me.

"I'm Dr. McCarthy," I said, and held out my hand.

She was roughly forty, with a fine-boned, olive-skinned face, gentle lines around her eyes. "I am Nicole Devereaux."

We shook hands.

"Would you come with me?" Her accent was elusive, but there.

I followed her to the flat-roofed barn. Inside a homemade box stall, a black mare was awkwardly cross-tied, with baling twine and a garden hose improvising an impromptu halter and ties. Behind the mare a five-gallon plastic bucket lay on its side.

"I found her this way," Nicole Devereaux said. "I have not touched anything."

Studying the mare, I noticed that she seemed calm and alert, no signs of distress or any abnormality. Rather, she gazed at me with a docile eye, apparently unperturbed.

I put a hand on her shoulder. The black coat was smooth and slick, without the slightest dampness. Pulse normal, respiration normal.

"She seems fine," I said.

"Yes, she is fine, I think." The woman sounded diffident. "But," she gestured at the mare's rump, "look under her tail."

I walked to the mare's rear end, patted her hip, and glanced to see that her expression was still docile. Lifting her tail, I looked underneath. Nothing seemed amiss, though there was a viscous substance smeared around her vulva. For a long moment I stared, then looked at the five-gallon bucket. It took me a minute, but I got it.

"You found her just like this?" I asked, glancing at the way she was tied.

"Yes, what do you think?" Nicole Devereaux asked.

"I see what you mean," I said slowly. "You think the bucket was used to stand on. Why didn't you call the police?"

"I have no wish to have the police here," she said.

"But if you'd think someone has, uh, sexually abused this mare, it's not a matter for a veterinarian."

"I just want another opinion. Do you think that is what has happened?"

Slowly I ran my eyes over the scene. This time I noticed more smears of the viscous substance, which did, indeed, look like semen, on the mare's rump. Shaking my head, I told the woman, "It seems that way. But if you want to know, I think you should call the police and let them do some analysis of that." I pointed at a smear.

"I don't wish for the police," Nicole Devereaux said. "Do you think she will be all right?"

"She seems fine to me. And if it's true that someone has, well, for lack of a better word, raped her, I can't see any reason why it would do her any harm. More likely to do him harm, I'd say. Does she kick?"

"No, never. She is very sweet." Rubbing the mare's forehead affectionately, Nicole Devereaux untied her and led her out of the barn.

I followed, watching as she put the animal in a small corral shaded by an apple tree. Looking around, I saw an old adobe brick house half-hidden behind a few more ancient fruit trees and a hedge.

"Do you live there?" I asked, pointing.

"Yes."

"Did you hear anything out at the barn last night?"

"No, but I am a good sleeper."

"Do you have a dog?"

"No." She smiled for the first time. "Cats."

I smiled back and wondered how to put it. "Ms. Devereaux, I'd call the police if I were you. Anyone who'd sneak out here in the middle of the night to do this is not someone I would want prowling around my house. Do you live alone?"

"Yes. I understand what you are saying. But I do not want the police. I just wanted to know if my thoughts were," she paused, "legitimate. I will be careful. Thank you. What do I owe you?"

I gave her the standard charge for an exam and a ranch call. Since it was a weekend, technically I should have added an emergency charge, but it just didn't seem reasonable, given the little I'd had to do.

"I will write you a check," she said.

I followed her as she walked toward the house, my eternal curiosity about people's dwellings and ways of living poking its head above the blanket of indifference I'd been under for months. Still a faint spark of the old Gail there, I thought wearily.

The adobe house was small and old and entirely charming. The whitewash flaked off the mud-brown bricks, leaving irregular dark patches on the mostly white walls, and the low, cedar-shingled roof was mossy. A five-foot-high adobe wall that matched the house surrounded what looked like a kitchen garden. Nicole Devereaux pushed open a wooden gate and walked up an uneven path toward a Dutch door, which stood with the top half open. An apricot-colored rose draped a long arm like an archway over the path.

I stopped to smell one nodding voluptuous blossom. The fragrance, rich and familiar, made me smile.

Nicole Devereaux stopped with her hand on the latch of her door and looked back at me.

Still holding the rose, I asked her, "Lady Hillingdon?"

"Yes. You are right. Do you know roses?"

"A little. I've been making a garden for the last two years and I've gotten interested in old roses. I grow this one at home; she's one of my favorites."

The woman smiled, an expression of pure and simple delight, such as you see on the face of a child. When it disappeared from her mouth it still remained in her eyes. "The rose is my favorite flower. I planted this bush, it is five years ago now." She smiled again, but more to herself. "Five years I have been in this house."

Opening the door, she stepped inside. I glanced around the enclosed garden before I followed her. Other climbing roses, some of which I thought I recognized, festooned the gracefully deteriorating walls. Mostly in shades of cream and gold and apricot—the colors I favored myself. Tea roses and Noisettes, I thought. Classic border perennials—delphiniums, pinks, Shasta daisies—blended haphazardly with weedy herbs and wildflowers in an untidy band around the base of the wall. The center was all roughly cropped grass, which looked as if the horse, rather than a mower, kept it trimmed.

Uneven slabs of slate had been laid to form a path from the gate to the door where Nicole Devereaux had disappeared. I followed her into the house.

Into the kitchen, it turned out. This truly was a kitchen garden. The kitchen itself was small and unfancy, with cracked tile on the floor and an old-fashioned refrigerator and sink. A table sat in a windowed nook that extended out into the garden, and light filled the little room, even on such a foggy morning.

An open archway on one side of the kitchen seemed to lead to the rest of the house. I couldn't see Nicole Devereaux anywhere, so I stepped through the archway and stopped abruptly.

"My God," I said softly.

TWO

The room beyond the archway was amazing. At least to me, who had never seen anything like it. Originally it must have been several rooms, given the age and style of the house. At a guess, dining room, front hall, and living room. Whatever walls had divided it had been removed, leaving one big open space.

The walls were whitewashed, with windows set deep in them; the floor was planked oak. A fireplace with a simple oak mantel filled one end of the room. Nothing else. No furniture, not so much as a camp stool. Only paintings.

Paintings everywhere—hanging on the white walls, on easels in the middle of the floor, leaning against each other here and there. One, which appeared to be a work in progress, was sitting on a particularly large easel by a window that looked out at the kitchen garden. On the wide window ledge were paints and brushes.

I stared at the paintings as if mesmerized. Brilliant, vivid colors—lapis blue, coral red, indigo violet—in great sweeps and strange shapes, somehow evoking landscapes, and yet like no landscapes I had ever seen.

I stared and stared, forgetting my purpose for being here, lost to everything but buoyant, yet demanding creations in front of me. The nearest one, dominated by a swirling topography of amber, revealed delicate black inking over what looked like watercolor. The closer I peered, the more intricate the detail appeared, revealing further nuances and possible meanings.

Stepping even closer, I felt as if I were entering the world of the painting, a tawny landscape as foreign as it was familiar. And yet, was it a landscape? I stepped back. Were these paintings abstract, impressionistic, surrealistic? I couldn't say. A unifying force seemed to bind them all, but neither it, nor they, could be easily defined.

Footsteps. I turned abruptly to see Nicole Devereaux enter the room from the other end. I felt shy, almost embarrassed. Had she meant me to see her work? Was I trespassing on her private space?

"You're an artist," I said, trying to fill the gap.

"That is true." Her expression was not unfriendly; she stood quietly in the middle of her room and watched me look around.

"I really like your work," I said.

"Thank you." She smiled, sudden and sweet, as she had when I commented on the rose.

"Is it it for sale?" I asked.

"Some is. It is how I make my living."

"Oh." I took that in and was impressed. I knew people who painted, of course. But I had never known anyone who made a living as an artist.

Nicole Devereaux continued to regard me pleasantly enough, saying nothing, seeming content with the silence and my obvious appreciation of her art.

As for me, I could hardly tear my eyes away from the paintings. For the first time in what seemed like years, and was certainly months, something was speaking to me again. With their deep and brilliant colors, these disembodied semi-landscapes were saying something I could hear. Not that I understood it. But it was a voice I recognized.

Tantalized, I stared around the room, wanting to explore, to look at each painting carefully and slowly. I brought my eyes back to Nicole Devereaux's face. "I might like to buy one," I said.

She smiled again. "Of course. They are very expensive." She said it simply; a matter of fact.

"Oh," I said.

"I work very slowly. And there is some demand now. I have been painting a long time. Ever since I was a girl."

"Oh," I said again, aware that I was proving a lousy conversationalist.

She watched me quietly.

"I would like," I said slowly, "to look at your work, and if I could afford it, to purchase a piece for my home."

"Of course," she said. "Would you like to set up a time?"

Belatedly it occurred to me that she had called me out here to look at her horse, not her paintings, and that she was, perhaps, busy with other things at the moment. She came toward me, then past me, into her kitchen. Reluctantly, I turned my back on the paintings and followed her.

Sitting at the kitchen table, she wrote me a check and consulted a calendar. "I have time in the evening next week," she said. "Most evenings."

"How about Monday, then?"

She made a note on the calendar. "At seven?"

"That would be great. Thank you." I put the check in my pocket.

A tortoiseshell cat jumped onto the chair beside Nicole and she stroked its head with a hand that was as finely boned as her face. "Yes, Ruth," she said to the cat. "What is it?"

The cat mewed, in that questioning, plaintive tone cats so easily assume.

"Yes, you can be fed," Nicole responded.

I stared at the woman, fascinated by the shape of her face and the cadence of her voice. This was the creator of those strangely symbolic paintings, those paintings that had seemed to reflect my own inner landscape. Vivid colors and the play of light and shadow on empty hills—something, something that was me.

And so, I wondered, gazing at Nicole, who was this?

Her angular face gave no clues. Dark brown hair pulled back in a knot, dark eyes, jeans and a faded shirt, sandals on her feet. A slender hand stroking a cat. Plenty of lines around the eyes. That was it.

I put my hand on the door latch. "Thank you," I said again. "And be careful."

"I will be. Thank you, also." A smile with a note of finality.

And then I was out the door and walking across the small garden to the wooden gate, in something of a daze. I found my way to my truck, wondering the whole time what had come over me. I'd never been particularly moved by a piece of art before. I'd admired, been repulsed, been intrigued. But never swept away, never inclined to spend major money. My little house was decorated with the few bits and pieces I'd either inherited or acquired, somewhat by chance. I was in no sense an art connoisseur.

Still, I was aware that I truly longed for the paintings in Nicole Devereaux's studio. Desire is a trap, I told myself. But what registered more was that I had felt desire at all. It had been so long, or so it seemed, since I had felt much of anything but weariness.

Pulling out of Nicole's driveway, I took a last glance over my shoulder. The adobe house was mostly hidden from the road by a big and untidy hedge of what looked like the rambling rose called Mermaid. I could see the black mare, munching hay in her corral under the apple tree.

The sight of the horse recalled the reason for my visit. Damn. Now that was a strange thing. In my half dozen years as a practicing veterinarian, I had never come across anything like that. I tried to imagine someone who would sneak into a barn in the middle of the night in order to have sex with a horse. Creepy. Nothing came to mind but adolescent boys, playing a prank. I hoped that was all it was.

I was on Harkins Valley Road now, driving through a particularly wet, dense fog. Despite the lack of visibility, I knew exactly where I was and what was around me. I had a lot of clients who lived in Harkins Valley; it was familiar turf.

In many ways, it was an odd area. A fertile little valley in the hills south of Santa Cruz, it had been settled by dairymen and farmers, and the terrain was still dotted with their fairly humble dwellings. At a guess, Nicole's house had been one of these.

However, in the last thirty years the inviting arable land had been bought up bit-by-bit by the increasingly wealthy folks who had begun to populate Santa Cruz County. Some had come when the university moved in, others had arrived when the once quiet, rural Santa Clara Valley, only a half hour away, had evolved into the heavily industrialized Silicon Valley. And a lot of these people wanted "a place in the country."

Harkins Valley was ideal for small horse properties, and it was now crowded with them. Ranging from remodeled farmhouses like Nicole's with an acre or so, to forty-acre white-board-fenced estates with five-thousand-square-foot pseudo-mansions plunked down on them—not to mention everything in between. And everybody had a horse.

Not surprisingly, the place was full of odd contrasts between new and old, shacks and spec houses. Even the landscape seemed to lend itself to this. The valley couldn't make up its mind whether to be open and sunny, or steep and shady. It wavered in and out along its length, billowing into wide, level meadows with oaks dotted decoratively here and there, and narrowing in places to shadowy canyons thick with redwoods.

It was in one of these redwood filled passages that I braked and pulled my truck into a driveway. My friend Kris Griffith lived here, in a house that she had purchased about the time I bought my own property.

Like Nicole, Kris was in the low-rent district of Harkins Valley. These sections of shady canyon were not nearly as popular, or as valuable, as the meadow ground. Although Kris had three acres here, barely an acre was usable; the rest was almost vertical hillside. And though the sun could slant invitingly through the trees on warm summer afternoons, on cold, foggy mornings like this, or long, wet winter days, life in a redwood grove was pretty dark and dank.

Still, I smiled as I always did when I saw Kris's house. A narrow little box of a place, sided only in weathered plywood and stripping, it still managed to look inviting. Maybe it was the smoke rising gently from the chimney pipe, or the old-fashioned French doors leading out to a deck overhung with jasmine. Or the border of foxgloves and ferns around a tiny lawn, with the redwoods towering up all around it. Who knew what alchemy caused some houses to work and others not? One thing was apparent: money couldn't buy it.

I knocked on Kris's door, thinking how pleasant it was to have at least one friend I could drop in on without notice. Kris and I had known each other for many years; since her divorce our relationship had evolved into what I, an only child, could imagine was a sisterly one.

It took awhile for Kris to open her door. Well, after all, it was Saturday morning. She had no doubt been out last night. Although it had taken her a year or so to recover from her divorce, at this point Kris was relishing her status as a divorcée and frequently regaled me with sagas of nights spent out at the bars and clubs.

Sure enough, her bleary expression when she finally opened the door was a definite tip-off.

"Gail, it's early," she said.

"Kris, it's after nine o'clock," I responded. "Were you asleep?" I added innocently.

"Of course I was asleep." Kris grinned. "I was out until two-thirty. Unlike you, who were probably snoring by nine o'clock. You should've come with me."

"Right," I said. "Then what would I have done when the answering service paged me at seven?"

Kris shrugged. Her blond hair, which reached her shoulders, fell in what I understood to be a stylish curtain around her face. Her slim body was covered—barely—by a close-fitting sheath of a black night-gown. It struck me that I never saw Kris lately when she wasn't wearing some sort of snug garment.

She had a good figure, no doubt about it. For a woman of forty, or a woman of any age. But when I had first met her, six years ago, near the start of my veterinary career, she had seemed relatively unconcerned with looks and clothes, interested solely in her family, her horse, and the competitive sport of endurance racing.

The Kris Griffith I had become friends with cropped hair short, wore eyeglasses, didn't bother with makeup. Though she always looked neat and attractive enough, it was clear she didn't worry about impressing anyone.

No longer. In the last year, Kris had undergone quite the transformation. Although her face was scrubbed clean at the moment, I knew from previous occasions what she would've looked like yesterday evening. Foundation to hide all wrinkles, much color on lips and cheeks, much blackness around the eyes. Not to mention the inevitable short, tight black skirt, skimpy top, and high heels. Kris had become very predictable.

"How'd it go?" I asked her.

"Oh, all right." Kris yawned and led me into her living room. "I didn't get lucky, though."

"Too bad." I was less than impressed with Kris's current mission in life, getting laid by as many attractive younger men as possible. Not to mention that my standards on "attractive" were pretty damn different from hers.

"We ended up at a bar called Moe's Alley, dancing to a great blues band. You would have liked it. You should have come," she said again.

"Uh-huh."

Kris was always trying to get me to go out with her and her other single girlfriends. She bemoaned my lack of interest in the dating scene and had told me, more than once, that I was wasting my best years.

Well, maybe she was right. I was thirty-six, no longer young. I'd never been married. The relationship with Lonny that had just ended was the only serious one I'd ever been in. And somehow or other, I just didn't have a flair for flirting with strangers.

Kris was heating water for coffee. She watched me over the open bar that divided her kitchen from an airy living area. "You need to get out more," she said.

"Why?"

"I don't know. You've seemed so down lately."

I said nothing to this.

"Gail, you're an attractive woman. Lots of guys would like to go out with you if you'd give them a chance. You don't have to mourn Lonny forever."

"I've got a date tonight," I offered.

"Who with? Clay?"

"Yeah."

"Jeez, Gail, don't sound so enthusiastic," Kris said sarcastically. "I'd love to be going out with Clay Bishop. The guy's good-looking, has some money, seems like he's real nice. What more do you want?"

"I like Clay," I said.

Kris shook her head and poured hot water over the coffee in the filter. "You still don't sound very enthusiastic."

I looked out through her French doors at the foggy landscape. "I know," I said. "But it's not Clay. He is nice. It's just me."

Handing me a cup of coffee, Kris sat down on her futon couch, next to the armchair I was sitting in. "So what's going on with you?"

"I don't know," I said.

"You're depressed," Kris said firmly. "I know, I was depressed for almost a year. Right after the divorce. It's not something you can shake off, or talk yourself out of. It's like having the flu. You actually feel physically shitty—all the time. And tired and like nothing interests you. Right?"

"You're right," I said, surprised that Kris had pegged my emotional state so exactly.

"I know," she said. "I went through it. You don't like to admit it to anyone, but sometimes you feel so helpless, maybe being dead would be easier. You start to realize just how it is people commit suicide. Am I right?"

"Yeah," I said slowly. "Though I'm not there, yet."

"No," Kris said. "But you let the thought cross your mind. I know; I did. And the worst part is, you know perfectly well there's no real reason for it. I knew I didn't want to be back with Rick. I knew my life was basically okay. I was depressed—clinically depressed. It's a disease, Gail."

"I know that."

"So you need to do something about it."

"See a shrink?" I rolled my eyes upward.

"Yes." Kris was emphatic. "That's exactly what you should do. You of all people should understand. This is a medical condition; your brain isn't making enough serotonin, or whatever they call it. Medication can help."

"I know, I know." I looked at her wearily. These were the very things I'd been thinking myself. But I couldn't seem to summon enough motivation to overcome my distaste for the idea of consulting a psychiatrist.

Kris looked at me sympathetically "It's not so bad, Gail. I'll give you the number of the guy I went to. He was very good. I'll bet he could help you."

"All right," I agreed, partly to get her off the subject.

"So where's Clay taking you tonight?" she asked, seeming to sense my discomfort.

"Some place downtown called Clouds," I said.

"Oh, Clouds is nice. What are you going to wear?"

"I don't know." Once again, I felt overwhelmed with inertia.

Kris was still gazing at me with a worried look in her eyes. "If you're not so excited about Clay Bishop," she said, "what about that guy you met last summer? You seemed to like him."

"Blue," I said. "Blue Winter. I guess nothing is going to come of that."

"Why not?"

"I don't know," I said again. It was beginning to sound like my mantra. "I went out to visit him once. He just didn't seem too interested."

"Did you tell him you'd broken up with Lonny?" Kris demanded.

"No. I wasn't exactly sure how to work it into the conversation."

"Jeez, Gail, you are lame. If he's a nice guy he's not going to ask you out if he thinks you have a boyfriend. Particularly if he knows the boyfriend. You've got to be a little more direct. Why don't you ask him out to dinner?"

"I could, I guess."

"Why not?" Once again, Kris was emphatic.

"I don't know why not," I said. "I'd just don't seem to have the energy or the interest."

"That's depression," Kris said. "Maybe Clay's the right guy for you and you just don't recognize it because you're depressed. Like I said, I wish I was going out with him."

"Give it a try," I told her. "I don't mind."

Kris laughed. "You're his type; I'm not. Clay's a nice guy; he wants to get married. I'm not into that; I'm into having fun. At least for now."

"You figure I'm the marrying type?" I asked her.

"You're the type that wants to get serious." Kris smiled. "Clay lived with his last girlfriend ten years. He's the serious type, too."

"Uh-huh." I knew this, more or less, as did all the rest of the local horse community. Clay Bishop lived in Harkins Valley, too, and his family owned the Bishop Ranch Boarding Stable. Clay and his brother, Bart, both good-looking single men, were the subject of much talk in horsey circles.

"Well, I like Clay just fine," I said firmly, "but I'm not sure I want to get serious about anyone."

"What? You mean you want to start going out with me and Trina?" Kris grinned.

"No." I laughed—sort of. "Oh hell, Kris, I don't know what I want."

"You need to see my shrink." Kris got out a piece of paper and a pencil, found her address book, and began copying. I let my gaze drift around the room.

Kris's house was two stories high—in the living room. This created a tall open area, which made the small room seem much bigger. A loft bedroom and bathroom over the kitchen completed the space. There was a spare bedroom over the garage that was used by Kris's teenage daughter, Jo, during the periods when she stayed with her mother. A simple house, but pleasant.

I liked this room. A collection of rugs from different lands covered the pine floor—all faded, all patterned. Dusty rose, burnt orange, plum—the soft old colors vibrant against the worn wood. An equally eclectic selection of art decorated the white walls—Japanese wood-block prints, a pen and ink by Heinrich Kley, an aboriginal painting, one of Maxfield Parrish's romantic landscapes. Staring at this last, I thought of Nicole.

"Do you know a woman named Nicole Devereaux?" I asked Kris. "She lives down the road about a mile, going toward Watsonville. In a little adobe house on the right that you can't really see from the road."

Kris shook her head. "I don't think so. In Lushmeadows?"

"No. Just past that."

I looked out through Kris's French doors. The fog was clearing—slowly. Just visible through a gap in the redwoods, Harkins Valley Road wound past manicured white-board-fenced pastures in a flat, open section of the valley. This was the Lushmeadows subdivision, a bunch of plots with great big houses on them, intended for the horsey crowd. Across the road sat the Bishop Ranch Boarding Stable, all that was left of the old Bishop Ranch, and home to my sometime companion Clay Bishop. The Bishops had sold the majority of their ranch land to the Lushmeadows Development Company in order to bolster their sagging finances. A situation that was becoming all too common in this county.

"I don't think I've met anyone around here named Nicole," Kris said. "Does she have horses?"

"One," I said. "A mare." And I told Kris the story of my odd call out to Nicole's. "It bothers me," I said. "It seems like such a creepy thing."

Kris shuddered. "That's the weirdest thing I've heard in years."

I shrugged. "Well, it's not as bad as raping a woman, if you think about it."

"I suppose." She shivered again. "But it's so strange. What kind of person would want to do that to a horse?" Abruptly she stood up and stuffed her feet into a pair of fleece-lined leather boots with rubber soles. Pulling a jacket off the rack by the door, she said, "Let's go feed Dixie."

"All right." I got up and followed her.

Kris's corral and barn, a prefabricated, portable metal construction, sat on a small patch of level ground outside her back door, providing enough space, barely, for one horse. Redwoods leaned over it, making it dark and muddy in the winter, and it was far from an ideal spot for a stable. But Kris had been determined to keep the little mare.

A world-class endurance rider for many years, Kris had given up the sport when her great gelding, Rebby, had crippled up with an obscure ailment called EPM. Kris had retired Rebby and he currently lived in a twenty-acre pasture at the far end of Harkins Valley, boarded with a couple of other retirees. Kris had acquired the little half Arab, half Quarter Horse mare she called Dixie mostly for her daughter.

Or so she said. In reality, I didn't think Jo was all that interested. It was Kris who rode Dixie, taking long rambles along the maze of trails that twined through Harkins Valley and the surrounding ridges. Even though her divorce had forced Kris to move from an elegant little horse ranch to this shady cabin in the woods, she had clung to Dixie and to horse-keeping with tenacity.

I understood. Even though she no longer had the time or money for competition, and Dixie, in any case, was not of that caliber, Kris needed to have a horse around. To feed, to brush, to take for rides. Just to provide that elemental presence, that unique connection to the natural world that horses are.

I felt the same way. Horses were unlike other pets; when you rode a horse you partook of his power, you put yourself at his mercy. Galloping a horse, you felt the force and the joy of speed and danger, given to you by this animal who in most ways was as dependent on you as a pet rabbit in a cage. And yet when you were on his back, you and he were in a sense partners; you trusted him to take care of you; he trusted you to take care of him.

Dixie nickered at us as we approached the barn and we both smiled. A horse's morning greeting is a reassuring thing. All's well with the world.

Kris put a flake of oat hay in Dixie's feeder, and we both watched the mare eat. A little golden dun without a white hair on her, Dixie was the color of toffee candy, with big soft, dark eyes like a Jersey heifer.

"She's sure a sweet little horse, isn't she?" I said to Kris.

"She's a doll. I only get around to riding her a couple of days a week, I'm so busy, but she's just as calm and quiet as can be. Even though she lives in this tiny pen."

"She's easy to handle and be around, too." My mind was following a different track.

"Sure." Kris looked at me. "What are you thinking?"

"I don't know. About Nicole Devereaux's mare, I guess. She said that horse is real sweet. And she doesn't live a mile away."

"That's a bad thought."

"Keep an eye out, Kris."

"For what?"

"I don't know." I shook my head. "Anything out of the ordinary, I guess. This woman, Nicole, didn't want me to call the police, so I guess I won't, but it does seem really weird."

"I agree." Kris wrapped her jacket more closely around her and turned back toward the house.

"I'd better get going," I said. "Today's housecleaning day. I'm so busy during the week I don't get much done."

"I hear you. Me, too."

"How's it going at work?" I asked her as I walked toward my truck.

"Good. Busy. It takes a lot of my time and energy."

"I can imagine." Kris had gone back to work post divorce, as a high school teacher.

"Just like your job." Kris smiled at me as I got in my truck. "Promise you'll call my shrink?"

"Sure." I smiled back as I shut the door and started the engine, but I was aware that the smile was merely pasted on.

Watching Kris in the rearview mirror as I drove away, I wondered. She stood alone in front of her small house, looking somewhat forlorn in her barn jacket and boots, with her nightgown clinging to her ankles. And yet the smile and wave she gave me were genuine, warm and unforced. Kris was all right.

Why her and not me? The comparison was inevitable. Kris had been through a difficult divorce after many years of marriage; she was currently short of cash and struggling; she lived alone; she had no boyfriend. In many ways my own situation, though similar, was better. I had more money, more security; Lonny and I had not been as deeply intertwined as Kris and Rick. But I was the one who was depressed.

Get a grip, Gail. I shook my head at myself. Kris had said she was depressed, too. She'd gotten help. That was what I needed to do. Get help. And soon.

THREE

Despite everything, I drove into my own driveway with a feeling of relief. Not the suprised joy I had once felt at owning such a lovely piece of land, not that, but a sense of quiet and safety. In two short years, this property had become home.

My two and a half acres were located on a sunny south-facing slope in the hills behind the town of Corralitos, and the topography of the land made the property unique. The lower acre was comprised of a grove of young oak trees, where my horse corrals were. The upper section was a small, round hollow in the hills, a natural bowl or am-phitheater. My house, which sat at the back of this bowl, was shielded on three sides by brushy hills; it looked out to the south, toward the bay. Though I was a mere quarter of a mile from a busy thoroughfare, I could see no other houses from my front porch.

I drove up the drive, past the horse corrals where Gunner and Plumber dozed under the oaks, past the little fenced vegetable garden, and up to the house. Excited yips from the dog pen greeted me. Roey was anxious to be let out.

I sat in the truck for a moment, staring out through my windshield. The corrals and barn and garden were my own creations; the house, though, had been bequeathed to me by a former owner. I couldn't imagine how I'd gotten so lucky.

The place had been built for a single woman in her fifties, a professor at the local university. As I understood the story, she had meant to end her days here, but, more or less on completion of the house she received a too-lucrative job offer on the East Coast and moved. Thus this house, my little house, had never been lived in by anybody but me.

The lady professor had shared my taste for small houses. In a place and time where the minimal size for a new house seems to be a couple of thousand square feet, she had built a seven-hundred-square-foot dwelling. I had smiled in surprise and delight when I'd first seen it, and its unmarketable (in the real estate agent's mind) size had been the reason I was able to afford this property at all.

The house suited me perfectly. My ideal has always been a little house with a big garden, and not only was this house the size I would have chosen, it had been built by someone with an aesthetic sense very similar to my own.

Shingled all over with cedar shakes that were already starting to weather, the house had a green tin roof, a big front porch, and many windows on the south side. It seemed to nestle into the hills behind it, and it was situated such that it overlooked the property and out toward the distant ridges to the south.

I knew the house's story in fairly intimate detail; it had been built by Clay Bishop. I had known Clay for many years as a client; I'd also known he made a living as a contractor. But it wasn't until I'd purchased this property that these facts had coalesced into a much closer acquaintance.

Upon learning that Clay had been the contractor who built my new home, I'd called him with a few small, specific questions and much general curiosity. He'd been friendly and helpful, and within a month I'd hired him to build my barn. That had been almost two years ago, and during that time we'd evolved into friends and then . . . what?

What, indeed. I stared at my house through the windshield of the truck, not seeing it. Clay had taken me out to dinner a half dozen times in the last few months. He seemed sincere, and steadily more romantic.

We'd kissed good-night last time, with much mutual curiosity, or so I thought.

And now what? It seemed to me that Clay wanted the relationship to progress, and me—I didn't know what I wanted. Clay was, as Kris had said, handsome, intelligent, and pleasant to be around. I didn't know why I wasn't more intrigued.

Except that I wasn't much intrigued with anything. Roey yipped again from the dog pen, impatient with me. I got out of the truck and unlatched the gate. The little dog burst out, going full tilt—alternately running, yipping, and chasing her tail.

Wearily I walked toward the porch, watching Roey romp around, and wondering, yet again, why I couldn't seem to enjoy anything anymore.

The dog was unaware of my malaise. Giving up tail chasing, she dashed down to the barn, found a bit of horse hoof that had been pared away by the shoer, and began playing with it—flinging it in the air, catching it, and racing around with it in her mouth.

At two years old, Roey still acted very much like a puppy. She'd been given to me by my friend Lisa Bennett, and I'd named her in honor of Lisa's two parent dogs, Joey and Rita. Roey had turned out to be very small for a Queensland heeler, and her size, combined with her red color and long, white-tipped tail, gave her a foxlike appearance.

Blue, the Queensland I'd owned for fifteen years, had been docked before I got him, and I'd grown accustomed to his short stump of a rabbit tail wagging his approval. But Lisa had declined to dock her pups, for which I didn't blame her, and now I was equally taken with my little red fox of a dog.

Actually, Roey tended to remind one of a whole selection of wild animals. Frolicking up and down the hill with her ears folded back and her mouth wide open in a happy pant, she looked just like a bear cub. Lonny had said she reminded him of a badger, with her stocky body, wide forehead, and wedge-shaped head. And Queensland heelers, Australian Cattle Dogs to dog show people, seemed to make a lot of folks think of coyotes, perhaps because of the sharply pricked ears. To top it off, someone actually had asked me once if Blue was a hyena.

Whatever it is they're reminiscent of, there's certainly something feral-looking about a Queensland. In Roey's case, as in Blue's, the wildness wasn't confined to her appearance. A more rambunctious, mischievous dog probably didn't exist in all of California. On top of this, she was smart—smarter than I was, I sometimes thought. The whole combination was hard to beat if you wanted charm and entertainment, but it could be exhausting. In my present mood, in fact, it seemed like too much.

Roey had ceased playing with the bit of hoof, located her Frisbee, and brought it to me. She dropped it on the ground at my feet, wagged her tail vigorously, and looked expectantly up into my face. From long experience I knew I would have no peace until the Frisbee was thrown; bending over, I picked it up and sent it spinning across the hollow.

Roey chased and leaped and caught and retrieved the Frisbee—over and over again. Her appetite for this game never waned. When she was panting and exhausted and I was dying for a little quiet, I called her and shut her back in the pen. She watched me with wistful eyes as I walked away, and I felt like a child beater.

I didn't seem to have enough energy to go around anymore. Stepping through my front door, I surveyed the gritty floor and groaned. How in the hell was I going to muster the oomph to get this house cleaned?

I used to like cleaning the house. Its small size and the beautiful surfaces and textures made it a genuine pleasure to tend. But now, now sweeping the floor was too much.

Still—I walked down the short hall to the living room and stared at the blank wall. Paneled in pine planks, nailed rough-side out, the wall stretched to the peak of the roof, unwindowed except for a small clear pane fitted into the apex. It was the biggest open wall in the house, and when I had first seen it, I knew that it it cried out for some sort of dramatic piece of art. One piece, I thought. Something that would somehow set the tone for the whole place.

Unfortunately, I had no such thing. My few bits and pieces were all too small and too mild. And I had been too busy with other pursuits to engage in a search.

So the wall remained blank. But now that I had seen Nicole Devereaux's work, I knew what I would put here. One of those big, intense, abstract landscapes—that was what the wall wanted.

For a moment I gazed at the room, trying to see it with fresh eyes. I still thought it beautiful, as I had when I had first seen it, but custom had perhaps staled my innate perceptions.

The room was twenty feet by twenty, and maybe twenty feet high from the floor to the peak of the open ceiling. It was paneled in rough golden pine, and floored with deep mahogany-red hardwood. In one corner was a gray stone fireplace, and in the opposite one, a small kitchen area with terra-cotta tile counters and silvery stainless steel refrigerator and stove. The third corner was filled with a built-in desk, and the fourth contained a round table and chairs. There was a small couch covered in a dark green Navajo-patterned fabric, placed where it faced the hearth and the big windows that looked out to the south. That was it.

The rest of the house consisted of the short entry hallway lined with bookcases, a bedroom, and a bathroom. Definitely an efficient living space.

I loved it. My previous house had been roughly six hundred square feet, and I'd become accustomed to the coziness of a little house, and inured to the inconvenience. Yes, if I didn't pick up for a few days there seemed to be junk on every available surface, and no, I couldn't go around buying furniture and artifacts wholesale.

This last suited me just fine. I hate shopping, and I really didn't have the time for it. I'd purchased the couch and a sturdy desk chair when I'd bought the house—nothing more.

Now, I thought, now I would finally get the piece of artwork that the room demanded and the place would look complete. I liked its overall bareness and simplicity, and didn't feel the need to add much clutter. One piece was what I wanted—the right one.

The thought caused a trickle of interest to creep into my mind, and I used this glimmer to push myself through the routine of straightening the house, cleaning the kitchen, sweeping and mopping the floors. I left dusting and scrubbing for another day.

By this time it was almost noon; the fog had thinned and cleared—

barely. I knew from long experience that an hour or two of feeble sunshine was all I was likely to get. Santa Cruz County went through occasional periods of nonstop fog every summer, and we were in the middle of one now. Since I lived back in the hills, the sun managed to break through almost every day, but it was a short-lived battle. As soon as the afternoon began to wane, the fog crept back in, blanketing the air with its wet chill.

Staring out my windows, I reflected that if I was going to do anything outdoors, now was the time. Or, on the other hand, I could just lie on the couch and doze. The thought caused alarm bells to go off in my mind. This was exactly what depressed people did, lie around and stare at the walls.

Do something, I told myself. Go outside. Just start.

I pushed my reluctant body to the door and out on the porch. The vegetable garden needed weeding, the grass needed mowing, the roses needed trimming and tying up. I stared at the garden morosely. I didn't want to do any of these things.

Lifting my eyes, I looked farther down the slope to where the horse corrals were. Both horses were watching me, ears pointed forward; they'd spotted me as soon as I walked out of the house.

"All right, all right," I told them. "I'm coming."

I was going to do something to make myself feel better. I was going to ride a horse.

FOUR

Despite the difficulty I had overcoming my reluctance to the logistical preparations for a ride, I still felt a little twinge of relief and enjoyment when I actually swung my leg over a horse. Over Plumber in this case. Gunner, my older horse, had developed a case of navicular, oddly enough in a back foot, and was on R and R.

Navicular disease, a degeneration of the small navicular bone in the horse's foot, is a fairly common problem in Quarter Horses, but it's usually seen in the front feet. As a vet, I was quite familiar with the drill for this problem. Shoe the horse with pads for cushioning, give him drugs to improve his circulation—lack of blood supply to the bones in question being thought to be a cause of the problem—and give him bute (horse aspirin) as needed. In Gunner's case, I was also giving him a six-month layoff.

This wasn't such a hardship for me. Two riding horses were actually more than I could keep going, given my quota of free time and level of emotional energy. It was all I could do to get one horse ridden two or three days a week. Since I kept both horses in a corral that was larger than an acre, where they could run and play as much as they wanted, I didn't feel that the lack of enforced exercise was a problem.

As I walked Plumber around the arena, I reflected on how lucky I was that he had an amiable disposition and a relaxed nature. Whether I rode him every day or once a month, he behaved equally well.

I warmed him up gradually—lots of walking, trotting, and slow loping—before I moved on to anything more ambitious. Daisy, the cow, watched us from one corner of the arena, her eyes alert. She knew what I was up to.

I'd acquired Daisy from my friend, rancher Glen Bennett; he'd used her for several years as a roping cow. The red-and-white corriente heifer had proved adaptable, as some cattle are; she'd learned the roping routine and seemed perfectly amenable to going through the motions. However, after two or three years she'd gotten very large, which had caused Glen to get rid of her.

"Best damn cow on the whole place," he told me. "She'll lope right out there, let you rope her, over and over again. You can lead her off; she won't drag. But those guys all think she's a problem because she's so big."

Staring at the red-and-white heifer, who probably weighed well over six hundred pounds, I could see why a roper might object if she was loaded into the chute. If such an animal did decide to resist and hang back on the rope, it would be brutal for the head horse who had to pull it.

"She won't drag, though," Glen said, sensing my thought. "I guarantee it. She'll do just what you want her to. We've had her around so long she's got a name. We call her Daisy."

I'd bought Daisy and hauled her home, and she had, indeed, proved to be just what I needed. I had decided to teach Plumber, my younger horse, how to be a rope horse; what was required was a cow that would allow me to rope it over and over and over again and not give up. Daisy was perfect.

Loping Plumber in circles, I planned the training routine for today. Nothing too strenuous. Just a little breakaway roping, enough to keep the horse progressing. Plumber loped underneath me with an easy rocking motion; he was short-strided but smooth. His mane fell neatly on the left side of his neck, his cocoa-colored coat was naturally slick and shiny. Even though I kept him turned out and didn't blanket him,

Plumber, a former show horse, always looked glossy and tidy; it was just his natural way of being.

Once Plumber was thoroughly warmed up I picked up my breakaway rope—a lariat fastened with a bit of slim wire that would come apart when pulled upon—and began to swing it. Plumber's ears went quickly back as the rope whirled around his head; he wasn't crazy about this. But I'd done it before, and he'd accepted it. After a minute, I could feel the tension seeping out of his body. Kicking him up to a lope, still whirling the rope, I headed for Daisy. The cow took one knowledgeable look at us and then headed off across the arena. Plumber followed her.

This part, on Plumber, was a no-brainer; he knew how to follow cattle. Plumber had been a hackamore horse when I acquired him; in the course of his training he'd been taught to "watch" a cow. He followed Daisy automatically; I swung my rope and tried to help him find the right position.

What I wanted the horse to do was "track" the cow—assume a position just to the left of her left hip and stay there. This Plumber was learning; in his former experience as a cowhorse, he'd been taught to go to the head and turn the cow.

Round the pen we went, following Daisy wherever she went, staying on her hip as she doubled back and spurted ahead. I spun my loop until my arm got tired.

Taking a deep breath, I waited until the cow was lined out and going straight, and threw. The loop settled around her horns, I pulled to take up the slack, dallied the rope around the saddle horn, and stopped Plumber.

He melted easily into the ground; he was a good stopper. For a brief second I felt Daisy's weight hit the end of the rope, felt Plumber brace himself, and then the breakaway rope gave way and the cow was free. She trotted off; I coiled the rope back up and patted Plumber's neck. "Good boy," I told him.

Looking up, I saw Plumber's brown ears pricked forward at the departing cow and realized that in this moment I was not depressed. Somehow the action, the motion, the interaction with horse and cow, had wiped my mind clean. Though I knew it wouldn't last, I felt a deep sense of relief that the darkness could lift, even if temporarily.

I roped Daisy another half dozen times and then put Plumber up. Giving him and Gunner a pat, I looked wistfully at the sky, which was already turning gray again. The fog was creeping back in.

I should mow the grass, I thought. The idea roused no enthusiasm. Maybe I would go inside and lie down for a while. It couldn't do me any harm to take a brief nap. Uneasily aware that I was sleeping more than I used to, I headed toward the house. I'd almost reached the porch when my pager went off.

"Damn." Even though I knew that I was on call this weekend, I always hoped (optimistically) to have my two-day window of free time uninterrupted. It almost never happened, though.

Crossing my fingers that this call wouldn't be some ignorant yahoo at the far end of the county who couldn't tell a real emergency from an absolutely normal horse, I marched into the house and called the answering service.

"A Mike O'Hara has a colicked horse," the woman told me. "He'd like you to come out."

Immediate relief. I knew Mike O'Hara. He was reasonably knowledgeable; if he said his horse was colicked, it no doubt was. Also, Mike lived in the Lushmeadows subdivision; he was only fifteen minutes away, if that. I would have plenty of time to take care of this call and get home and get ready for dinner with Clay.

Letting Roey out of her pen, I held the truck door open so that she could jump in and hop on the seat next to me. She'd spent enough of the day incarcerated.

Not very many minutes later, I was back in Harkins Valley. I cast a mildly curious glance at the Bishop Ranch as I drove past it, wondering if Clay was home. Then I turned between the big stone pillars with the ostentatious sign, and I was in the midst of suburban glitz.

Let's face it, I'm prejudiced. I hate subdivisions of any kind. My childhood home, a small apple ranch in the hills north of here, had been bulldozed out of all recognition by a developer, and was now covered with cheek-by-jowl stucco houses. The development I was driving through, though far more pricey and upscale, was, to my eyes anyway, equally ugly. These big lots had bigger spec houses on them, that was all.

Mike O'Hara's property was not one of the more deluxe. He had a two-acre parcel, neatly fenced, with a classic ranch-style home plunked down in the middle of it. The barn and corrals were out back. The whole place was relatively characterless, but it was neat and tidy and well tended.

Mike was waiting for me at the barn. A vigorous man in his fifties, Mike had graying hair, a strong chin, and a body that was still trim and hard. He shook my hand firmly when I got out of the truck— old-fashioned manners were part of Mike's personality.

"Hello, Gail. Thanks for coming so quickly."

"No problem. So, how's the horse?"

Mike was leading me toward the barn as we spoke. "He's not doing too bad," he said.

Mike owned an older gelding, a retired ranch horse. Sonny, a bay with a striped face, was tied to the hitching rail behind the barn. As I watched, he started pawing the ground.

"He's been like that for a few hours," Mike said. "Not bad, but he doesn't quit doing it. I thought maybe a shot and some oil would put him right."

"Looks like it might," I said. The horse wasn't sweating, and he appeared calm. In all likelihood, he wasn't very seriously colicked.

Colic was, in reality, a generic term for any sort of digestive disorder in a horse. Since horses can't vomit, an upset stomach is a potentially lethal problem, with complications ranging from twisted intestines to ruptured guts. However, many colics, and this appeared to be one, are fairly mild bouts of gas, easily treated and cured. Taking Sonny's pulse and respiration, I ascertained that both were only slightly elevated.

"I think you're right, Mike," I said. "I'll give him a shot of pain-killer, and oil him up. I think he'll be fine."

Mike nodded and patted the horse's neck. He wasn't a talkative man, or particularly friendly, but he always seemed fond of his horse.

Once I'd given Sonny a shot of banamine, and pumped mineral oil down his throat to speed the passage of whatever was in his gut at the moment, I took my leave, telling Mike to call me if the horse showed any further signs of colic. With any luck at all, I thought, the com-

31

bination of pain relief and subsequent relaxation, and the laxative effect of the oil, would fix this guy right up. I was halfway to my truck when Hannah, Mike's wife, called to me from the door of the house.

"Gail, would you like a cup of tea?"

"Sure," I said without thinking. It was always my impulse to respond affirmatively to offers of hospitality, even when, as in the present case, I really wanted to get going.

Instead, I followed Mike through the back door of the house and sat down at the kitchen table while Hannah made tea. She was a chatty, outgoing woman, a good example of that well known type, the church lady. Hannah and Mike were both very involved members of the local Bible Church, and Hannah was one of those people who took her religion seriously. She didn't preach or push, but I was aware that she made an effort, in all she did, to follow the tenets of her church and set an example.

She put a plate of homemade cookies and a cup of tea in front of me; I felt unexpectedly grateful. I'd forgotten to eat today, something that was happening to me more and more often. My appetite seemed to be gone; sometimes the first clue I would get that I was hungry was a feeling of unexpected weakness.

Tea and cookies were comforting, and filled the hole I had just noticed in my stomach. Mike and Hannah sat at the table with me and chatted. She talked about baking; he talked about riding his horse on the trails that rambled through Harkins Valley. I listened and ate cookies. I'd known these people ever since I'd first started practicing as a veterinarian. They were, if not friends, old acquaintances.

Suddenly Mike shifted the subject. "I hear you're going out with Clay Bishop."

"Once in a while." I looked at Mike in surprise. It wasn't like this dignified older man to make a personal comment.

"Would you accept a fatherly warning?" Mike leaned forward in his chair.

"I don't know," I said. "You can try me, I guess."

"Just be careful," Mike said. "I've known Clay and Bart quite a while. They're neighbors. I don't think either one of those boys is trustworthy."

Hannah sighed. "They have a very fast lifestyle, Gail. Mike and I have noticed."

"Well, okay." I wasn't sure what to say. Clay's brother, Bart, was known as something of a womanizer. But a fast lifestyle, to people like the O'Haras, might mean that beer was openly drunk on the porch, or that women were known to stay the night.

"You're a nice girl, Gail. I wouldn't want to see you get hurt," Mike said.

"Well, thanks." Once again, I sounded awkward. I had no idea how to receive this unlooked-for advice.

"I hope you won't be offended."

"No, I'm not offended. Thanks for thinking of me." I ate one more cookie and stood up. "I need all the help I can get. And thanks for the cookies and tea. Let me know if Sonny gets worse."

Mike stood up. "I will."

Hannah gave me a concerned smile. "Take care of yourself, Gail. You look a little tired."

I wondered if this innocuous woman, almost a stereotype with her short gray hair, flowered dress, and too-plump body, had some God-given gift to divine what was in people's minds.

"I will," I said again. "And thanks."

Mike walked me politely out to my truck. As I climbed in he said, "You won't forget what I told you, now."

I stared at him, trying to decide what to make of this. In the end, I gave a mental shrug. I just didn't have the energy. "No," I said. "See you later."

I started the truck and rolled out the driveway, watching Mike in the rearview mirror. He stood erect, shoulders back, in front of his barn, reminding me somewhat of an Old Testament prophet of doom. What in the world did Mike O'Hara have against Clay?

I regarded the Bishop Ranch even more curiously as I drove out the gates of Lushmeadows. The entire ranch property was now a mere five acres or so, and all the old barns and sheds that had once been part of a turn-of-the-century dairy had been reorganized as a boarding stable. This was run by Clay's brother, Bart, who lived in the big ranch house with his mother. Clay had a small house at the other side of the property. I couldn't see his truck in its driveway. Various people could be seen here and there, riding or leading horses; however, I couldn't pick out Clay or Bart. It was a cheerful scene despite the fog; all the old buildings and houses were painted barn-red. The big outdoor arena was full of riders, exercising their boarded horses, no doubt.

I drove on past, thinking of what Mike O'Hara had said. Granted that Bart, who was the horse trainer of the family, was known as a flirt and usually had some pretty client in her twenties on his arm, it still seemed odd to me that the normally reticent Mike would go to the trouble to warn me off.

Passing Nicole Devereaux's place, I could see the black mare in her corral; instantly my mind went back to this morning's call. Kids, I told myself. Seventeen-year-old boys, no doubt.

Only the roofline of Nicole's house was visible behind the dense hedge of rambling roses. I could see a curl of smoke coming out of the chimney. I pictured Nicole at work in her big room, a fire in the fireplace, perhaps some music on. Maybe jazz.

Kris's house was just ahead; I contemplated stopping by for the second time in one day, but gave up the idea. Afternoon was creeping toward evening; I needed to go home and get ready.

I had a hot date. With the slightly ominous, or vastly desirable Clay Bishop, depending on your point of view.

FIVE

Twenty minutes later, I stared at my naked body in the mirror, thinking morosely that this was all a big mistake. I'd showered and washed my hair, which hung lank and wet and dark around my face. All my physical flaws were glaringly apparent. Too much extra flesh on my waist and hips and thighs, increasing lines around the eyes, and worst of all, a dispirited expression in the sag of my mouth. Shit.

I straightened my spine, put my shoulders back, lifted my chin. Sucking my stomach in, I cocked one hip slightly and smiled at the mirror. Better. My breasts hadn't sagged yet, and posed this way, my body looked strong and curvy. With a smile pasted on it my face wasn't so bad—well-shaped, nearly blue eyes under dark brows, high cheekbones, wide mouth. The wrinkles were smile lines, I assured myself.

A moment of this and I rolled my eyes and let my body sag. This sort of classic feminine posturing only went so far with me. It was time to get down to reality.

Still, I watched myself out of the corner of my eye as I dressed. I liked looking at myself and the room, reflected in the slightly flawed glass of the antique mirror over the old dresser. This dresser and the matching bed, with their baroque, scrolling lines and deep mahogany-red wood, lent a certain dignity and gravitas to my otherwise very plain bedroom.

It was a simple room, a small, square box with one window, the walls painted soft white, the floor a grayed-white Berber-weave carpet. But the old bed with its carved headboard and footboard and the ornate dresser seemed, if anything, more resonant than they had ever been against the gentle, even cream. Picking up on the idea, I'd purchased undyed linen sheets and a cotton comforter in warm white, and let the furniture, which I'd inherited from my parents, speak for itself.

My mother's jewelry box, a beautifully crafted bit of rosewood with brass fittings, sat on the dresser. I opened it and took out a string of turquoise and lapis beads, transported back in a flash to a small girl who had loved to play with her mother's jewelry.

Fastening the beads around my neck, I paused. How often had I watched my mother do this, looking into the same mirror? I could see her vividly, as she had been shortly before she died, her neatly cropped brown hair just showing gray, her functional glasses perched on the end of her nose. For a woman who, in most ways, was a hardheaded, pragmatic sort, she'd loved personal adornment—clothes, makeup, jewelry. And despite my somewhat humble lifestyle, I felt I'd inherited a bit of this from her.

I stared at myself. It had been a long time since the image of my mother had come to me so powerfully. She, and my father, had died in a car crash in my eighteenth year. Suddenly I missed her. If she were alive, would I feel quite so lost?

My eyes filled with tears. I blinked them away and sat down on the bed, overwhelmed by the need for some sort of unconditional love and acceptance.

I have to get some help with this; the words repeated themselves in my head. The bit of paper Kris had given me was on the dresser where I'd unceremoniously tossed it. I stood, picked the scrap up, unfolded it. Dr. Alan Todd, it said. And a phone number. I put it back.

You haven't got time for another maudlin wallow in self pity, Gail. Get dressed.

Five minutes later I surveyed myself with a glimmer of satisfaction.

36

The amethyst-colored knit dress clung and flowed in all the right places; the scooped neck and scalloped edging on hem, neckline, and cap sleeves were subtly flattering. This dress, and the little black wool sweater that went with it, had cost a fortune by my standards, but I had to admit, I felt better about myself every time I wore it.

Black stockings against the fog's chill, comfortable black suede flats, and a slight application of eyeliner, lip gloss, and blush, and I was ready. My hair, mostly dried by now, waved and curled about my face. I ran my fingers through it and let it alone. Kris had encouraged me to wear it this way. "It looks sexy," she said. I seldom did so, but I was going to follow her advice tonight.

Roey's excited yaps alerted me to Clay's truck pulling up my driveway. Grabbing my favorite jacket, a woven silk blazer in a soft charcoal-black, I headed for the door.

Clay Bishop was getting out of his pickup in a slow, deliberate fashion, which was typical of him. He smiled at the leaping, barking Roey, ran his eyes over the house and garden, glanced down the hill at the horses. He'd seen all this before, of course, but it was like Clay to look at everything in this quietly appraising way. The more I got to know the man, the more I was aware of the level thoughtfulness hidden behind a serene exterior. Clay Bishop was a force to be reckoned with.

I liked this. Had I been feeling even a little more engaged by life, I probably would have liked Clay quite a bit. As it was, however, I felt tepidly pleased by his company and was content to leave it at that. I wasn't sure Clay was, though.

"Hello, Gail." Clay's smile was instant, warm, upon seeing me in the doorway.

I smiled back. "Hi, Clay."

No doubt about it, this was a handsome man. At roughly six foot, Clay was tall enough for my taste, which runs to large in men. He was slender, though, verging on thin, despite the well-developed muscles visible under the short-sleeved polo shirt. It was his face that made him so attractive; the high, hard cheekbones and nice blue-green eyes under strong brows were the perfect contrast to the blond mustache and the brownish-blond hair almost equally spangled with sun-bleached gold and premature silver. If his chin was a little weak, and his mouth a little soft, the mustache mostly hid it.

Clay held the truck door open for me, and I smiled to myself as I managed, only semi-awkwardly, to clamber in without revealing an undue amount of thigh.

However I looked at it, Clay was a good deal. Trouble was, I wasn't in a shopping mood.

Tonight's program was supposed to be dinner out and an early evening. I'd declined Clay's initial invitation to dinner and a movie on the grounds that I was on call. He'd amended it to dinner, with the understanding that he'd drive me home at any minute. How could I complain?

Riding beside him in the truck, I was happy to be quiet. The nice thing about dating someone to whom I was reasonably indifferent was that I didn't feel any big need to entertain the guy. If Clay found me boring, so be it.

You weren't indifferent to that guy you met last summer; I could hear Kris's voice in my mind. It was true, too. I had been a long way from indifferent to Blue Winter. The thought of him caused a little prickle to run down my spine, even now.

Tomorrow, I promised myself, tomorrow I'll go visit Blue. See if there are any sparks left.

"So, have you ever been to Clouds?" Clay's voice broke into my thoughts.

"No, I haven't. I've heard it's nice."

"I think you'll like it."

"I'm sure I will." There I went, murmuring conventional social chitchat. But I was damned if I knew what else to say.

"How's your horse doing?" I asked Clay. When in doubt, stick to horses as a topic; everybody loves to talk about their horses.

"Oh, Freddy's fine," Clay said easily. "I've been riding him back in the hills, some after work. That's his best lick. He's real good outside."

Unlike his brother, Bart, Clay's involvement with horses was minimal. He kept his bay gelding, a ranch horse he'd bought in Nevada, in the family stable, and rode him occasionally, but that was it. His only other contact with the family business was as a handyman. Clay repaired the old barns and fences, built retaining walls where they were needed, wired sheds for electricity . . . etc.

"Have you been riding much?" he asked me.

"When I can. I worked Plumber a little bit on the cow today."

"How'd he go?"

"Oh, he did fine."

Clay nodded. Once again we were quiet. The silence didn't seem entirely comfortable, but I simply couldn't think of anything to say. It was Clay who initiated conversation once again.

"I'm sorry I'm not being very good company. I just got back from a funeral; I guess it upset me a little."

"I'm sorry," I said. "Whose funeral?"

"A neighbor. A woman who lived down the road from us. She was my age; we'd been friends since we were children."

"That's too bad. She was young. What was her name?"

"Marianne," Clay said slowly. "Marianne Moore. I can hardly believe it." He looked across the truck at me. "She was murdered."

"Murdered?" I was startled. Murder wasn't what I'd expected to hear. Cancer, maybe. But not murder.

"Yeah," Clay said. "They found her out in her barn. Somebody had hit her over the head and killed her."

"That's grim."

"I know. She was a real sweet woman. We all felt terrible."

"It's hard to believe," I said. "Does anyone know why?"

"That's the weirdest part. There doesn't seem to be any motive. The cops are completely stuck. It's pretty terrible. I guess it's got me down."

"I understand."

We both lapsed back into silence, which lasted all the way to the restaurant.

Clouds turned out to be in downtown Santa Cruz, a place that was familiar to me from my childhood. In those days the little villages that dotted the county had boasted a grocery store, a gas station, and a restaurant or two, at best. For all major purposes, one had to go to "town." Which meant either Santa Cruz or Watsonville.

And the big store in downtown Santa Cruz was Leask's. This was an old-fashioned department store, family-run, a place where they had everything. Everyone shopped at Leask's.

Things had changed. Various malls sprawled about the countryside, a 7.2 earthquake had nearly demolished downtown Santa Cruz, and Leask's had folded. But change hadn't stopped there. The downtown area had been rebuilt, slowly and steadily, in a much slicker, more urban style, and was once again popular. And the space that had housed Leask's was now a movie theater and Clouds.

As we walked through the door of the restaurant I told Clay, "This is where I used to buy my shoes when I was a kid."

He smiled. "I remember. Me, too. This *was* the shoe department, wasn't it?"

I smiled back at him. This was one of the ties Clay and I had—we had been born and raised in Santa Cruz County. That was unusual; most folks who live in Santa Cruz, like the rest of California, are transplants from somewhere else. To be a second-, or in Clay's case, third-generation resident was uncommon, and it created a subtle bond.

Looking around Clouds now, I was struck by the strong urban flavor. This was no funky beach-town restaurant; this was a sophisticated, upscale, big-city bar, with an elegant little raised restaurant seating area alongside. My dress felt right at home.

"Would you like to sit down at the bar and have a drink?" Clay asked.

"I'd love to."

We settled ourselves on bar stools, me with a sigh of satisfaction. I like bars. Or rather, I like the restful and yet convivial atmosphere some bars seem to have, and Clouds, despite its sleek mahogany and stainless-steel exterior and trendy track lighting, had a good and friendly feel.

The bartender approached with an inquiring smile. "What'll you have?"

I ordered a vodka tonic; Clay chose a beer. She made my drink; I watched the deft, competent motions, no action wasted. When she placed the drink in front of me she gave me a friendly grin. I smiled back, thinking that maybe I would have been better off as a bartender. A lot less stress than being a veterinarian.

The woman poured and brought Clay's beer. "How's it going?" she said as she set it down. Judging by her tone, she knew him.

"Real well," Clay said. Looking at me, he added, "Gail, this is Caroline. Caroline, Gail McCarthy."

"Nice to meet you." The bartender and I got the words out at about the same time.

"Caroline's the best bartender in town," Clay said.

The woman grinned; she was instantly likable. Though I was sure that a certain outwardly friendly stance was an integral part of her job, she had a sparkle that seemed genuine.

"So how do you like this job?" I asked her curiously.

She smiled again; she'd learned to smile.

"Well . . ." I watched her think, fingering a charm hung around her neck. She was about my age and had wavy brown-blond hair that fell to her waist, confined in a simple ponytail. No makeup, eyeglasses, her one concession to the dressy style of the restaurant being an all-black outfit. But while the waitresses wore skimpy tube tops and tight low-waisted pants, she wore a simple fitted black shell and black jeans. Plain, professional, somehow elegant.

"It's a job," she said at last. "I've been doing it for ten years. I like this place," she added. "They're good people to work for." Then she grinned again. "But I'm not exactly using my education." Her hand moved; I saw that the charm she'd been fingering was a Phi Beta Kappa symbol. She was educated enough, then.

"What do you do for a living?" she asked me.

"I'm a horse vet."

I saw her eyes widen slightly; the mobile face became even more friendly. "Really?" Her eyes moved to Clay. "And you have horses, right? Is that how you met?"

Clay smiled, a quiet, self-deprecating smile, mostly in the eyes. "Yeah. Gail's my vet."

Another man sat down at the bar; Caroline moved in his direction.

I watched her go, thinking that her animated, fair-skinned face had an unusual quality. She wasn't exactly pretty—her features were a little too strong for that—but she had a lightness and a vivacity that were unique and perhaps more attractive than mere physical beauty.

"She's nice," I said to Clay. "Do you know her well?"

"Not really." Clay gave me that quiet smile. "Just from coming in here. She's friendly."

I nodded, picturing this handsome man sitting in the bar alone. Naturally Caroline would chat with him. Which is what you ought to be doing, I reminded myself. Good manners demanded it. Yet I found it difficult to make conversation with Clay. He responded easily and was always polite and friendly; still, I had a sense of a deep inner reserve.

"So, how are things going at the boarding stable?" I asked.

"Pretty much the same as usual. Bart's always got some new problem." Clay began to recount his brother's latest horse-training saga; I listened with half my brain. The other half was roaming around the restaurant, watching Caroline tend bar, checking out the various patrons.

Several women dressed in glamorous, big-city clothes sat together, laughing and talking. A blond girl in a white blouse and a silver-haired man, obviously a couple, leaned toward each other at the bar. A good sprinkling of single men, most of whom looked like young stockbroker types—a few of these were chatting in a desultory way.

As usual, and despite my overall mood, I found myself intrigued by watching people. The little details of face, hair, and clothing, the small nuances of how each chose to present him- or herself, were endlessly fascinating. And a bar was the perfect venue.

Clay had come to the end of his story. I smiled at him. "I like bars," I said.

"It's better then watching TV, anyway."

"Damn right," I said, with more emphasis than I'd intended. "TVs have ruined the neighborhood bar."

Clay's laughed. "That sounds pretty funny."

"I know. But I think it's true. People used to go out in the evening, have a drink with their neighbors, pass the time of day in a social way. Now they stay home and stare at that stupid machine, which proceeds

42

to mold their thought processes into a conventional pattern. It's a double evil."

"You think going out drinking is better?"

"Yes, I do," I said firmly. "Though it would be good if people walked or rode their bikes to the pub, like they would in a village."

"Or their horses," Clay added.

"That's right. I think having a drink and talking to people is a good thing, it's a slice of real life. It's," I stumbled a little, "it's living your life instead of absorbing this vicarious experience someone else has orchestrated. I think TV is terrible for people's minds. What they find attractive, what they want, how they look at the world, is all ordained by what they see on the stupid TV." I laughed. "I know I'm ranting on about this; it's a pet peeve."

"I'm surprised you don't have a 'Kill Your TV' bumper sticker on your truck," Clay teased.

"I would if I were the bumper sticker–type. I don't have a TV, I've never had one, so I never got to kill it."

Clay was smiling at me as if he thought I was amusing; I decided to put the ball in his court. "How about you? Do you have a TV? Do you watch it?"

"I guess I'd better watch my step here." Despite his words, Clay sounded relaxed and confident, unworried by my peccadilloes. "Yeah, I've got a TV. I watch it. I like the news; I like to rent movies, watch the occasional sporting event. That's about it."

"Well," I said, feeling mollified, "I do understand why people have them, but I still think the world would be a better place without TV."

"What do you do in the evenings when you're home alone?" Clay asked curiously.

"Read a book, play music, send e-mail," I replied promptly. Brave words. These days I mostly laid on the couch and stared at the wall.

"So why is the computer so different from a TV?" Clay asked.

"It's interactive. You have to use your mind." I was beginning to feel I'd gone on about this subject long enough. My drink was finished. "Are you hungry?" I asked Clay.

"Of course." He stood up and motioned to Caroline. "We're going to sit down at a table and have dinner."

"Right." Caroline gave me that engaging grin as I climbed off my bar stool. "Nice to meet you, Gail."

"And you," I said.

Clay had reserved a table for two in the corner, I found, and we were waited on by the owner of the place. The food was excellent, the wine also. Clay kept the conversation going smoothly. As we drove home, I reflected that it had been what you might call a perfect evening. My pager never even went off.

So, why then this sense of inner malaise, this apathetic distress?

When Clay pulled up in front of my house, I readied myself for the inevitable kiss. Not that I dreaded it. I just didn't feel much of anything about it, one way or the other. But instead of putting his arm around me, Clay sat quietly behind the steering wheel, looking through the windshield at my door. "How about a cup of coffee?" he said.

Uh-oh. A cup of coffee after a date . . . even I knew this was code for, "Would you like to go to bed?" And I was not, by any means, up for that.

"I'm sorry, Clay," I said. "I'm tired." Honesty compelled me to add, "It's not that I don't like spending time with you. But I'm not sure I'm ready for anything else."

Clay absorbed this without a flinch. Then he did put his arm around me. "How about a good-night kiss?"

I kissed him willingly enough; his mouth felt soft and warm. As I started to climb out of the truck, he took my hand and held me back a moment.

"I just want to tell you something."

I looked at him.

"I'd like to get to know you a lot better, and I'm willing to be patient."

"Well, thanks," I said awkwardly, swinging my legs out the door. "I enjoyed this evening."

Regulation words, but true enough. I shut the truck door and waved; Clay started the engine. In a minute he was gone. I stood on my porch, alone, wondering what possessed me. Why didn't I want to have a little fun with Clay?

Roey yapped at me from the dog pen. I let her out, then went to the barn and fed the horses and the cow. Then the dog and cat got their dinners, and at last, I could peel my clothes off and climb into bed.

Lying there, all alone in the dark, I could feel tears on my cheeks. Why was I crying? I didn't know, exactly. Just this endless sadness.

You have got to get some help with this; it was the last thought I had before sleep blotted everything out.

SIX

I awoke to sunlight and the sound of my banty rooster crowing. The sun poured into my bedroom through the uncurtained window facing east, spreading butter-colored patches over the cream of the walls and bedspread. The little rooster's slightly hoarse crow was as cheerful as the light.

Jack, the rooster, was somewhat unreliable as an alarm clock. He was apt to crow at two in the morning, or, as now, when the sun was already well above the horizon. I had no idea what went on in his tiny brain, but I liked his cocky crowing, and the sight of him and his mate, Red, pecking around the barnyard.

Looking out the window, I could see unfettered blue sky, for once. Inexplicably, the fog had vanished. Suddenly I wanted to get up.

All the morning chores were more pleasant in the summer sunlight. Rich red tints gleamed in the mahogany floor as I carried my cup of coffee onto the porch. Roses nodded brightly on the grape stake fence around the vegetable garden. This morning, I thought, I'll tie them in.

Contemplation of the day ahead brought an immediate wave of disconcerting disinterest. Chronic depression was such a boring thing, so damn repetitive. Once again, for reasons I didn't understand, the wheel was taking me back down. One minute I was reaching out in tentative enjoyment toward the sunny morning, the next I felt like going back to bed.

Forcing myself to my feet, I took my coffee down the hill and fed the horses and the cow. Then I walked around the vegetable garden, surveying the roses, trying to see them truly through my disenchanted haze. How beautiful they were, with their seductive subtle shades, romantic associations, and long history. Madame Alfred, a cream-colored flower just flushed with warm coral, tangled with the apricot Lady Hillingdon. Buff-yellow Rêve d'Or wound its way through the more intensely copper Crépuscule. Roses had become a passion of mine in the last year. I longed for them to lift my heart as they had once been able to do.

Roses made me think of Blue Winter, who grew them for a living. I had promised myself I'd go out to the rose farm this morning. For lack of any excuse not to, I decided to follow through on it.

I tied the Tea roses into the fence and weeded the tomatoes. Then I poured another cup of coffee and thought about getting dressed. I could hardly go traipsing out to the rose farm wearing my battered sweats.

Wear something sexy; I could hear Kris's voice in my head. Shutting it out, I chose jeans and a white tank top with just a little lace trim. A denim shirt worn open as a jacket, and my hair woven back into a French braid, and I was done. I had met Blue Winter on a pack trip last summer; he probably wouldn't recognize me out of jeans.

Driving toward Watsonville, I wondered what I'd say to the man. That is, if I even saw him. My last trip out here hadn't been very productive. Blue had been too busy to say much more than hello.

But today was Sunday. Surely if Blue was around at all, he'd be a little more free.

Why, just why, was I doing this? I felt like a teenager with a crush, not my favorite feeling. Clay Bishop was pursuing me avidly enough. What did I need with the apparently uninterested Blue Winter?

Who knew? He appealed to me. And what do you have to lose, my mind said in a detached tone. Nothing much.

By now I was pulling into the rose farm driveway, feeling like a complete fool. I wasn't exactly sure what I was here for. To look at roses, I assured myself. You like roses. I could see the display garden up ahead, roses draped everywhere, the big, vigorous vines and shrubs splashed with the vivid colors of the blossoms. Crimson, magenta, gold, pink . . . mingling in somehow harmonious profusion. I could smell the heady scent all the way from the parking lot.

Beyond the garden were the greenhouses, where the roses for sale were grown. And beyond the greenhouses, somewhere out of sight, was the trailer where Blue Winter lived.

I had never seen Blue's home, but he'd told me once he lived "out back." I stared around. At the moment, I didn't see anyone. The sign in front said the place was open. Next to the garden, a small office building sat quiet; no hints of life visible there. I got out of my truck and walked toward the garden.

Inside the gate, the roses invited me. Each one different from the others, as unique and individual as a horse, or a person. Here was the exquisitely formal cream-colored Madame Hardy, grown by the Empress Josephine. I bent to smell a blossom. This rose, this very plant, since roses are propagated by cuttings, had pleased Napoleon's lover.

A darkly golden rose with a mandarin-orange blush caught my eye and I stopped to search for the name tag.

"Lady Fortviot."

I looked up. Blue Winter stood on the other side of the fence, looking down at me from his six-and-a-half feet. "I saw you drive in," he said. The dog by his side wagged her tail.

Caught by surprise, I gaped up at him, at a loss for words. This tall, red-headed man appeared, as he had the entire time I'd known him, quietly composed. His steady gray eyes watched me thoughtfully from under the brim of a fedora hat. I couldn't tell if he was glad to see me or not.

His spotted dog, on the other hand, greeted me with more tail wags and a curvaceous little wiggle. Everything about her, from the ingratiatingly laid-back ears to the wildly waving white tail said that she, at least, was happy to find me here.

"Hi Freckles," I said. "Hi, Blue."

Another few seconds of quiet, and he seemed to sense my discomfiture. "Would you like a tour?" he asked me.

"Sure." What was it about this guy that rendered me so awkwardly tongue-tied? Some quality of inner stillness that he had made normal chitchat seem frivolous.

Whatever it was, I followed him about the rose garden more or less mutely, listening to his descriptions of the roses and asking occasional questions, the dog trailing in our wake. He took me through the greenhouses and explained the growing operation, showed me the shade houses with the retractable roof where the young plants were acclimatized. When we were done, he asked, "Would you like a cup of coffee?"

"Sure," I said, expecting to be led toward the office. To my surprise, he headed off in the other direction; I almost had to trot to keep up with his long, loping stride.

In a minute we emerged from behind the last greenhouse into an open field on the edge of a bluff. An unobstructed view out over the Monterey Bay rendered the grassy slope dramatic. In the foreground was a travel trailer under a small tin-roofed pole barn, the whole structure almost smothered with an exuberant wealth of climbing roses. Two wooden chairs sat outside the trailer door, under an arbor draped with rose vines. I stopped short with a smile. "Is this where you live?"

"Yes."

I could see corrals out back, with horses in them. One big dun gelding and one small sorrel mare. I recognized them from last summer's pack trip, Dunny and Little Witch. Blue was leading me toward the trailer. I followed him through the door.

Once again, I could feel a smile breaking out on my face. The trailer was old and the interior looked like the cabin of a boat, the walls and ceiling paneled in warm teak-colored wood. It was windowed on all sides and full of light. A couch, an old-fashioned desk in one corner with a computer on it, and a stout armchair were the only furniture. Blue walked into the minuscule kitchen and began making coffee.

"This is great," I said.

"It's little." He put the water on the stove and lit the burner.

"I like little houses. You should see mine. It's not a whole lot bigger."

"I'd like to." Blue smiled, showing crooked teeth and that unexpected sweetness I'd felt when I'd gotten to know him last year. I was reminded of the reason for my visit.

I watched his graceful hands as he poured the grounds into the filter, remembering the slender wrists, the red-gold hairs like fine copper wire on the long forearms. The surprising delicacy in such a big man. Artist's hands, I thought.

Staring at them now, I felt the same pull, an intense physical draw. Blue Winter's fair skin was roughened by sun and wind, and his eyes were lined. A strong jaw and a straight nose made his face handsome enough, but he had none of Clay Bishop's male prettiness. And yet I longed to feel those hands touch me.

Blue handed me a cup of coffee and our fingers brushed. Sure enough, I felt it all the way down in my stomach. The current was still there.

"Shall we sit outside?" he asked.

"Okay." I settled myself in one of the wooden chairs under the rose arbor; Blue sat in the other. The spotted dog lay at his feet. A peach-colored rambler draped a casual arm over my shoulder.

Blue caught my look. "Treasure Trove," he said briefly. Then, "So how have things been going for you since last summer?"

Now was my chance. "Well, I broke up with Lonny." Nothing like being obvious, Gail.

"That's too bad." Blue took a swallow of his coffee.

"Yeah, in a way. But we were both ready to move on. We're still good friends."

"That's good." Once more, Blue seemed remote.

"How about you?" I asked.

"I'm fine. Working hard out here, mostly." The distant tone in his voice sounded like a rebuff, but last summer's pack trip had created a subtle but intimate undercurrent between this man and myself, and I could feel it now. I sensed that Blue Winter was shy rather than aloof, and if I'd learned anything about him, it was that if you wanted to know something, you had to ask. He didn't volunteer much. So, I'd ask.

"Anyone new in your life?"

"No, actually. I'm pretty solitary."

"By choice?"

"More or less." He glanced over at me. "I'll tell you why, if you're interested."

"I'm interested."

Blue took another swallow of his coffee. I could feel him thinking. "I've been in two long-term relationships," he said at last. "Both of them lasted around seven years. The first woman I was married to, the second not. Both of them left me eventually. The last woman I lived with left me in about six months. That was a couple of years ago. I decided I was meant to live alone."

"Do you like it?"

"In some ways. I can do it. I traveled a lot when I was young, mostly alone. I'm used to being solitary." He glanced over at me again. "I'm used to feeling lonely."

His tone was detached, but I could feel the sadness.

"Do you plan to live alone for the rest of your life?" I asked him.

He shrugged slightly. "I think so. For a while, when I was young, I trained to be a Buddhist monk. I sort of see myself like that now, I guess."

I smiled at him. "That's too bad. I'd kind of planned on asking you out to dinner. Are all Buddhist monks celibate?"

He actually laughed. "It depends," he said. And then, "I'd go out to dinner with you."

I sipped my coffee with an inward smile. This was going better than I'd expected. Maybe Blue would be an antidote for depression. One thing was for sure, I really liked this man.

I was about to open my mouth when my pager went off, unpleasantly shrill. I hushed it and looked apologetically at Blue. "I'm on call. I need to phone the answering service."

"Of course." He stepped through the trailer door; in another minute he handed me a phone.

The woman at the answering service was brisk. "A Linda Howard has a horse that's very lame; she's afraid it's broken a leg."

"Give me the phone number," I said. Blue was already handing me a notepad and pen.

Number taken, I hung up. "This sounds serious," I told Blue. "I need to call this woman right away and get going. Maybe we could finish this conversation another time." I wrote my phone number down on a slip of paper and handed it to him. "Give me a call sometime, if you want."

"I'll do that." Blue folded the paper and put it in his jeans pocket.

I dialed Linda Howard's number. Her name was familiar, but I didn't know her. I thought she might be a regular client of my boss, Jim Leonard.

Sure enough. My "Hello, this is Dr. McCarthy," elicited "I'd like to speak to Jim, please."

"I'm sorry, I'm on call this weekend. Jim's not available."

The woman's voice was strained and angry. "Look, this is my best mare, and she won't put any weight on her right fore. Jim's been my vet for fifteen years, and I want him out here."

"I'm sorry," I said again. "Jim's off today. I'm sure he'll be happy to come out tomorrow."

"Dammit. I need him now. I've been a good client for a lot of years; why the hell can't you give him a call?"

I shut my teeth on the anger rising inside me. This situation came up occasionally; it was inevitable. Many of Jim's regular clients preferred to use him, and there was no denying he was a more experienced veterinarian. However, what some of them, like this lady, failed to recognize was that Jim had a wife and four kids and a private life of his own. Like most veterinarians, he deeply valued his free time; he would have shot me if I'd passed an emergency call on to him on his day off, merely because the client demanded it.

Patiently, I tried again. "I'm sorry, ma'am. Jim's policy is that only the vet on call is available during our off-duty hours. You can have me now, or you can have Jim tomorrow morning."

"Fuck." The expletive came out loud and clear; I held the phone away from my ear. Blue Winter winced.

Linda Howard sounded somewhere between rage and tears. "I need someone out here right now. I'm afraid her leg might be broken. I need Jim, dammit."

"Do you want me to come out or not?" I was getting tired of this.

"I guess so. It's 6380 Spring Valley Road." And she hung up the phone.

Great. I looked over at Blue, who was regarded me sympathetically. "I'd better go," I said.

"Not much fun for you."

"No. This happens some. I'm used to it. Believe it or not, I actually have a few regular clients who prefer me, and most of Jim's people don't mind me; I've been with him seven years. But there's still a few. This lady's going to be a ball, I can tell. But what can I do?" I stood up. "Thanks for the coffee."

"You're welcome." Blue stood, too. "I'll walk you out to your truck."

We walked in silence, Blue slowing his long stride to match mine. When we reached my pickup he gave me that unaffected smile.

"I'll call you. Maybe we'll have dinner sometime."

"I'd like that." I smiled back, realizing how much I hoped he meant it.

"See you later, Stormy," he said.

I started the truck. Linda Howard and her mare awaited me.

SEVEN

Two hours later all the good feelings I'd had on seeing Blue had evaporated in the chill of Linda Howard's hostility. Her mare had turned out to have what I thought was a bowed tendon rather than a broken leg, a vastly more fixable problem. But Ms. Howard was not placated by the good news. She watched me critically as I palpated, flexed, and eventually wrapped the leg, and listened with obvious disdain to my instructions for treating the mare.

"I'll call Jim in the morning," was all she said. No thank you, no apparent relief that the horse wouldn't have to be destroyed.

What the hell. It was part of the job. Now I was home, sitting on the porch, feeling like shit. Even the weather seemed in league against me.

The morning brightness had faded, and clouds came and went across the sky, alternately hiding and revealing the sun. Light and shadow played somberly over the ground. A restless little wind moved the air around, and I could feel the weight of my own mortality hanging heavy on me.

I stared out over my hollow in the hills, not cheered at all by its magic. I'd created a space of beauty and tranquillity here, all right, but for what? For the fleeting pleasure it gave me? Right now that seemed too transitory to be of any importance. I simply didn't know what I was doing it all for.

What is wrong, I asked myself, not for the first time. What is it that's missing in my life? Some sort of true-love, happily-ever-after scenario? I'd never expected or needed that before. Or was it some kind of spiritual grounding that was lacking? Again, this had never bothered me in the past. My job, my animals, my various interests had been enough. So what was so different now? I didn't know. I only knew I felt shitty.

The impulse to go inside and lie down on the couch, turn my face to the wall, was strong, but I fought it. I'd been a fighter all my life, struggling to put myself through college and vet school after my parents died, battling stress and monetary worries in my first few years working for Jim. Now, automatically, I fought the insidious lethargy of depression, pushing myself to keep going, keep doing, despite the lack of inward motivation. You are not going to give in to this; the words chanted in my brain.

I walked slowly down the slope toward the horse corrals. Plumber watched me coming and nickered. I could see the two banty chickens scratching in the straw outside the hay barn. Jack, the little rooster, was a silver lace, very elegant with his white feathers all edged in black. Red, his mate, a more pedestrian commoner, was just a little red hen.

Despite my mood, I smiled at the sight of them. Chickens are cheerful creatures, pecking and clucking around. Without thinking, I checked the big water trough where I kept water lilies and goldfish; sure enough, several tiny goldfish fry wiggled into the weeds as I peered; they'd been born in the last few days.

Plumber nickered again and came trotting up the hill toward me; Gunner ambled behind him. Life teemed and thrust everywhere around me. Once again, I turned to the natural world, in its constant effervescent liveliness, to comfort me.

I saddled Plumber, smoothing the nice wool Navajo blanket in shades of steel blue, black, and cream over his back. I'd bought the saddle blanket years ago to go with Gunner's bright bay coat, high white socks, and one blue eye; now Plumber had inherited it. It looked just fine against his smooth light brown hair, the color of coffee with cream in it.

Once Plumber was saddled, I shut Roey in the dog pen, gave Gunner a pat, and climbed aboard. I could hear Gunner's neighs behind us as I rode down the driveway; no horse likes being left alone. However, I knew from past experience that Gunner, a sensible animal, would settle down once we were out of sight.

The grass along the verge of the drive needed mowing, I noted. Just when was I going to get to that? One of the things I hadn't thought about in my desire to acquire a country property was the amount of steady work it would entail. I always seemed to be behind.

I rode out my front gate, Plumber walking calmly along the edge of the somewhat busy country crossroad I lived on. He was used to traffic, and unconcerned with the noisy automobiles that hurried past him. Still, I kept a cautious eye out for bigger trucks with flapping tarps, or other potentially horse-eating vehicular monsters.

In a little while we reached the crossing I was aiming for; I waited patiently by the side of the road, looking for a large hole in the traffic. Plumber stood quietly; one of the things I liked best about the little horse was his willing and cooperative nature. Eventually a gap opened up and we crossed the road, Plumber stepping confidently across the pavement. I smiled to myself, recalling the first time I had crossed this street on Gunner; my older horse had balked and refused to step over the white line, seeming to regard it as some sort of terrifying obstacle. But Gunner was a spook—not so Plumber.

Winding our way up the trail on the other side of the road, I thought about my two horses. How individual they were, in their reactions and temperament. And yet there was a basic sameness, that prey-animal mentality that differentiates horses from companion animals such as cats and dogs. Despite its size and apparent strength, a horse is always something small and vulnerable inside; its first reaction is flight rather than fight.

Hills rolled away on both sides of us, slopes of wild oats bleached gold in the fitful June sunshine. Clumps of tangled brush—greasewood, manzanita, sage, blackberry—broke up the grassland. Everywhere was the movement and scurry of the wild things, going about their business.

Quail scuttled along the ground, clucking to each other, cottontail rabbits sat up to listen and hopped away. A lizard ran up a nearby fence post. Louder crackling in a patch of dense brush fifty yards away was probably deer, though I couldn't see them. Plumber cocked his ears, unperturbed. He was used to deer.

These brushy California coastal hills were alive with wild animals; since I had moved out here, I had seen more varmints, up close and personal, than ever before in my life. A raccoon broke into the cat food bin almost every night; a bobcat had taken one of Jack's previous two wives right in front of me; a red-tailed hawk had gotten the other. Roey had twice been thoroughly skunked, and a big six-point buck regularly pruned most of my rosebushes.

Living in the brush meant living with wild animals—a joy and a trial. I was vexed with the deer's habit of preferring rosebuds to all other vegetation, and I wept over the two little hens; still, there was nothing like the sight of a gray fox skylined on the ridge, staring down at me with that peculiar intense stillness in its eyes. Or the time a coyote had parked itself under an oak and watched me ride my horse for half an hour. Or the day I had seen two Cooper's hawks mating in the top of a Monterey pine at dawn.

On and on it went, with every day full of these interactions, bright and sad, this endless dialogue with nature. I watched the sunlight on the shining wild grass, saw a red tree squirrel pick its way from oak top to oak top, following a highway I would never know. Plumber's ears moved forward and back, forward and back, as he walked along the trail.

Now the ground was growing steeper; we entered a grove of redwoods, the terrain instantly and dramatically different. Deep shade under the trees, a chill in the air, ferns clustered on the bank above the trail. It was quiet here, almost hushed, compared to the life and motion of the brush country.

Plumber walked; I let my gaze drift. An occasional shaft of sunlight slanted through the shadows under the trees. The air had a rich, loamy smell. The trail wound through the forest, leading upward. I knew where we were, and where we were headed. Upward, ever upward, toward the ridge.

I could see light through the trees; in a minute we emerged from the forest into more open country. Grass and brush, scattered clumps of madrone and oak. We were fairly high now—a tapestry of hills, like a cloth tossed down into folds, lay on all sides of us.

Rolling, gentle hills, the golden-eyed California Coast Range. Not steep and severe and dramatic, not intense as the Sierra Nevada Mountains were. No, this country was different, these brushy, brambly curves a complete contrast to the sharp silver granite edges of the mountain range where I'd spent my last vacation.

The Sierra Nevada—the range of light. I thought nostalgically of green meadows full of wildflowers and clear mountain lakes. The wind riffled through a clump of pampas grass by the trail with a paperlike rustling, and Plumber cocked a watchful ear.

Everywhere the brush country crowded around me, nearby slopes golden and olive and brown, more distant ridges fading to a misty gray-blue. The trail picked its way through a thick stand of ceanothus, arching over us like a tunnel. This wild lilac would have been a blaze of blue-violet, sweet-scented bloom in March; now, in early June, it was just a tall green shrubbery.

On we went, and up. The trail grew narrower, found its way through a grove of madrones, their graceful red-barked trunks like a curving, sinuous group of young dancers. Ahead was an opening, a small meadow crowning a hill.

I rode on, aiming for the high spot. Big vistas opened up where I could see through gaps in the trees that fringed the trail. Hills, rolling and tumbling away to the blue half moon of the Monterey Bay, visible now in the distance. In a minute I was on the crest, looking out over the coastline as a Spanish conquerer might have done.

These hills would not have been so very different then, I reflected, had such a one come here on horseback. These trees, obscuring and revealing that blue curve of water, these fields of dried grass flashing silver and gold in the breeze . . . all this would be the same. But to the invading army they would have appeared unknown and challenging, rather than friendly and familiar. How the hell are we going to get from here to there, they probably thought.

Good question, when you're on horseback in uncharted country. This little meadow was the destination I'd had in mind. Off to my right I could see a trail disappearing into a clump of oaks, a trail I knew would take me back home. I'd ridden this loop many times before. But off to my left was another trail, one I'd never explored. Today, I decided, is the day.

The new trail was steep, and it headed rapidly downhill through heavily forested country that blocked out all views. Plumber picked his way cautiously, bracing himself against the slope. I leaned back and concentrated on avoiding long poison oak vines that reached out across the trail. No use itching for the next two weeks.

Down and down we went, descending the other side of the ridge. I knew roughly where we were, but I had no idea where this trail was headed.

We bottomed out in a little valley, which had obviously at one time been a farm. I could see the remains of a homestead at the upper end, and most of the open ground was planted in apple trees. Neglected now, with brambles growing between them, the trees still survived, twisted and old and wild. Small green apples adorned the branches; I made a mental note to come back here in the fall.

Skirting the apple orchard, I picked up the trail, or a trail, on the far side, headed uphill. It looked reasonably well made and as though it were traveled some. I followed it. It took me up and over another ridge, and then followed a canyon deeper into the hills. Then, once again, upward through dusty open fields and clumps of scrub.

Here it was warmer, and Plumber was getting tired. He plugged on up the hills like the little trooper he was, but his neck was wet with sweat; I stopped often to let him rest.

Time to head back, I thought. The question was how.

I wasn't exactly sure where I was, though I could guess the general area. I had hoped that this trail would eventually take me in the direction of home, but it had not, and now I wasn't sure that it would. It led on inexorably inland, east, and I lived more or less due north.

On the other hand, I was bound to end up somewhere, I reassured myself. There just wasn't enough open land in this part of the world to get really lost in. Sooner or later I was sure to pitch out on a street or road, which I would no doubt recognize. The big question was when and where.

My horse was tired and I had no desire to end up on a major thoroughfare and have to follow it home. Even though Plumber was relatively unbothered by cars, the mixture of horses, traffic, and pavement is not a good one. Automobiles are just too big and heavy and plain-old lethal, especially driven by ignorant yahoos who think it's funny to spook a horse. And pavement is slippery and too damn hard to take a fall on. No, I didn't want to ride home along a road.

So just where the hell were we? The trail was going downhill again, plunging abruptly into a very deep redwood-filled gorge. Down and down we went, steep switchback after switchback, descending through the trees, toward what?

I could go back, I thought. I could always retrace my steps and go home. But that would be a long ride, and defeating as well. I wanted to see where we would come out.

So far the trail had been good, which was a relief. One of my worst nightmares is having a trail peter out in rough country. Usually by the time you realize the thing is truly impassable, you've struggled through some pretty tricky stuff, so retracing your steps is also scary. Not to mention, turning around can be damn near impossible. I was always very leery of this situation, and apt to turn back if trails begin to look too much like deer paths. But this one was still clear and apparently well-traveled. I saw the occasional hoofprint in the dust and now and then a pile of dried manure. Horses came this way, then. It was a passable trail.

But just where did it go? I was getting quite interested in the answer to this question. So, I was sure, was Plumber. If he could have spoken, I knew he would have said, "So, are you lost, or what?"

Well, I wasn't. I just didn't exactly, specifically know where I was, that was all. I still knew which way home was, and I knew that if I kept going in the current direction, I was bound to strike a road in the reasonably near future. That was good enough.

We'd reached the floor of the canyon—an awesome place. Redwoods towered up around us, somber dark pillars in a dim cathedral. Not a ray of sunlight penetrated down here. Far, far above, lacy green branches wove a tapestry with the blue of the sky. The walls of the canyon rose abruptly and vertically on each side; a little creek ran down the middle.

It was quiet, mysteriously quiet. Even though I knew this hushed silence was the nature of a forest, it could still give me the creeps. I always had the feeling someone was hiding, watching me. I infinitely preferred open grassland, or the lively scrub.

On we went, following the little creek through the dark canyon. I kept expecting to stumble on an old bootlegger's still, circa 1920, or for that matter, one of Joaquin Murieta's outlaw camps. The place had that kind of feeling. Hidden.

Finally the trail found a rift in the canyon wall, on the opposite side from the direction we came in, and began to climb. It was terribly steep.

Plumber literally scrambled to clamber upward, trying to find traction. I leaned forward over his withers, clinging to his mane, trying to put my weight where it was easiest for him to carry. I let him trot up each rise, and then breathe for several minutes on the switchbacks. Even so, his flanks were heaving. If this goes on much longer, I thought, I'll have to get off and lead him.

One more scramble and we topped out. Our trail T-ed into a trail that ran in both directions along a ridge, lit with late-afternoon sunshine. So which way to go?

I stood still for a few minutes and let Plumber catch his air, then chose the left-hand and more downhill direction. I thought civilization might be closer that way. And downhill was better than uphill. Always go downhill when lost. I wasn't lost, I assured myself, just confused. And Plumber was certainly tired. Downhill was better for him.

We hadn't gone fifty feet when I heard a distinct rustling in the brush ahead. Plumber heard it, too. He stopped, ears pricked sharply forward. Leaves crackled in a clump of greasewood to the left of the trail. Let it not be pigs, I prayed.

Wild pigs lived in these woods; I'd often seen signs of their digging and rooting. But I had never run into the actual animals, which was a good thing. Most horses are instinctively and majorly frightened of pigs; why, I don't know. But I had no reason to believe Plumber was an exception to the rule. Lad, the otherwise docile and well-behaved horse I'd owned as a teenager, had nearly killed me once when I tried to ride him through a pig farm. I could still remember the ungovernable fear that had sent him rearing straight up in the air and almost over backwards. I distinctly hoped I was not going to get a repeat of this.

Plumber's body stiffened; he raised his head. I could hear a stick breaking in the brush where the animal was. Maybe thirty feet away.

"It's just deer," I said out loud, in a voice meant to be calm. "Just deer, that's all."

More crackling—Plumber grew tenser. I shortened my reins, took a good grip on the saddle horn with one hand, and bumped him gently with my legs to remind him I was there and in charge. Plumber snorted. The brush rustled.

I stared; the horse stared. A branch of greasewood dipped; I saw motion, and what I thought was a hair coat. Tan, not black. Not pigs, then. But somehow I didn't think it was a deer. All four of our eyes, equine and human, were locked on the moving brush. And a cat stepped out on the trail. A big cat.

For a second, all my senses reeled. Not a bobcat. Too tall—the ears were rounded, the tail long and thin. The same brownish-gold, though. A cougar.

My God.

The mountain lion was about the size of a golden retriever dog. He stood in the trail and looked at us calmly, perhaps a little arrogantly, the tip of his tail twitching slightly. The horse and I were frozen.

For my part, I wasn't sure if I was more scared or thrilled. I'd always wanted to see a mountain lion in the wild. But I couldn't help remembering all the disconcerting stories that had been in the news recently.

The lady jogger killed by a couger up near Auburn, the young male hiker who had been chased by a cat here in Santa Cruz County—the animal had followed him all the way to a major road. My neighbor believed a cougar had taken his dog, and not too long ago I'd been called out to treat a horse that had been jumped by a big cat. The bloody, gaping bracelets around his neck came back to me in an instant.

I'd been told that cougars had chased horsemen before; I'd certainly been followed by coyotes when I was on horseback. There was no certainty that this wild animal would not attack us.

On the other hand, we were pretty big as a twosome. And I was man, master of technology, the creature who had dominated the world. Don't forget that, Gail.

One second more I stared at the big cat, memorizing the sight of that lithe and powerful form, the stare of the greenish-yellow eyes. Then I unbuckled and pulled my belt from around my waist, whirled it around my head, and kicking Plumber in the ribs, yelled at the cat, "Go on!"

Plumber started; he didn't exactly step forward, but he moved. The cougar flashed us a quick glance and leapt rapidly up into the brush and disappeared. Just like that.

But . . . I pondered the trail ahead. Did I really want to ride between those two banks, knowing the cougar was up there somewhere? No.

I turned Plumber, and looking over my shoulder, began walking back the way we had come. Well, jogging. Plumber jigged and pranced with agitation, not happy at all about the big predator behind him. I didn't blame him. Keeping a firm hold on the reins, I let him stretch out in the long trot, still looking back over my shoulder.

Nothing. The woods were empty and quiet. Too empty and quiet. Suddenly I'd had enough of solitude and this ramble through the hills. I was ready to see some people again.

Trouble was, none were in sight. We topped one hill, then another. More woods. Then some open ground. Then I spotted a downed barbed wire fence on one side of the trail. It was flat on its side, but this had once been a pasture.

Another rise, dropping down into brush. The trail was wider, almost a dirt road. Up we went, yet again, through walls of greasewood, ceanothus, madrone, Scotch broom. Over the crest, a sharp bend in the way, and suddenly I saw a house.

I almost felt like cheering. "We made it," I told Plumber.

Just an innocuous brown house off in the forest, not familiar to me, but it meant we were back in civilization. Sure enough. The dirt road went past the house, took another bend, and became paved. I could see a fenced pasture and more houses; I recognized the road in the distance.

Now I knew where I was. I'd ridden to Harkins Valley.

EIGHT

Harkins Valley wasn't all that far away from my house as the crow flies—obviously enough. It took me fifteen minutes to get here in my truck, mostly because of the route I had to follow to stay on pavement. But going cross country on horseback, I had simply ridden up and over the small range of hills that lay between the valley and my place, which was maybe five miles, if that, to the north.

Well, I thought, gazing around. Here I was. I'd emerged at the back of the Lushmeadows subdivision. I was now on familiar turf. I could see Mike O'Hara's place from where I stood; I started Plumber in that direction, following a trail that ran by the side of the road.

Lushmeadows had been built for horse people; these little bridle paths crisscrossed the whole housing tract. It wasn't a bad idea, and very convenient to me now, but I still found the place repulsive.

It was the basic sameness of everything that revolted me, I thought, looking at the houses. These houses had all been built by one man— the developer. They had no doubt been designed by an architectural firm, and though there was some variation, that in itself was repetitive. Here was a fake Tudor, here one with Greek pillars, here the ubiquitous Mediterranean-type with a tiled roof. Then a smaller, plainer ranch-style house (Mike O'Hara's), for those with less dollars, and back to the fake Tudor again. Yuck.

Even though many of the houses were so large and expensive that they qualified as mansions in my book, even though the parcels were a couple of acres at minimum (often much larger) and the land itself was beautiful, I thought the whole place was tacky.

What I wished for was a law that said a person could only build one house at a time—for him- or herself. No more characterless spec houses, created only to make a profit. Sure, some houses would still be generic, others would be downright ugly. People have different tastes. But at least each house would reflect the views of an individual, if only in which particular architect he or she selected. It was the lack of quirkiness in these big, dull, ostentatious houses that was so alarming. Houses like libraries, a friend of mine had once called them.

Mike O'Hara did not appear to be home. No car in the driveway; no sign of life. His bay gelding grazed in the pasture; Sonny looked fine. That was a good thing.

I rode on. Up ahead the street forked; I aimed for the big gate that was across the road from the Bishop Ranch. The houses were larger and more palatial along here, if such details as inappropriate colonnades and porticoes can make a spec house look palatial. This was prime territory. And just ahead was the extremely large and downright gaudy dwelling of Warren White, the developer-contractor who had created the Lushmeadows project.

I knew Warren; like everybody else out here he had horses, and I'd been called out to treat his Arabians once or twice. Kris had dated him for a while a few months ago as well, but that seemed to be over now. Still, as I passed his driveway I saw Warren and two other people out at the barn, talking, and one of them was Kris. They all looked my way.

I pulled Plumber up and waved, and Warren motioned me in. It was like him, I thought, to use an arrogantly curt hand gesture that seemed to leave no options other than to do as he asked. Though I had no doubt that Warren meant to be friendly, even his hospitality had didactic overtones.

Warren was rich. Not that being rich turns every man into a bossy little prince, but it sure seemed to have had that effect on this one. He was also blond, handsome in a superficial way, and single, and as one might expect, he considered himself God's gift to women. I couldn't imagine what Kris had ever seen in him.

Now, now, Gail, I chided myself as I walked my horse up the verge of the long concrete driveway, don't be so nasty. So you and Kris have different taste in men—so what? I hadn't liked Kris's ex-husband, Rick, either—another good-looking, wealthy, pompous ass, in my humble opinion. Well, maybe not so humble.

I passed the house—immense, rococo Mediterranean, painted an orangey pink with many palm trees around many porticos and colonnades, perhaps my least favorite house in the whole subdivision—and approached the little group standing by a white-board-fenced corral out at the barn. Kris, Warren, and a dark man I didn't know.

"Hi," I said.

Kris grinned. "So what are you up to?"

"Hello, Gail." Warren White was cordial. "Out for a ride?"

"That's right." I glanced curiously at the dark man.

He was the type to make you glance. Of medium height and strongly built, with wide shoulders and a narrow waist, he had dark olive skin and dark hair and eyes. He wore the hair fairly long, and he had good bones and a sort of young, healthy animal vitality that contrasted pleasantly with a face so classic it looked as though it might have been etched on an old coin. He was younger than I was—I'd guess late twenties or early thirties—and I suspected, of southern European origin. Italian, Greek, Spanish maybe.

Warren White followed my gaze and said, "George Corfios, Gail McCarthy. George works for me; Gail's my vet." Having placed both of us neatly in relationship to himself, he looked away.

"George just moved out here." Kris said this with a look at George that was quite plainly interested, or so I thought. So this was her latest boy toy. Or potential boy toy, anyway.

George himself said nothing, though his eyes went to me and he smiled briefly. It wasn't apparent whether he was aloof or merely shy.

"Where are you living?" I asked him.

"In Warren's barn." He looked directly at me as he spoke; I had a sense of strength reined in.

"George is one of my carpenters," Warren said. "He has a horse and needed a place to live, and I had this apartment over the barn and could use a caretaker."

Kris smiled at George again. "That's George's horse." She pointed to a gray gelding, plainly mostly Arab, trotting along the back fence, tail held high.

George looked back at me. "Perhaps we will be getting to know each other, since you are a vet."

His voice had just the slightest trace of accent; from his name I imagined that he was probably Greek.

"Well, I hope not too soon," I said and smiled. "If you take my meaning."

"I do." George smiled back. He was certainly handsome enough.

"Nice to meet you, anyway," I said. "Good seeing you guys," to Kris and Warren.

"Are you riding home?" Kris asked me.

"Maybe. Right now I think I'll ride over to the Bishop Ranch."

"Oh," she grinned. "Say hi to Clay for me."

Warren and George absorbed this exchange without comment and I smiled back at Kris. "I will. Have fun." I turned Plumber and started back down the driveway.

Five minutes more and I was across Harkins Valley Road and riding up the Bishop Ranch entry drive. Horses were everywhere, in wooden pens alongside the old barns, in portable metal corrals set up wherever there was space, in stalls with their heads hanging out over the bottom halves of Dutch doors. Clay had once told me that the Bishop Ranch boarded over a hundred horses.

The place was popular, I believed, partly because it was relatively cheap. Unlike some of the fancier boarding and training stables in the area, the Bishop Ranch boasted no covered arenas or mechanical horse walkers or extra warm-up pens. One large central arena, and access to the network of trails that ran through Harkins Valley—that was it. And, a more subtle distinction, the place had no particular orientation.

Many of the stables in the area were run by a trainer who had achieved a certain amount of recognition in a given field. There were dressage stables and jumping horse stables and cutting horse stables; there were stables that catered to the owners of Arabians who were into endurance riding. In contrast, the Bishop Ranch Boarding Stable was more generic, providing basic pens, stalls, and feeding at a reasonable rate to a motley collection of animals. Although Bart, the proprietor, did train horses, he had never competed much in any particular event; his expertise lay in breaking colts and retraining problem horses.

That is, if he had much expertise, of which I was not entirely sure. Horse trainer is a self-proclaimed title. Those who have tested themselves in the show ring can be said to have proved their abilities to the world; trainers like Bart, on the other hand, have merely hung out a shingle, and some of them, I had reason to know, caused as many equine problems as they solved.

I had no idea if Bart was in this category; I saw him occasionally when I was called out here to treat horses, and he always appeared reasonably competent; that was about all I knew. I had heard both good and bad about him through the client grapevine, but this was typical. No horse trainer can please everyone all the time, and as much bad-mouthing goes on in the horse business as in any other—some legitimate, some not.

Riding up the gravel road, I kept an eye out for Bart or Clay, but didn't see either. A blond woman came walking toward me, leading a paint horse.

I smiled and asked her, "Are Bart and Clay around?"

She gestured over her shoulder. "They're up at the big barn, mending a stall."

"Thanks," I said.

She smiled and kept walking.

Pretty girl, I thought, probably in her twenties. The majority of the people who kept horses out here were women, ranging from teenage girls to grandmothers, and these provided a seemingly inexhaustible pool of dating material for brother Bart. Hard to blame him, I supposed.

I'd reached the big barn, the largest structure on the ranch. Clay had told me it had once housed the dairy cattle. Since then the interior had been chopped up into several rows of box stalls. I dismounted and led Plumber inside.

Clay and Bart were about halfway down the main aisle; it looked as though Clay was rebuilding the door of one of the stalls. Bart stood there talking to him.

The two brothers didn't look much alike, I observed to myself. Clay was fairly tall and slim, of medium coloring; his brother Bart, on the other hand, was more short and stocky, with very dark hair, clear blue eyes, fair skin. Bart's chin was square and his nose was straight; he carried himself with his shoulders back and his spine a little rigid, whether because he wanted to look taller or had a bad back, I didn't know.

They were both handsome man, but to me Bart had that faint and indefinable air of arrogance that is an instant turn-off. Not so Clay.

"Hi," I said.

Both men looked at me; Clay smiled instantly and put down his tools. "Hello, Gail."

Bart's face registered neither pleasure nor dismay. He nodded in greeting.

"Did you ride over here?" Clay stood up from his job and walked over to me, patted Plumber on the shoulder.

"Yeah, I did. But not exactly on purpose. To put it bluntly, I got lost, and this is where I ended up."

Clay laughed. "I've done that."

"On top of which, I saw a mountain lion."

Both brothers looked immediately interested; this was news.

"Where?" Bart asked.

I described the spot, and he shook his head. "Damn," he said, "that's too close."

"Surely your horses aren't in any danger here, confined the way they are?"

Bart shrugged.

"I saw one not a month ago, riding through these hills," Clay said. "Jumped into the trail ahead of me and stood there for a minute. At

70

first I thought it was a big yellow dog and then it dawned on me what I was seeing. Pretty spooky, when you're alone."

"That's for sure," I agreed. "I turned around and went the other way, I can tell you."

"Are you planning to ride back?" Clay asked. "I'll saddle Freddy and go with you."

"Well," I looked at Plumber, who was snuffling his muzzle along the barn aisle, picking up bits of alfalfa hay, "I think my horse is pretty tired. I was wondering if I could beg a ride home in the stock trailer."

"Of course." Clay glanced over at Bart. "It's all hitched up, isn't it?"

"Yeah." Bart wasn't looking at Clay, he was looking at Plumber. "I wouldn't let him do that if I were you," he said to me.

I stared at the man in surprise. Granted that many horsemen prefer their horses not to nibble on things when they're on the lead line, it still struck me as an odd thing for Bart to say.

"I don't mind," I told him. "This horse is pretty well-mannered. I treat him like this because I like him to be relaxed." I tugged Plumber's head up; he complied willingly enough. "He doesn't need to eat your hay if you don't want him to."

Bart looked straight at me. "That's not the point. You need to teach that horse to pay attention to you."

I shrugged. "I don't agree." Turning to Clay, I said, "You don't mind driving me home?"

"Not at all," he said.

"Great, I appreciate it." I turned my back to the two men and started to lead Plumber off. "I'll wait for you outside," I said.

Jeez, what an asshole, was what I thought. Brother Bart, that is. To make the assumption that I was ignorant enough not to know the conventional rules of horse etiquette and the further assumption that I needed to be enlightened by the mighty trainer, argued a degree of arrogance that bordered on insolence, in my opinion. I was beginning to be sure I didn't care for Bart.

I led Plumber out of the barn, tied him to the hitching rail, and leaned against it. It was late afternoon and the sun was resting on top of the western ridge. In another fifteen minutes it would be out of sight, and I could feel the chill of incipient fog in the air. I was glad I'd asked Clay to drive us home.

Watching as the two brothers checked out the dually pickup and stock trailer, it struck me that Bart was constantly posturing dominance in his body language and speech, always trying to be in charge. Clay seemed inured to this, or at least he didn't react to it. Yet I didn't have the impression he was submissive, merely indifferent.

Everything being pronounced in working order, Clay pulled the rig up in front of the barn.

Bart opened the stock trailer door. "Want me to load him for you?"

"That's all right. I'll load him," I said.

I led Plumber into the stock trailer, and he followed without hesitation; he'd been hauled many miles in his lifetime. Tying him in the front, I walked back out. Bart shut the door behind me and latched it.

"If you ever want to take any lessons on that horse, just let me know," he said.

"If I do, I will," I said, hoping that I didn't sound as curt as I felt. I had no wish to antagonize this man, but he was really getting on my nerves. That reflexive, defensive need to prove himself superior—it was a trait I'd run into in other men, and it was not a quality I was particularly patient with. "Thanks for your help," I added, trying to be polite.

"No problem." Bart looked to me as though he sensed my antipathy and returned it. Oh well.

I climbed in the passenger side of the truck and let out a small sigh of relief as Clay pulled out of the Bishop Ranch driveway and on to Harkins Valley Road.

We passed Nicole Devereaux's house; I saw the black mare in her corral under the apple tree. Then we were winding up the canyon toward Kris's place. Clay was good at hauling a horse trailer, I was pleased to find. He didn't take the curves too fast, and Plumber was riding quietly.

"Thanks for doing this," I said. "I really didn't want to ride home."

"I know how you feel," Clay said. "I've gotten myself lost back there before."

"What did you do?"

"Wandered around until I found my way back out." Clay smiled. "It's not that big of an area; it's pretty much impossible to get really lost."

"That's what I was telling myself," I said.

Clay smiled again. "When I'm exploring trails back there it always reminds me of gathering cattle with the rancher I bought Freddy from. He runs a lot of cattle up near Winnemuca and I used to go out there in the fall and help him gather. We'd be pushing some group of steers along and a few of them would break away and take off, headed for somewhere else. I'd always get all excited and think I had to take off after them, but that old man would never turn a hair. He never got out of the trot, either. He'd just look at me kind of tolerantly and say, 'Relax, son. They got the Pacific Ocean on the left and the Atlantic Ocean on the right. Where they gonna go?'

"So that's what I tell myself as I wander around in the woods. You got the Pacific Ocean on the left and the Atlantic on the right. How the hell are you gonna get lost?"

I laughed. "I'll remember that," I told him.

Clay pulled the rig up my driveway and I unloaded Plumber and put him back in his corral. It was late enough that I fed both horses and the cow. Clay stood there, looking indecisive. I'd already thanked him for bringing me home; now I wondered if I should invite him in for a beer. I didn't really want to; I wanted to flop down on the couch with a glass of wine and relax. But maybe politeness demanded I be more hospitable.

I was about to open my mouth when the phone rang, making my mind up for me. "Thanks again," I said hastily to Clay. "Got to get that. See you later."

Dashing up the hill and through the door, I managed to grab the phone before the answering machine picked up. "Hello," I said breathlessly.

"Hi, babe," said a voice both friendly and familiar. Lonny.

"Hi." I sat down on the couch and began unlacing my boots, holding the phone between my shoulder and my ear.

"I just called to say hello, see how you were doing." Lonny sounded cheerfully upbeat, his usual tone.

"I'm doing okay," I said. "How about you?"

"Not too bad. I finished building the house last week. Good to have the construction crew off the place at last."

"How's everything going otherwise?" I asked him.

"Real well. I've been going roping a lot." Lonny's voice was friendly and familiar all right, and at the same time distancing, the pleasant voice of an old acquaintance, all intimate undertones gone.

"What's going on in your life?" he asked.

"Not too much. Work. I've been riding Plumber some," I said guardedly.

"You doing okay?"

"More or less. I've been a little down, I guess. How about you? Seeing anybody new?"

"Oh, there's a woman around here I go out with from time to time. Nothing serious. And you?"

"The same." I pictured Lonny's rough-featured face as I spoke, remembered how this older man had been a rock of strength and comfort for me. "I miss you." I said spontaneously.

"Me, too." Lonny sounded sincere, but still quite cheerful. It was not his nature to let much of anything get him down.

"Actually," I said cautiously, "I *have* been pretty down lately. I think I'm going through a real depression." If I couldn't tell Lonny, who could I tell?

"Don't do that, Gail. Your life is good. Don't let yourself get depressed."

"It's not something I'm choosing," I snapped. "Depression's not like that. It's something that's happening to me."

"Hogwash. Tell yourself you're happy and you'll be happy."

I said nothing. Lonny meant to help me, I knew. I also knew he took his own advice, and to be fair, it worked for him. No doubt Lonny had never been depressed a day in his life. He had no understanding of the way I felt.

"How are your horses doing?" he asked cheerfully.

"They're fine. How's Burt and Chester and Pistol?"

"Doing good. Pistol's lame, of course, but he's happy, out in the pasture."

More conversation followed, along pleasant, innocuous lines. I made no more attempts to talk about my problems. Lonny and I had never dealt with these kinds of issues very well when we were together; why had I imagined it would be different now?

I managed to end the conversation on a positive note, sincerely wishing Lonny well, and promising to call soon. I hung up the phone knowing how fond of him I still was, and sure that he'd always be a part of my life. At the same time, another part of my mind acknowledged how much I had wished this call was from Blue Winter. And yet another part just plain didn't care much at all, about anything.

I finished pulling my boots and socks off and got up and poured myself a glass of wine. Sitting back down on the couch, I thought sadly that it was true that I missed Lonny. I missed the security and comfort of my life with him, and in many ways I still loved him. But there was no going back.

NINE

I drove to work the next morning on automatic pilot, trying to put my thoughts and emotions on hold and devote all my energy to getting done what needed to be done. It was a struggle. But my heart did lift a little when I drove into the office parking lot.

There it was, the new sign that had been put up only a month ago. SANTA CRUZ EQUINE PRACTICE. DR. JIM LEONARD AND DR. GAIL MCCARTHY. My boss had made me a partner in the firm. I was on the sign, after working here for almost seven years.

It was a good feeling, in the midst of a lot of difficult ones. Jim was not an easy man to work for, but I'd achieved a decent professional relationship with him, and along the way, earned his respect, or so I thought. Given his demanding, perfectionist tendencies and the short history most of his junior vets had enjoyed, I was proud of what I'd done.

I was less proud five minutes later as I stood in Jim's office discussing Linda Howard's mare. Knowing Jim's habit of coming into work an hour early, the woman had called him at seven o'clock sharp, and he had, in the ensuing hour, been out to see her mare and come back.

"That mare had a fractured splint bone, not a bowed tendon, Gail. And she needs surgery to remove a bone chip."

I stared at Jim wearily. He was, no doubt, right. Jim was a virtual wizard with equine lamenesses, what those in the trade called a "good leg man." His knowledge was almost intuitive; Jim could look at a lame horse and know instinctively what was wrong with it, though sometimes it was difficult for him to explain exactly how he knew. Long years of experience in treating horses had created a backlog of useful mental images that Jim could access at will. Having many fewer practicing years under my belt, I was at a distinct disadvantage when it came to diagnosing more obscure problems, or correctly interpreting delicate nuances.

"How did you know?" I asked him.

"It's subtle," he said charitably. "When you saw the mare she was probably so swollen that it was hard to tell. But once she'd been wrapped for twenty-four hours and the swelling was down, I could feel that the tendon was fine, and it was easy to palpate a big lump on the inside of her cannon bone." Jim shrugged. "It was an understandable mistake."

"I see. I'll bet Linda Howard didn't say anything nice about me."

Jim said nothing.

"She likes you," I said. "She was pretty unhappy when she couldn't get you out yesterday."

Jim still said nothing. I knew that he knew that some of our clients preferred him to an extreme degree. There was little either of us could do about it. But I hadn't done the office any favors by making a mistake with an already hostile client.

I sighed. "Sorry," I said.

"It was a tricky one." Jim didn't sound particularly upset. "I could have made the same mistake if I'd seen her first."

"Thanks," I said. But I was pretty sure that, in fact, he would not have. Jim wasn't often wrong. I'd learned an incredible amount in the years I'd worked under him, and I was still learning. Even at the worst of times, when long hours, low pay, and Jim's sometimes derogatory attitude had really gotten on my nerves, his abilities as a veterinarian had always been such an inspiration that I'd only become more determined to stay the course. And now, now I was committed.

This was my practice, this was my life. Jim and I had worked out a deal in which he would retire in ten years and I would, at that time, become the sole proprietor. It was what I had always wanted, and I had finally made it happen.

So how come I didn't feel better about it? My reverie was interrupted by the receptionist, who came through the office door and said, "Gail, June Jensen has a newborn foal. She wants you to come out right away and imprint it. She says Gordon's out of town."

"Oh," I said. I looked at Jim. Imprinting a foal was something clients normally did themselves, and it would take me at least an hour.

Jim shrugged. "Go ahead and do it. I'll handle anything that comes up. Make sure she pays for it, though."

"How much?"

"A ranch call, an emergency call, and a full exam charge."

"Okay." I started for the door.

Jim's voice trailed after me. "Get back as soon as you can. I'm doing a surgery this morning, and I want you to help me."

"Okay," I said again.

June Jensen lived in the Soquel Valley, in my old neighborhood, in fact. Driving to her place on Olive Springs Road, I went right past the little cabin I'd lived in for five years. There were flowers in the window boxes; it looked like the new owner was taking care of the place. I smiled at it affectionately as I passed, but felt only the mildest of nostalgic twinges. My property in Corralitos had become home.

June and Gordon Jensen had a pretty little spot that was bounded by Olive Springs Road on one side and Soquel Creek on the other. Their older farmhouse had been remodeled just enough to be clean and comfortable and not so much that it had lost its character. Behind it, a small barn and corral occupied the patch of meadow next to the creek.

June came out of the house as I drove in. A woman of about my age, she was a little plump and distinctly unglamorous, prone to wearing jeans and baggy sweatshirts. She was also not a horse person; it was her husband, Gordon, who owned the bay mare that produced a foal every year.

"She foaled two weeks early, Gail," June was already talking as I got out of the truck. "Gordon will be back tomorrow, but that's no help now. And you know how he feels about imprinting these babies."

"Is the foal doing okay?" I asked.

"I think so. I came out this morning to feed, and she was standing there, nursing. I almost dropped the grain bucket, I was so surprised. Tiz usually foals right on schedule."

June was leading me toward the horse corral as she spoke; I could see mama and baby ahead. Everything looked reassuringly normal.

I knew Tiz, the bay mare, well. Gordon Jensen had owned her for many years. A registered Quarter Horse with a fancy pedigree, Tiz was well made and kind-natured. Every year Gordon bred her to a different stallion, raised the baby up to weaning age, and sold it. He made a small profit on the colts, enough to pay for his horse-keeping expenses, which was important to him, I knew. Gordon and June didn't have a lot of money.

"How do you want to do this?" I asked June.

"I'll hold Tiz," she said promptly, "and you imprint the baby. I do this with Gordon every year. I'm used to hanging onto the mare."

"I take it she's okay with this." I looked questioningly at June. Some mares were extremely protective of their babies and could be downright violent.

"She gets a little upset," June said, "but not bad. She's never tried to bite or kick us or anything."

"Good," I said. "Do you want to catch her?"

"Could you do it?" June glanced at me diffidently. "I'm not all that used to putting the halter on; I'll probably fumble it. I can help you corner her."

"Sure." I took the halter she handed me. I was fairly used to catching clients' horses. It wasn't my preferred method, but I often ran across this situation. Since I knew Tiz, it wasn't an issue, but I'd nearly been flattened last week by a brown gelding that belonged to a teenage girl who couldn't catch him.

Shaking my head at the memory, I slipped between the boards of the horse corral, halter in hand. June followed me. Setting my emergency bag down on the ground just inside the fence, I started toward the mare.

Her head came up as soon as she saw me, and she placed her body protectively between me and her baby. The foal, a sorrel filly, moved restlessly on her long legs, not sure whether to be curious or alarmed.

"It's okay, Tiz," I said reassuringly. "You know I'm not going to hurt your baby."

Tiz was having none of it. Even though she produced a foal a year, and this process was undoubtedly familiar to her, the brand-new creature by her side brought out all her maternal instincts. At some level she understood that I was not really a threat, but her genes told her to keep her vulnerable foal safe from any possible predators.

I walked toward the pair, June following me, and Tiz trotted away, tail held high, nickering at her baby to follow. The baby whickered back and trotted, then loped, after her mother. Even though I had seen it many times before, I smiled in delight at the sight of the several-hours-old filly manipulating her long legs into the rhythm of a canter, looking remarkably coordinated and confident.

Horses were amazing this way, I thought, as June and I began walking Tiz into a corner where she could be more easily caught. Like other large prey animals, deer for instance, their newborn young were ready to keep up with the herd in an hour or so.

This filly was pretty damn lively. She galloped alongside her mother, moving with little apparent effort over the ground.

"Nice strong foal," I said to June.

She smiled. "I hope Gordon will like her."

At this point we had Tiz in a corner. The mare stopped, once again placing her body between us and the baby.

"Come on, Tiz, you know we've got you," I said calmly, and walked quietly towards her.

Tiz's head came up, but I could see a certain acceptance in her eyes. I walked to her shoulder and patted it, then slipped the lead rope around her neck.

The mare nickered anxiously to her baby; I used the lead rope to control Mama as I put the halter over her nose and behind her ears. Once the halter was buckled in place, I relaxed. Tiz was safely caught. Now for the baby.

Handing the mare's lead rope to June, I walked around Tiz's body and approached the filly. Head up, eyes big, the little horse watched me. Stepping slowly toward her, I held my hand out. A diminutive muzzle stretched in my direction, delicate and whiskered. The baby sniffed my hand curiously. Then she scooted away.

Tiz neighed again and stomped her front feet. June bumped her with the lead rope and said, "Whoa." I began following the filly. It took me about five minutes to catch her, but once I had my arms around her body, she struggled for only a few seconds and then held still.

Imprinting a foal is an interesting process that has recently become popular with some of the more enlightened horse breeders. The idea is to handle the colt a great deal in its first few hours of life and accustom it to a wide variety of things—having its body confined, its feet picked up and worked on, a halter put on its head and used to lead it, other routine handling. The theory behind all this is that a horse will take an imprint of these actions, and in later life, will be much more relaxed and confident in the breaking and training process, and thus much easier to handle.

Imprinting worked, as far as I was concerned. It didn't change the basic personality of the horse; some imprinted colts were more lively and fractious than others. What it did was dramatically decrease a horse's instinctive fright at having its body confined in any way. As a prey animal in the wild, a horse's major defense is its ability to get away and run—fast. Thus horses react very unfavorably to anything that diminishes their chance of doing this—being controlled by a lead line, having their feet held up. Imprinting seems to give horses some security in these areas; just as they bond to their mothers in that first hour, so they also absorb the message that this confinement is okay.

For the next hour I went through the imprinting procedures that I knew; June told me a few more that Gordon regularly used. I held the filly and picked her up so that all four legs were off the ground; I lifted each foot in turn and tapped on the bottom of it; I put my fingers in her ears, nose, and mouth; I draped a soft rag over her back and fanned her gently with it; and I put a halter on her and led her a few steps. I also put a little iodine on her navel to prevent infection and noted that the placenta, which I found nearby, looked complete.

The baby responded well to my efforts; once she tried to kick me, but she gave in fairly easily and I felt she had taken the imprint. Stroking the dainty arched neck, curved like a seahorse, with its fine ridge of curly baby mane, I said to June, "I think this is enough. We don't want to exhaust her. Have Gordon catch her and do this stuff again a couple more times when he gets home. I think she'll be fine."

"Thanks, Gail." June slipped the halter off the mare and turned her loose. Tiz moved away a few steps and then stopped; immediately the filly began to suck.

"How much do I owe you?" June asked me as we walked out to my truck.

Calculating rapidly in my head, I charged her for a ranch call and an exam, purposely neglecting the emergency charge Jim had told me to add on. This call would be expensive enough for the Jensens without that, and I hadn't really spent that much time here.

I could hear Jim's voice in my head. "Don't be such a soft touch, Gail. We're in this to make a living, you know."

Rebutting it with a mental, "The practice is doing real well, Jim, and it's not good business to overcharge people," I accepted the check June wrote out for me and said my good-byes.

I wasn't in the truck two minutes before the car phone rang. The receptionist sounded a little frantic. "I've got two calls for you, Gail, and both of them are saying they're emergencies. One is a horse that's been sick for a week and Jim's been treating it, but he isn't sure what's wrong with it. Today the horse is a lot worse and two other horses in the barn are sick.

"The other call is a woman who says her horse has pigeon fever, she thinks. She wants the vet out right away. And Jim's off dealing with a colic."

"I'll see the client with the horse that got worse," I said. "Pigeon fever's not really an emergency. Call the woman and tell her that, and that I'll be out later today."

So it went. The sick horse turned out to have a case of what we called bastard strangles. The only reason I was able to diagnose this was that the two other horses that had just come down with the disease were exhibiting the more normal form of strangles, characterized by a snotty nose, a mildly elevated temperature, and abscesses under the jaw. Occasionally strangles went underground, so to speak, and the abscesses were internal. Such cases were hard to diagnose, the horses tending to show few symptoms other than fever and general malaise.

I diagnosed and treated this group; the man who owned them wasn't happy at all. "Dammit, if I'd known this was strangles I would have isolated the first horse so the others didn't get it. Jim told me he thought it was some sort of internal infection and not contagious. So I left the horse in the barn with the others. Now the whole herd's going to get strangles."

There wasn't much I could say. The man was probably right about the whole herd getting the disease. Since he raised Morgan horses and had somewhere between twenty and thirty head on his place, this was a fairly major problem.

"I'm sorry," I told him. "Bastard strangles can be hard to catch. We can vaccinate the ones that aren't sick yet; they might not catch it."

"How much will that cost?"

"Twenty-four dollars a horse."

"Shit," the man said forcefully. He was mad, I knew, not at me, or even at Jim, but just at the whole situation. Strangles is a real nuisance of a disease.

He eventually agreed to vaccinate the rest of his herd; I gave them the nasal injections and took my leave.

Driving away from yet another unhappy client, I called the office to see what was most pressing. The receptionist sounded even more stressed. "Gail, Jim wants you back here right away. He's ready to do that operation."

Back to the office, where I helped Jim take a bone chip out of a polo pony's ankle. Then out to a colic—by far our most frequent emergency call. Then another lame horse, followed by one with a cut on its forehead that needed to be stitched. It wasn't until the end of the afternoon that I made it up to the little mountain town of Boulder Creek to see the horse with pigeon fever.

Sure enough, this Peruvian Paso mare had the characteristic swelling on her chest. And her owner was mad as hell.

"I called early this morning and said I wanted somebody out here right away," she snapped.

"Did the receptionist call you back and explain that this isn't really an emergency?" I asked.

"In your opinion." The woman wasn't mollified.

"We often don't even treat this," I said. "Once the abscess bursts, you can clean it out every day with some hydrogen peroxide. But this one isn't ready to open yet," I added, feeling the swelling gently. "As long as this mare is eating and drinking well, there's nothing to do but wait."

"That's neither here nor there. When I call your office and say I need a vet right away, I do not expect to wait eight hours. What if this horse had been dying of colic?"

"Then I would have come as soon as I could. I made the judgment that your horse could wait, based on what you said was wrong with it. And I was busy all day treating horses with more immediate problems."

"I'm not impressed. I think your behavior is totally unprofessional, and I will write Jim a letter saying so."

"Fine." I climbed back in my truck. "Do what you need to do."

This did not improve the situation. The woman was still working on an irate tirade when I shut the pickup door. I'd just plain had enough.

Wearily, I drove back toward Santa Cruz. This kind of thing happened. It was inevitable; it was part of the job. No need to let it get me down.

But it did get me down. Everything got me down, or so it seemed. The least little bit of stress and/or adversity sent me reeling. Tears leaked out of my eyes as I drove the truck back toward Santa Cruz. It just isn't working, I thought. I am just not doing okay.

I made it back to the office feeling tired and defeated and sad, very sad. Sitting down at my desk, I stared at the phone. I didn't want to go on feeling this way; I wasn't sure I *could* go on feeling this way.

Reluctantly, I dug the scrap of paper out of my pocket. Dr. Alan Todd. Kris had said he was good. I hoped she was right.

84

TEN

I was lucky. Dr. Alan Todd had a cancellation. He would see me tomorrow evening at five. Wonderful. And yet, despite my reservations, I did feel better. At least I was doing something about this damn depression.

Right now I was on my way to Nicole Devereaux's, and I was feeling pretty good about that. I'd grabbed a quick dinner at Café Cruz, and I was about to arrive right on time.

I was looking forward to seeing Nicole, I realized, looking forward to spending some time studying her work. The paintings had left an imprint on my mind, one I hadn't forgotten.

Pulling into Nicole's driveway, I parked next to the rambling rose hedge and looked around. No front door was evident. The one time I'd been here I'd gone in the back door. Tentatively, I started in that direction.

Nicole came out the garden gate. She smiled when she saw me. "I see you were remembering the way in."

"Yes," I said. "Is that the only door?"

"Yes, there was a door on this side," she gestured toward the road, "but I had it covered over when I turned the house into my studio. The rose hides it now."

"Oh." I followed her toward the kitchen garden. "It's your house then?"

"No, it belongs to a friend. She allowed me to do the, how do you say it, remodel."

We followed the path toward the Dutch door, and I glanced automatically at the roses. A graceful cream-colored beauty weaving its way between sky-blue spikes of delphiniums made me ask, "Is that Devoniensis?"

"Yes." Nicole smiled quietly.

I made a mental note to someday acquire that rose for my own garden.

Then we were in the house, and I was once again entering the room of the paintings. With a jolt of recognition and delight, I stared around, my eyes resting on one intense wash of color and then another. The paintings were all that I remembered; brilliant, evocative, and mysterious, they beckoned, inviting me closer.

Seeing, I suppose, my rapt expression, Nicole said, "Take your time. Look as much as you would like. Would you care for a glass of wine?"

"That would be lovely."

"I have a Pinot Gris that is open."

"Wonderful." I could not take my eyes off the painting in front of me. It was the one I had noticed when I was first here, predominantly tawny amber in color, undulating like hills, with areas of warm olive green and a central shape of deep cobalt blue. As in all the paintings, a delicate tracery of black inking rendered the work subtly shadowed, coaxed me to examine it more closely.

I stepped forward. Intricate as a garden spider's web, the faint lines somehow evoked leaves, and yet the patterns were almost geometric. And that deep, pure blue, like a body of water.

Nicole handed me a glass of chilled white wine. I took a sip. "Do you mind if I ask you a lot of very naive questions?" I asked her.

"Of course not." Once again, she smiled. "I am hoping you will ask me questions."

I gestured at the painting. "Does this represent a landscape, or is it abstract?"

Nicole thought. A long pause ensued, in which I could see her thinking. "It is both," she said at last. "If you would like, I will tell you a little about the paintings."

"Please."

"This one," she looked at the painting I was studying, "and most of the others that are here, were, how would you say, inspired by a particular time and place in my life. Then, I lived in a town called Cadaqués, on the Costa Brava, in Spain." She looked at me inquiringly.

I shook my head. "I've never been to Spain."

"Cadaqués is very beautiful," she said. "The landscape is very austere and rocky, and the sea is lovely colors. The little town is whitewashed, with small, crooked cobblestone streets. The artist Salvador Dali lived and painted there."

"So is this," I gestured at the painting, "a scene from Cadaqués?"

"In some ways. I think you would say that it is inspired by the landscape around Cadaqués—the hills and olive trees and sea. But it is not of them, really. It is a vision in my head that came from them. An interior landscape, perhaps you could say."

I nodded and moved around the room, looking at paintings. Another undulating sweep of hill shapes in sandstone reds, reminding me somewhat of Georgia O'Keeffe. And then a lovely tumble of ocher and coral with a brilliant lapis-blue curve in the lower right-hand corner.

"Did you paint these when you lived in Spain?" I asked.

"No, these were all painted here. It is a strange thing." Nicole smiled. "When I lived in Spain, I painted things in my head from Amsterdam, where I lived for many years. I did not paint Spain at all. Now I do." She smiled again. "For me, I think, it is necessary to distill the experience before I can paint it. I need to have some distance from it. As I am saying, I do not paint the thing itself, but the vision it has produced in my mind."

I stared at a darker painting, all indigo-blue and violet, shot through with flashes of scarlet. Over all, the delicate inked shapes, particularly dramatic on white areas.

"So, do you always do the ink lines? I've never seen that on watercolors before."

"Yes. That has become my signature. I think I originally started because when I was very young I always drew line drawings with pen

87

and ink. When I began using watercolor, the paintings looked incomplete, too soft. I began inking on the ones that I did not like, that I had given up on. And then, gradually, it grew to be an important aspect of what I was doing."

My eyes shifted to Nicole as she was speaking and I took a sip of wine. I'd been so absorbed by the paintings that I'd barely looked at my hostess or touched the drink in my glass; I'd even neglected my usual habit of gazing around a room to try and pick up its character. Nicole didn't seem to notice. She was probably used to this.

Now, for a minute, I studied the woman who had made the paintings, and this space. She was dressed much as she had been when I'd first seen her—jeans and a chambray shirt with paint stains on it, hair simply tied back in a ponytail. Work clothes, I surmised. Her face was without affectation, both in its clear, open expression and in the lack of makeup or artifice. In many ways, she could be said to be beautiful: the delicate, finely drawn bone structure, wide mouth, and big dark eyes all lent themselves to that. And yet, in some lights, in certain glances, she could appear very plain.

I took another sip of wine. "You said you've lived in Amsterdam; are you in Dutch, then?" I asked the question tentatively, uncertain how she would respond to subjects other than her art.

"My mother was Dutch; my father is French. I was raised in Amsterdam, very close to Anne Frank's house. Perhaps you know it, or know of it."

"Know of it. I've never been anywhere outside California." I felt a little ashamed when I said this.

Nicole smiled, that simple, guileless smile. "Perhaps you will go someday."

To this I said nothing.

"I went first to France when I left home. A little village called Valery. And then, later, to Cadaqués, in Spain."

"And then here?"

"And then to the United States," she agreed. "First to San Francisco, and then here. I came with a boyfriend," she added. "He was to study at this university. But then he left." Once again the smile. "And I stayed."

"Do you like it here?"

"In some ways. It is a good place for me to paint. I have done much since I have lived here. My work now supports me entirely. But I do not know people here, as I did in Europe. I miss going out to the cafés in the evening sometimes with friends. It is a very different world there.

"Even so, this place is special to me. This house, this room that I have made."

It truly was a remarkable room. Open and airy, filled with paintings, the room had a clarity, almost a purity, that was hard to put a finger on.

Nicole saw my eyes travel around the space. "The windows are mostly on the north side," she said. "This makes a light that is good for painting. It is, how do say it, indirect."

"So do you paint in this room every day?"

"Yes. At least a little. Sometimes I work in the garden. Sometimes I take the horse for a ride. Once in a while I clean." She smiled again. "But not very often."

I smiled back at her. I thought her a charming human being.

Bringing my eyes back to the paintings, I asked her, "How do you go about making these?"

Nicole's smile illuminated her face. "First I have an idea. An image in my mind of color and shape. Perhaps I do a sketch, perhaps not. When it is clear in my head what the painting must be about, I begin putting the washes of color on the paper, reserving the areas I wish to remain white."

I imagined her, standing before the big easel near the window, brush in hand, contemplating the work before her.

"This can take several days," she went on. "Each day I place the colors and shapes that I see the painting needs. Then I wait until it appears balanced. Or not. Some paintings never work out."

"Does the inking come last?"

"Yes. Once the painting has the balance I look for, I begin the inking, to give it force and life."

"How long does it all take?"

"It depends. A big work can take two or three weeks, even a month."

"I see."

"That is why they are so expensive," she said. "That, and that there is some demand for them now."

"How much is expensive?" I asked.

"The larger ones are several thousand dollars. The smaller are less."

It figured. What I wanted for my wall was one of these big ones. I stared at the painting in front of me now; approximately three feet by four feet, it balanced curvaceous and yet also angular burnt orange shapes against swirls of aquamarine and grayed violet. This would fit my wall. And yet I was not sure this was the one I wanted.

I wandered to the next, a very vivid work, with a strong blood-red cleft dividing areas of apricot and yellow-green. And then another in tawny tones with turquoise billows and coral rivulets.

I looked back at Nicole. "I can't decide," I said helplessly. "I do want one, but I don't know which one."

"It may take some time," she said simply. "Sometimes people are struck instantly, and they say, I must have that. Other times they must look and look and then one painting in particular speaks to them more and more. You can come back, if you'd like," she added.

"I would like to," I said, looking at my watch. I'd been here an hour. Good manners demanded that I not take up too much of this woman's time. Finishing my glass of wine, I said, "When would it be convenient for me to come back?"

"Most evenings this week I am free."

"Could I come Wednesday evening then, around the same time?"

"That will be fine." Nicole smiled as she said it, and I had the sense that she did welcome me, that my presence was not an intrusion.

She went with me to the door. Once we were outside, in the garden, I looked over the low wall toward the barn.

"Do you ride much?" I asked Nicole.

"Perhaps two or three times a week," she said.

"On the trails around here?"

"Yes."

"And how is the mare doing?" I asked idly.

"She is okay, I think. But this morning I found her tied in the barn again. As you saw her the last time."

90

"You did?" Startled, my mind went snapping back to the original reason I'd come out here. My God. Though I'd more or less forgotten Nicole's strange problem, caught up in my interest in her paintings, the sordid little scene came back to me now in a rush.

"Damn," I said. "I don't like that. I really think you need to call the police."

Nicole stopped short and looked straight at me. "Gail," she said, "is it all right if I call you Gail?"

"Yes, of course," I said.

She smiled. "I am Nico to my friends." She pronounced it "Neeco."

"All right."

"So what I am telling you now is to a friend."

"All right," I said again.

"I cannot call the police. I cannot have anything to do with them. I am here illegally, and if it is found that I am living and working here, I will be forced to leave. Deported."

"Oh," I said. "I see."

"So I cannot call the police."

"I understand. But," I stared at her in the last light of the summer dusk, gray shadows all around us, "it seems like it might be dangerous, someone coming here at night like that."

Nicole was quiet for a moment. Then, gently, "That is your worry, Gail, not mine. I am not busy with that."

Feeling rebuked, but in a kind way, I nodded. "Okay," I said.

Still, I climbed in my truck not sure at all what I was feeling. Only that I thought Nico looked very alone, walking back toward the lighted windows of her house.

ELEVEN

My next day of calls went relatively smoothly, sans irate clients for once. My mind drifted back to Nico as I drove from place to place. To her paintings, her house, her presence. And to her problem.

It was such a dark and powerful image—a strange man sneaking into a barn at night to have sex with a horse. What sort of man would do such a thing? Perhaps a teenage boy, I thought again. But the fact that the act had been repeated bothered me.

I thought about it off and on all day, without reaching any conclusions about what to do. Nico had asked me specifically not to call the police, and clearly her reason was a good one. And yet, I was worried. I would not want someone creeping into my barn at night to rape my horses.

Thank God I've got geldings, I thought, and had to laugh. When you looked at it one way it seemed almost ludicrous. Turn it another and it was ominous. I didn't know what to think.

What I did know was that I liked Nico. I felt drawn to her, as I was to her work, and I felt an odd kinship between us. What it was composed of was unclear still, but I had the sense that something in her direct, forthright manner found an echo in me.

I had noticed this quality before in Europeans, and had occasionally wondered whether I might feel more at home, in some ways, in Europe than America. That simple, uncluttered habit of saying clearly what one thought and felt, without false social niceties or a pretense of being other than one was, seemed natural to some German, French, and Dutch women I had known. As natural to them as it seemed foreign to many Americans.

I had always found it difficult to connect with women. The friendship I'd formed with Kris had been built up over years of time and trials, and probably never would have become close without her divorce. The few friends I'd made in high school and college seemed relatively distanced from me now. I wondered suddenly if Nico and I might become friends.

One thing was for sure. Nico and her work had aroused my interest as nothing else had done in six months. I found I was hoping we would become friends, become part of each others' lives.

I was hoping for something. The fact of it was immensely cheering. Perhaps I was getting over this damn depression. Perhaps I didn't need a shrink.

But I had an appointment with one. Reluctantly, at five, I presented myself at his office, which turned out to be not all that far from my own.

An innocuous little beige stucco building with a hedge in front of it, Dr. Alan Todd's place of business was neither imposing nor, in any sense, impressive. It was downright humble.

I entered a very conventional-looking waiting room, and was startled to find myself the only human being in it. No desk, no receptionist. No other patients. Just a couch, two armchairs, a table with magazines, and some regulation scenic photographs on the walls. There was a door at the other side of the room, firmly shut, and a light switch on the wall next to it with a printed sign over it. "Dr. Alan Todd," it said. "Flip switch to 'on', to indicate your arrival."

I flipped the switch. A small red light beneath it glowed. I stared. That was it, it seemed. At a guess, now I waited.

Sitting down on the couch, I picked up *The New Yorker*. Still, I found myself a little too anxious to concentrate on reading. What was this going to be like? I had read about shrinks and seen them portrayed in movies, but I had no firsthand experience. I hoped I wouldn't have to lie on a couch while the shrink sat behind me. I also hoped he wouldn't just sit quietly waiting for me to say something. What in the hell should I say, anyway?

I was chewing this over in my mind when the door by the light switch opened and a man stepped into the room. A tall man, somewhat older than I, perhaps fifty or so, with graying hair, a Nordic face, clear blue eyes. He wore conventional East Coast–preppy clothes—dark blue slacks, loafers, a long-sleeved shirt with a maroon V-necked wool vest over it, a tie. Still, he looked somewhat casual and untidy; the clothes were a little rumpled: there was a small but obvious hole in the vest, the tie was an odd yellow-and-chartreuse pattern.

Taking all this in as quickly as I could, I stood up. The man held out his hand and smiled. "Dr. Alan Todd," he said.

I shook his hand. "Dr. Gail McCarthy." I smiled, too, somewhat amused. I seldom introduced myself as Dr. McCarthy, other than to clients, but I seemed to have an impulse to place myself on an equal footing with this man.

"Nice to meet you." Dr. Todd smiled again and held the door open for me. I preceded him down a short hall with doors on each side. "It's the first door on your left," he said.

Following his directions, I stepped through the open door of the office and looked around curiously. A very ordinary office, it seemed, much like the waiting room. A desk in one corner, various bits of stuff tacked on the walls, a shelf full of books. There were several seating options, including a couch, a couple of armchairs, and the desk chair. I wondered if I would be evaluated on where I chose to sit.

I selected an armchair across the room from the desk, avoiding the couch. Patient fears intimacy; I could just imagine the mental note.

Quit being paranoid, Gail, I told myself. And besides, that's what you're here for, anyway. You want him to evaluate you. Be that as it might, it was still uncomfortable. I felt like a bug on a pin. And here was the botanist, bending over me.

Shoving the image away, I watched Dr. Alan Todd settle himself comfortably into the desk chair, turning his back to the desk so that he faced me. He placed a file folder in his lap and glanced at it, then back at me. Folding his hands quietly over the folder and leaning back in his chair, he said, "So what can I do for you, Dr. McCarthy?"

I decided to be blunt. "I'm depressed," I said, "and it's beginning to interfere with my life. My friend, Kris Griffith, said you helped her with a depression. I was hoping you could help me."

"What form are you picturing this help taking?" he asked.

"I'm not sure. I've never seen a shrink, I mean a psychiatrist, before. I know there are antidepressant medications; I wondered if some of them might help me."

Dr. Todd regarded me steadily. "Tell me about this depression," he said.

At this, I had to think. What was there to tell? "I'm not sure exactly what caused it," I said. "I have a lot of new stresses in my life, but there's nothing going on that's really negative. My boss made me a partner recently, and I moved from one place to another. About six months ago I broke up with my boyfriend, but that was a mutual decision and I still think it was the right thing to do."

"And when did your depression start?"

"About six months ago."

"I see," he said.

I realized that he was doubtless linking my breakup with Lonny to the onset of depression. Well, let him link. It did seem to have happened like that.

"What are the symptoms of your depression?" Dr. Todd asked.

"I'm not interested in anything anymore. Not my job or my horses or my garden or the man I'm dating. I'm tired all the time, I don't have any appetite, I cry for no reason, and I'm always wanting to sleep. Sometimes I even feel like I'd rather be dead than go on this way." That was as accurate a description as I could come up with.

"Sounds like you're depressed." He smiled at me in a friendly way, as if being depressed was no big deal, a minor problem that we could solve together. I sure as hell hoped he was right.

"Have you been depressed before?" he asked me.

"Not that I'm aware of. Not like this." I hesitated, the words bringing up some memory I couldn't place.

95

"When you were a child? In the past?" The shrink watched me closely.

"I don't remember. I was a very solitary child," I said slowly, "but I don't remember being depressed."

"Tell me about your childhood," he said.

"I was an only child," I began, wondering what to put in and what to leave out. "My parents were both what I think you'd call introverts; they seemed happy together but they didn't have a lot of friends. My dad was an only child and his parents were dead from before I could remember, and my mother's family lives in Michigan. So there weren't any grandparents or aunts and uncles and cousins around. I was raised out in the country on an apple farm, and I learned to entertain myself."

"Were you lonely?" he asked.

"I don't remember being lonely. I think now that I was just used to feeling lonely, maybe. It seemed like the norm to me. My parents didn't pay a whole lot of attention to me; they mostly left me to my own devices. I read a lot. I made up stories and games. My animals were my friends."

The shrink watched me quietly; I had no idea what thoughts were going on behind the steady blue eyes.

"So you don't remember having any feelings of sadness and depression?" he asked.

"No, I don't. I was sad when my parents died, of course."

"When did they die?"

"When I was seventeen, about to turn eighteen." I went on, trying to meet his eyes. "They were killed in a car crash on the highway. Overnight I went from being secure to having to fend for myself. Our home had to be sold to pay debts and taxes and whatever; by the time it was all said and done there wasn't much money left. My aunt in Michigan offered to let me live with her, but she was a virtual stranger, and I didn't want to do that."

"It must have been a difficult time."

"It was. I'd always wanted to be a veterinarian, and I decided then that I would make that happen. I quite consciously meant to create a new security for myself, one that wasn't founded on other people.

"It wasn't easy, though. I had good grades in high school and I was able to get a scholarship, but I still had to work in order to pay my bills. I worked full-time as a waitress to put myself through college and vet school."

"Were you depressed then?"

"No. Not that I can recall. I was too busy to be depressed, I think."

"You say you were sad when your parents died. Would you call that a depression?"

"No. Actually," I thought for a minute, "I was sad, of course. But I can't remember crying much, or feeling terrible. I was mostly shocked. And just like later, there simply wasn't any space for me to fall apart. I needed to make arrangements, pay bills, get myself accepted to college, rent a room. . . . You see what I mean? I couldn't let myself be too sad. I had to function. No one else was going to take care of me. I had to do it myself."

I leaned back in my chair and let out a deep breath. That was the most I'd ever said about myself to any human being. In general, I tended to keep my feelings and struggles to myself. Still, that was the point of coming here, wasn't it? To unearth buried problems. Dr. Alan Todd continued to watch me quietly; he seemed to be thinking.

"So, what's your diagnosis?" I asked flippantly.

"Oh, you're depressed, certainly," he answered in a similar tone. "I'm just wondering how we can most usefully help you. I'm not sure medication is the way."

"Did you give Kris antidepressants?" I asked him.

He studied me. "I really can't talk about other patients," he said at last. "However, I can say that I don't normally prescribe antidepressant drugs for someone who is in what I would call a situational depression."

"What's a situational depression?" I asked.

"When something has happened to cause the depression. A specific situation, like the breakup of a marriage, or a death. Essentially, the depressed person is really grieving; it's a natural process. Quite different from a person who suffers from chronic depression."

"So, what about me?" I asked.

"Your situation is a little different," he said. "In my opinion, and of course it is just an initial guess at this point, your depression was probably triggered by the breakup with your boyfriend. But part of the problem is the loss of your parents. You didn't grieve then, as you explained, and the grief is still there inside. This most recent loss has touched those old, and very deep, feelings of loss and grief."

"So, I'm really depressed about my parents' deaths?"

"Possibly. I surmise, too, that even when they were alive, you felt somewhat cut off from them, somewhat isolated and unconnected, and that your depression is about this, also."

I sat quietly, thinking. The words rang a bell. I had long been aware of my inability to connect easily with other people. Over the years, I had rationalized that it was simply part of my personality. But now I wondered. Had I always been lonely? Was I sad about that?

And what about Lonny? He had been the closest I'd come to warmth and intimacy, and yet I had always held myself apart from him. I'd never wanted to take that final step, make a commitment, give up my autonomy. Since my parents' death, my autonomy had been my security. Not needing anyone was my defense against being hurt.

Was it time to make a change?

I stared at Dr. Alan Todd, wondering what to say. What came out was, "I don't know if I can change."

"Yes," he said simply.

"It's a long habit and it goes very deep. To hold myself apart, separate, invulnerable."

"Yes," he said again.

"Do you think it's behind this depression?"

"It's possible."

"What can I do?"

"I think," he said slowly, "that the best thing we can do is to talk about your parents and your childhood. We need to go back to the time when they died, as well as the times when you were a little girl, and you can perhaps let yourself experience your feelings of grief and loneliness. Depression is about depressing something. You're holding feelings down inside where you can't feel them, because you're afraid to feel them. You perceive them as too painful. If you let these feelings come up to your conscious mind and allow yourself simply to feel them, to accept them, oftentimes they will cease to trouble you.

"There's an old Zen saying, 'What you resist, persists.' " Dr. Alan Todd folded his hands in his lap.

What was this, a Zen shrink? I had the impulse to say, "Yes, master." Still, his words were hitting home. Somehow when he spoke about my parents, I felt an emotional resonance—like a bell that has been struck. Deep in my heart, I believed he was right.

"You don't want to prescribe some drugs?" I asked him.

He regarded me. "No, I don't think so," he said. "Not yet, anyway." Another level look. "Perhaps we could meet again in a week?"

"All right," I said.

He stood up; I did likewise. Apparently our interview was at an end. By my watch, it had taken almost an hour.

"How do I pay you?" I asked him as we walked down the hall.

"I'll send you a bill," he said cheerfully.

Remembering that he had taken my address and phone number when I'd first called him, I said, "Okay. And thank you."

"You're welcome." Giving me another cheerful smile, Dr. Todd disappeared back into his den.

I stood alone in the waiting room, which was still empty. Perhaps I was the last patient of the day. The thought made me feel odd. Here I was, the patient of a shrink, not a role in which I had ever envisioned myself. And yet, I found I believed that he was right, that he might help.

Whatever I was, I assured myself, I was not a quitter. Dr. Alan Todd had set me a task—to understand myself and my relationship to my parents. If that sort of understanding would help with this depression, I would work at it.

99

TWELVE

By the following morning, I wasn't feeling so optimistic. My first call had turned out to be deeply frustrating—a horse who had gone down and wouldn't get up. This problem can have a number of causes, and in this particular case, I had found myself completely stymied when it came to diagnosing what was wrong.

The horse, a fat, gray Quarter Horse gelding, lay on his chest in the stall, obdurately refusing to get to his feet. His pulse and respiration were only mildly elevated, and he didn't seem to be in much, if any, distress.

"He's been like that since yesterday," his owner, a woman in perhaps her sixties, said tearfully.

I stared at the horse. I'd already tried to get him up by the simplest methods; I'd run a rope from his halter over the rafter beam, and had his owner haul on it as hard as she could while I tugged with equal force on his tail. No go. The horse lunged upward and collapsed, seeming to lack control of his legs.

The only useful piece of information I had wasn't helping me much. The gelding was positive for HYPP, sometimes known as "Impressive" syndrome, as it often occurs in horses who are descended from the well-known Quarter Horse stallion Impressive.

Trouble was, the symptoms this horse was displaying didn't match up with HYPP.

Normally HYPP horses have seizurelike signs and obvious distress, and this horse had none of that. I'd already pumped some fluids into him—the classic treatment for HYPP—but so far I'd seen no results. At this point, I'd been here two hours. It was time to call for help.

I wasn't crazy about asking Jim to bail me out of difficult cases; let's face it, it hurt my pride. But I knew that it was in everybody's interest, let alone it was my moral obligation that I do the best I could for this horse. And right now that meant finding somebody who knew more about this situation than I did.

Unfortunately, Jim, when I finally got him on the phone, sounded genuinely puzzled. "I don't know, Gail. I've never seen an HYPP horse go down like you're describing. And if he is HYPP, there isn't much to do except run fluids into him and let him rest."

"I've done that. He's been down twenty-four hours now," I said.

"Better get him up," Jim said unhelpfully, and hung up the phone.

Great. I considered my options. Finally, I told the woman, "I think we need to make a real effort to get this horse on his feet."

"What can we do?"

"I think we could try a tow truck with a boom."

"Well, all right." She was dubious but accepting.

Between us, we managed to make arrangements. An hour later the tow truck arrived, driven by an aging hillbilly in a dirty ball cap and low-slung jeans, who was sporting the worst-looking set of teeth I'd ever seen. He was friendly and helpful, though, and jockeyed his truck into the necessary position with a quiet competence that was reassuring.

Fastening the wide nylon webbing strap under the horse's belly, I instructed our driver to raise the animal at my signal. Once again, I steadied the gray's head and held the lead rope taut so he could brace against it.

"All right," I said.

Slowly and inexorably the boom lifted. In another minute the horse was on his feet. He stood there, swaying slightly. But he stood on all four feet. He had no broken legs, no dislocated joints, nor badly strained tendons. We all watched him.

After a few more minutes had passed, I unfastened the strap from around his belly. The tow truck driver was just climbing back in the cab when the horse collapsed, stumbling forward into the breezeway of the barn and settling almost calmly onto his belly.

"Damn," I said forcefully.

Now what? The gray still seemed remarkably quiet, but I felt he was beginning to show minor signs of stress. The woman who owned him was crying silently, tears running down her cheeks.

"Look," I told her, I hoped evenly, "this isn't going too well. In my experience, horses that go down and won't get up don't have a good prognosis. Horses aren't built to live lying down. If this guy doesn't get up in the next day or so, I'm afraid he'll probably die."

"But what's wrong with him?"

"I don't know," I said helplessly, even as various ideas spun through my head. Cancer? EPM? Heart failure? Nothing seemed to fit these specific circumstances.

"What should I do?" the woman asked.

"You've got three choices, basically. You can haul him to an equine hospital where they have more resources than I do, you can put him down, or you can wait and see."

"How long can I wait?"

"Another day, maybe," I said, feeling even more helpless. The truth was I simply didn't know.

"What would you do if it was your horse?" The woman swallowed a sob.

I hesitated. I hated this question, and I got it all the time. It was so terribly subjective. What I would do might be entirely unworkable for her.

"Haul him to the nearest equine hospital," I said at last. "They can put him in a sling, so he'll stand, and they'll probably be able to figure out what's wrong with him. But it will be expensive."

The woman stared at her horse, lying on his chest in the barn aisle, breathing heavily "All right," she said, "but how?"

I motioned to the tow truck driver who had been standing by his truck during our consultation. "We need to get this horse in a horse trailer," I said.

He nodded, already calculating the logistics of the problem.

"I can put him all the way out," I said.

He pointed at a large piece of plywood leaning against the barn wall. "If we can get him on to that, I can drag him out of the barn, like he was on a sled."

"Yeah." I looked at the owner. "This may not be pretty," I told her, "but we need to get him in the trailer, and it won't hurt him."

She nodded silently.

"Is there anyone who could help?" I asked. "What we could use is a few good, strong men."

"Maybe the neighbors," she said doubtfully.

An hour later we were more or less organized, with two neighboring men pressed into service. By now it was past noon, and my frustration was growing. Taking a deep breath and reminding myself to stay quiet and calm, I gave the gray horse five cc's of ketamine, which would put him all the way out for fifteen minutes or so.

The minute his nose was touching the dirt of the barn aisle, I nodded to my crew. "Let's go."

As we had prearranged, the five of us, using ropes and what strength we possessed, managed to lever the gelding onto the sheet of plywood, which had been attached by chains to the boom of the tow truck. As soon as he was on, more or less, the tow truck driver leaped into the cab and hauled him out onto the driveway where the horse trailer was ready and waiting.

Now came the tricky part. Thanking God the woman had a stock trailer rather than a little two-horse trailer, I helped the truck driver fasten a second chain to the boom. Once again he lifted the horse, looking for all the world like a carcass on a board, and we pushed, pulled, shoved, and dragged him into the trailer.

Just in time. We no sooner got the door latched than he snorted and lifted his head.

I tranquilized him, gave the woman more tranquilizers and directions for her journey, thanked everybody, and got back in my truck. It was two o'clock in the afternoon, I'd dealt with all of one call, and I was both sweating and starving. I called the office.

The receptionist sounded tense. "Jim's had a couple of emergencies," she said, "and he's way behind on his appointments. He was supposed to see this one woman at noon; he wants you to get out there as soon as you can."

"What's the matter with the horse?"

"It's too thin. She doesn't know what's wrong with it. She made the appointment earlier this week."

"Who is it?"

"Her name is Jeri Ward, and the horse is out at the Bishop Ranch. She's been waiting there since noon."

"Call and tell her I'll be right there."

I hung up the car phone, wondering. I knew a Jeri Ward. She was a detective with the Santa Cruz County Sheriff's Department. But it couldn't be the same person. The Jeri Ward I knew did not look like the type to own a horse.

I was wrong. When I pulled into the Bishop Ranch twenty minutes later, the woman who greeted me was indeed Detective Jeri Ward.

Parking my truck under the big cottonwood tree in the barnyard, I got out. Jeri Ward in jeans and a T-shirt looked remarkably different from the sleekly professional woman I'd met in the course of a murder investigation, many years ago. She also looked disconcertingly similar.

Even in her jeans, she appeared poised and well put-together; the white T-shirt unsullied, the short blond hair neatly groomed, the face calm and somewhat aloof. The sight of her brought back a rush of memories, most of them distinctly unnerving.

"Hello, Dr. McCarthy," she said, with just the faintest trace of amusement in her voice.

"Hello, Detective Ward," I replied. Belatedly I realized that she had made an appointment with Jim, not me, and that my presence was perhaps unwelcome. "Jim had an emergency," I said.

"No problem." Jeri Ward seemed quite unperturbed.

"Sorry about the wait," I added. "I was working on another emergency call."

"I understand," she said.

She probably did. As a cop, unexpected emergencies would be an everyday matter, just as they were for us vets.

"So what can I help you with?" I asked.

She smiled. I'd never really seen her smile before, I thought.

"My husband gave me a horse for my fortieth birthday," she said.

"Is that right?" I said stupidly. I'd always assumed this woman was single, that her cool professionalism reflected an austere nature; I would have bet she was solitary by choice. Apparently I was wrong again.

Jeri Ward began walking toward a shed row that led off the main barn; I followed.

"I've always wanted a horse," she went on, "but I thought I was too busy and they cost too much. But Kevin decided I ought to have one. One of his friends is a team penner, and he had a seventeen-year-old horse he wanted to retire. He said the horse would be perfect for me. He gave him to Kevin, just so the horse would get a good home."

"Sounds ideal," I said.

She smiled again. "Wait till you see him. Anyway," she went on, "I don't know much about horses, but enough to know that an older, gentle horse that I can ride through the hills is what I need, so in most ways this guy fits. There are just a few small problems, though."

She stopped outside a pen and we both stared at the horse inside.

"Is that him?" I asked incredulously.

"I'm afraid so." Another smile.

This had to be the funniest-looking horse I'd ever seen. He was little, with abnormally short legs and an equally abnormally long back. He looked like a dachshund. Added to this, he was high-headed, with a long, skinny, giraffelike neck, and he had a blind eye on the right side. Not to mention, he was thin as a rail.

"See what I mean," she said. "We picked him up last week, after I made arrangements to board him out here, and he really is gentle to ride, and he seems to be sound. But everything else aside, he's so thin; I thought I ought to have a vet check him, despite the fact that he's a gift horse and all that." Another smile.

"Okay," I said. "Let's get him out."

Jeri took a halter off a peg and walked into the pen with the sorrel gelding, who allowed himself to be caught with no difficulty. "Come on, ET," she said.

I had to laugh. "Is that his name?"

She smiled back. "Fits him, doesn't it?"

"It sure does." We grinned at each other companionably; I was remembering our last encounter, and how annoyed she had been at me for getting involved in a murder investigation. Apparently she was a different creature off duty.

I checked ET out as completely as I could; he was a perfect gentleman throughout. He did indeed appear to be sound; in fact, he was one of the cleanest-legged older horses I'd come across. Judging by his teeth he was closer to twenty than the reputed seventeen. Jeri just shrugged.

ET's pulse and respiration were normal and his heart sounded good; his gut made typical noises. He was definitely blind in the eye that was glazed blue; by my reckoning he had no vision in it at all.

"Do you know how that happened?" I asked. "It looks like the result of an injury."

"No, the guy didn't say. Just told me to be careful not to surprise the horse when he couldn't see me, and that other than that, he was perfectly gentle. And he does seem to be."

I nodded. "Lots of one-eyed horses do just fine," I said. I looked at the horse some more. "I really can't see any reason for his degree of thinness. Sometimes that can be caused by sand in the gut, but his gut sounds normal. Another possibility is heart problems, but once again, there's no sign of that. Have you wormed him?"

"The day I brought him home."

"And his teeth look fine, no corners or sharp edges." I ran a hand over the gelding's ribs. "What are you feeding him?"

"All the alfalfa hay he can eat."

"You might try oat and alfalfa pellets, and put a tub of alfalfa meal and molasses in the pen with him, so he can nibble on it free-choice. That is, if you can arrange it with the stable."

"She can do anything she wants." The voice came from behind me; even before I turned I knew it was Bart Bishop. That quasi-friendly tone thinly overlying an essential aggression—it had to be him.

It was. Bart flashed his teeth at me in the form of a smile. "Dr. McCarthy."

"Gail," I said automatically.

"And Detective Ward." The same brief baring of teeth. "This lady gets the deluxe treatment," he said.

"That's good," I said.

Jeri Ward nodded civilly.

"We wouldn't want to alienate the newest member of the Santa Cruz County Sheriff's posse."

Jeri gave him a short smile and said, "Can we arrange to feed this horse oat and alfalfa pellets and free-choice alfalfa meal and molasses?"

"Can do," Bart said crisply. "Of course, it will cost you a little extra."

"How much?" Jeri asked.

"Twenty-five dollars a month, and the cost of the pellets and meal."

"All right," she said.

"So, Dr. McCarthy," Bart was watching me. "What's wrong with this horse?"

"I don't know," I said. "There's nothing obvious. Maybe his former owner didn't feed him enough. Maybe he's just a hard keeper. If he doesn't show signs of gaining on this regime, I'll run some blood tests."

"Did you check his teeth?" Bart asked.

I stared at him. Did the man really mean to imply I was a totally incompetent veterinarian?

"Yes," I said shortly. Checking the teeth was a routine first step with a thin horse.

"No problem there?" Bart was pursuing it.

"No," I said, and stared right at him, willing him to walk away. This guy was sure different from his brother. I'd already glanced in the direction of Clay's house and ascertained that his pickup was gone.

"I'll start him on his new feed tonight." Bart was looking at Jeri now. "Is that okay with you?"

"Fine," she said. I had the impression she found Bart as annoying as I did.

He smiled at her with a glint in his eyes that I was sure he meant to be charming, but which struck me as merely obnoxious. With that handsome face and the mystique of the trainer's mantle on his shoulders, he was clearly used to bowling women right over. He probably found it annoying that neither Jeri nor I appeared impressed.

107

"Shall I put him back?" Jeri asked me, ignoring Bart.

"Sure," I said. "I'm done with him."

Taking his cue, Bart gave us both a nonchalant wave and moved off down the barn aisle. I resisted the urge to roll my eyes at the slight swagger in his departing butt.

Putting the horse away and hanging the halter back on the peg, Jeri accompanied me back to my truck.

"Call me if he hasn't gained some weight in a month," I said.

"All right." Jeri looked as composed and distant as ever. I have no idea what prompted me to say what I did next.

"Have you ever run into the problem of a man having sexual relations with a horse?"

Jeri stopped dead, as well she might, and looked at me. "No," she said. She looked at me some more. "It's a crime, you know. Bestiality. It's still on the books." She wrinkled her nose. "That's nasty."

"I think so, too. I have a client who thinks it may be happening to her mare. Someone is sneaking into her barn at night. She doesn't want the police involved, but I was just wondering what you thought."

Jeri shrugged one shoulder. "I think she should call us. A thing like that can become compulsive, like rape. Pretty soon the person has to do it. He won't be stopped. Such a person can be dangerous."

"That's what I thought," I said. "I'll tell her."

"Try and get her to call us," Jeri said.

"I will. And call and let me know how ET does."

"I will," she repeated, and smiled. "Thanks, Gail."

I climbed back into my truck feeling mildly pleased that Jeri Ward and I were now on reasonably friendly terms. A phone call confirmed that I had no more appointments or emergencies, so I headed back to the office. It was now four o'clock.

The last client of the day turned out to be a man with a young stallion who couldn't figure out the mechanics of breeding a mare. Jim had told the guy to bring the two horses in, and we would assist.

The stallion was a three-year-old Arabian, still a little uncertain about the sexual act. The mare, also an Arabian, was older, and the owner assured us she had been bred before. "She's quiet enough," he said. "I tie her in the barn and lead him up to her, but he just can't seem to figure it out. She's in heat now, and I really want to get her bred before she goes out."

"Hmmm," Jim said.

I watched him as he teased the mare, leading the stallion up to her and letting him sniff her, watched as the young stud nipped playfully at the crest of the mare's neck. We all looked hopefully at the stallion's genitalia.

Sure enough—he was responding appropriately.

Jim gave orders. "You hold this mare over here, where she's down in a hole and easier for him to get on," he said to the owner. "I'll handle the stud, and Gail, you help him get it in."

Great. Now this was one of my odder cases.

Jim led the stallion up to the waiting mare, who did, indeed, stand quietly. With an eager nicker, the stallion clambered up, his front legs hanging over the mare's hips, as he struggled to find the spot.

I put him in. Not too difficult, really.

We all stepped back as he pushed, finally getting the idea. Mission accomplished.

Watching as the stallion thrust into the mare, an image as powerfully erotic as it was innocent as a flower blooming, I felt mildly confused. The two men watched with me; outwardly we all looked detached, but I wondered what sort of thoughts were chasing around their brains.

Flowers are the sexual organs of plants, after all, was what I was thinking. This young bay stallion, just now completing the act of passion, was in some ways the equivalent of a full-blown tea rose. And yet there was the forcefulness of his thrusting; the male intensity of his desire.

I thought of Nicole and her mare and the man who came to her barn at night. Thought of the man secretively thrusting into the mare, as the stallion was doing. The image was deeply disturbing in ways I couldn't fathom; I shook my head abruptly to chase it away. When I did I shivered, and Jim looked at me.

I met his eyes and shrugged. "A goose walked over my grave," I said, and unaccountably, I shivered again.

THIRTEEN

Friday night I went out with Kris. I'd been to visit Nico on Wednesday, drank another glass of wine, and narrowed my choice down to one of three paintings. Nico reiterated that I should come back as often as I liked. Thursday and Friday had both passed relatively uneventfully, so when Kris called me at work late Friday afternoon, I had no ready excuse.

"All right," I said finally, yielding to her urging.

"And wear something sexy," she added.

"Right." I hung up the phone, and went back out to look at a horse with a pulled groin muscle.

Two hours later, as I showered and readied myself to go, her often-repeated advice came back to me. Wear something sexy.

Well, there was that dress. The blue velvet dress that I'd never worn. I'd bought it in a fit of something, right after I broke up with Lonny. A fit of what, exactly? Not pique or rebelliousness, but something like that. I was tired of looking like a conservative little country girl in my jeans and silk blouses. I wanted to appear sophisticated for once.

The upshot of all this was that I'd never brought myself to wear the new dress, either out on a date or anywhere else. It looked too overtly come-hitherish, and I never felt comfortable in it. Maybe to-night, I thought.

Taking the dress off its hanger, I pulled it on, or rather, I wriggled into it. The dress had a low-cut neckline and spaghetti straps; it fitted as tightly through the torso, waist, and hips as stretch velvet could manage, and flowed from there in a sweep to midcalf. A deep midnight blue, which looked black in the shadows and had a sheen of sapphire in the light, the dress bared most of my back and a lot of my chest, and had a glamorous, 'forties-type ambience—for all the world like something Myrna Loy might have worn in *The Thin Man*.

I stared at myself in the mirror. This dress was not me. It didn't reflect either my taste or my style, and yet, it looked good on me. What the heck. Tonight I'd be a vamp. There was no harm in it. I'd made Kris promise that it would be just us two, and if she happened to find a man she liked, she would arrange to meet him later and take me home.

I wasn't interested in picking up strange men. Let alone the fact that it wasn't my inclination, I also thought it was dangerous. Slipping on the high-heeled black shoes I'd bought because the dress demanded them, I studied my reflection. Then I opened my mother's jewelry box and picked out a piece of hers I almost never wore—a two-carat topaz pendant on a braided gold chain. It hung perfectly in the deep neckline of the dress.

Pulling my hair up in two combs, and adding a little extra eyeliner and lip gloss, I decided that I was almost unrecognizable as Gail Mc-Carthy, the horse vet. What I looked like exactly, I wasn't sure.

I could hear Kris's horn beeping as she drove her Mazda Miata up the driveway; Kris was always impatient. Putting my black silk jacket over my shoulders, I told Roey to be a good dog and stepped out the door.

Kris rolled the window down and gave a long wolf whistle. "Look at you," she said.

I grinned. "Well, is this sexy enough for you?"

"Yes, ma'am. You look great."

Folding myself into her little car I said, "I did it for you, pal."

Kris reversed handily down my hill and said, "You should do it for yourself."

Then we were off, with Kris running through the gears in her usual hasty fashion. I often thought that this snappy little black sports car was the perfect reflection of her current state of mind.

We'd agreed on Clouds as a destination for drinks and dinner; Kris cut a good five minutes off our time getting there. As we entered, I noticed that Caroline was behind the bar again tonight. The next thing I noticed was Clay Bishop—sitting at a small table with a woman.

The sight gave me a funny feeling. I'd thought myself indifferent to Clay; I'd also thought him devoted to me. Obviously I was wrong on both counts. It disturbed me.

The woman he was with was tall and blond, wearing a goodly amount of makeup and several earrings in her ears. She was about my age, slim and fit-looking, with a pretty face, and she had an indefinable air that I could only describe as Southern Californian. A little too obviously dyed-blond, a little too showy. She was talking vivaciously to Clay while he listened, looking absorbed.

I poked Kris in the ribs with my elbow and jerked my chin infinitesimally in Clay's direction. Kris raised an eyebrow and walked purposefully toward the bar. I followed. Clay turned his head and saw us. His eyes widened and for a brief moment he looked truly stunned, whether at my appearance or at seeing me when he was out on a date I couldn't tell.

He got somewhat clumsily to his feet. "Hi, Gail. Hi, Kris."

We both greeted him. The blond woman looked at us curiously. "This is Sue," he said. No further explanation seemed to be forthcoming.

I smiled, said, "Nice to meet you," and walked on by, finding a seat on a stool at the other end of the bar. Kris trailed after me.

"What a rat," she hissed.

"What do you mean? He's not committed to me. He's got a perfect right to date anyone he wants."

"Yeah, but all those protestations of devotion."

I shrugged. I had told Kris what Clay had said at the end of our last date. "He doesn't owe me anything," I said firmly.

112

"Well, I don't think much of his taste," she sniffed.

We both surreptitiously studied the woman, who was talking again. I had to admit I agreed with Kris. The blonde had a superficial prettiness that seemed applied all over, like a gloss. The patterned, somewhat shiny pants and top she was wearing were a little too loud for me.

Of the other hand, I smiled to myself, Kris and I probably looked like two ladies of the evening. Kris's backless black halter dress hit her at mid-thigh and was more than a match for my cocktail outfit. We were definitely a pair to draw to.

Caroline interrupted this reverie by asking what we'd like to drink. Kris chose a martini, I went with my usual vodka tonic. Caroline made the drinks with a ready smile.

"So, what's new in your life?" I asked Kris, firmly avoiding the sight of Clay and his date.

"Well, George," she said simply.

"Is he your new guy?"

"Almost." Kris grinned. "I'm working on it. He rode over to see me yesterday evening."

"Rode? Like on his horse?"

"Uh-huh. Those trails go everywhere through the hills. There's one that takes you up the bank behind my place and right over to Lush-meadows. He came that way. I thought it was romantic."

"Kris, what exactly do you know about this guy?"

"He works as a finish carpenter and builds furniture on the side. He's Greek. And he's sexy as hell."

"That's it?"

"What more do I need to know?"

"Shit, Kris." I took a long swallow of my drink. "Maybe he's a rapist in a past life. Might be nice to get to know him a little better before you jump in the sack."

"I know," she teased, "it would take you six months, minimum. I'm different."

"Well, maybe not six months," I said.

Kris looked over her shoulder. "They're leaving," she whispered.

I looked. Clay and his tall blonde were indeed exiting the bar. Clay gave us a casual wave and a smile. The blonde had a good figure. I was being surprised by how much it bothered me.

"So ask that other guy out," Kris said, seeming to read my mind.

"Blue? I went and saw him and made my interest plain. If he doesn't call me, he's just not interested. I don't want to hound the poor guy."

"Why not?" Kris finished her martini and looked for the bartender.

"Don't forget you've got to drive home," I warned.

Caroline approached. "How's it going, Dr. McCarthy?"

"Real well," I said firmly, knowing she would have seen Clay and the woman. "This is my friend Kris, this is Caroline."

"Hi." Both women said it at once.

"Like another?" Caroline asked.

"You bet." Kris grinned at me. "And then no more, I promise."

"How about you, Gail?" Caroline asked.

"All right. One more."

She made the drinks while we watched; I was struck again by her graceful competence and interesting, lively face.

"How are things going with you?" I asked her as she pushed our drinks across the bar.

"Oh, not so good." She smiled at me. "My least favorite customer was just in."

"Oh?" I looked a question at her.

"This guy. He's stalking me. I can't stand him. He comes in here almost every day I work, sits at the bar, and just stares at me. He leaves me soppy notes, he asks me out constantly, he's a royal pain in the ass."

"Must be one of the hazards of bartending," I commented.

"Uh-huh. But this guy's worse than most. I've told him I don't want to go out and he just won't quit."

"Do you know who he is?" Kris asked.

"Kind of. Your friend over there," she gestured at the table where Clay had been sitting, "knows him."

"What's his name?" I asked curiously.

"Warren. I don't know his last name."

Kris and I looked at each other.

"What's he look like?" Kris asked.

"Medium height, blond-haired, a mustache, pretty good-looking, snazzy dresser, gives the impression he has money."

"It couldn't be Warren White, could it?" I said, half to Kris, half to Caroline.

"Sure sounds like him," Kris said.

"The guy says he has horses," Caroline contributed.

"If it's him," Kris said, "he used to be after me. I knew him pretty well."

"Like real well," I added.

"So, what's the deal with him?" Caroline asked.

"A lot like you're saying," Kris said. "He pursued the hell out of me until I went out with him, and after a couple of dates, he just sort of faded away. The pursuit is what he likes, I think."

"How was he?" I teased her.

She shrugged. "It never happened," she said. "He sort of backed off at the last minute. If you want my guess, I think he's impotent."

We all absorbed that.

"It would explain why the pursuit is the big deal to him," I agreed.

"And why I get such a creepy feeling from him," Caroline added. "The guy must be totally sexually frustrated."

We all nodded sagely. As women of roughly forty, we'd all been around the block enough times to be familiar with the emotional problems triggered in men by any kind of impotence, however temporary. Guys just did not deal well with this situation.

"I don't know how you'd discourage him," Kris volunteered. "Maybe you should go out with him a few times. Then he'd let you alone."

"Yeck," Caroline said emphatically. "He gives me the creeps. Pushy little bastard."

I nodded sympathetically. Warren gave me the creeps, too.

Kris finished her drink in a long swallow. "How about dinner?" she said.

"Okay."

We ended up eating at the bar, sharing several salads and appetizers, which made a lovely meal. Caroline chatted to us occasionally throughout, though the subjects of Warren and Clay were tacitly avoided. When we left the bar, an hour later, Kris and I told her good-bye.

"Are you sober?" I asked, as Kris climbed into the driver's seat of her sports car.

"As a judge," she said.

"So don't scare me," I told her.

"You scare easy," she said, but she drove home considerably more sedately then she'd driven out.

I felt a twinge of the old depression as she dropped me off at my empty house. It was becoming harder and harder for me to enjoy my solitude; sadness seemed to creep in the moment I was alone, these days.

I walked the dog and fed her and the other animals. I'd just begun stripping off my clothes when the phone rang.

"Hello," I said dully.

"Gail, please, come quick, oh hurry, my God, it's Jo." It was Kris, or I thought it was Kris. Her voice was very nearly incoherent.

"What's the matter?" I said, thoroughly alarmed.

"I found Jo knocked out, at the barn. Oh, Gail, I . . . just hurry."

"I'll be right there."

FOURTEEN

Kris's house, when I got there, was not the scene of full-blown disaster I expected. No ambulances in sight. The lights were on, though, and I lost no time running to the front door.

"Kris!" I yelled, as I opened it.

"Here," came the response.

Kris and Jo were sitting together on the couch, Kris's arm around her daughter. In my first glance I registered that Jo looked basically okay—awake, alert, not bloody.

"What happened?" I demanded.

Mother and daughter stared at me blankly. Kris's face was as pale as Jo's, and neither seemed to know what to say.

I squatted on the floor next to them. "What happened?" I asked, more gently.

It was Jo who answered. "Someone hit me over the head, I think." She touched the back of her skull gingerly. "Out at the barn."

"When?" I asked.

"I'm not sure, not really." Jo looked down at her hands. She was a sweet child, and despite turning thirteen this year, had not yet acquired the rebellious insolence typical of adolescents. Her long, silky blond hair, very like her mother's, was tied back in a simple ponytail, she wore a baggy T-shirt and jeans, and I had never seen her use makeup. Her quite pretty face still held a candid, childlike expression. Perhaps, given Kris's current lifestyle, this somewhat tenacious attachment to childhood was Jo's form of rebellion. Whatever the cause, Jo was a remarkably easy teenager to get along with, and I liked her very much.

"Do you remember anything that happened, sweetheart?" I asked.

"A little," she said. "I was here in the house, watching TV, and I heard Dixie neigh. She doesn't usually neigh at night, so I thought it was kind of weird. Then I heard more neighing, so I thought I should go see if something was wrong. I got a flashlight, and I turned the outside lights on and I went out to the barn. Then," she stopped and looked at her mother, "I don't really know what happened. Something hit me I think. All I remember is waking up with Mom bending over me."

Kris nodded, looking, if anything, more scared than Jo.

"I came home, walked in the house, called Jo's name, and didn't see her. I could see that the barn lights were on, so I went out the back door and started out there. That's when I saw Jo. She was lying outside the barn, face down. I can tell you, Gail, I panicked pretty bad."

Kris stroked her daughter's hair gently. "I bent down and turned her over and she woke up. After I figured out that she was basically okay, nothing broken or anything, I brought her back in here and called you."

"How about her head?" I asked.

"There's a big lump and some swelling," Kris said.

"You should have a doctor look at her, in case of concussion." I peered into Jo's face. "Her eyes look all right. She's probably not concussed."

I thought a minute. "Stay here," I said. "I want to go have a look at the barn."

"Gail," Kris said nervously. "What if he's still out there?"

"He won't be. First you came home, then I drove up. Whoever it was, he's long gone."

Brave words. Still, I went out to my truck first and got Roey out of the cab. She was a friendly dog and would probably not recognize an intruder as an enemy; still, with her more acute senses, she would spot a stranger in the night sooner than I, and would no doubt run up to him, barking and wagging her tail.

However, Roey ran about the barnyard, sniffing happily, and showed no signs of spotting anything. I waited awhile; nothing happened. I couldn't see Dixie in her corral. The barn was brightly lit; after a minute, I stepped inside.

For a second I stared, not really comprehending what I was seeing. Dixie was cross-tied in the stall; an overturned feed bucket lay on the ground behind her.

"Oh, shit," I said softly.

Dixie looked at me, calm and curious. I rubbed her forehead and walked around behind her. I lifted her tail. It was possible. Some sort of mucousy substance was smeared on her vulva.

"Shit, shit, shit," I said again.

Giving the mare another pat, I shut Roey back in the truck and rejoined Kris and Jo.

They still sat huddled on the couch; their faces had more color, though.

"We need to call the cops right away," I said. Some urgency in my voice got through to Kris.

"What did you find out at the barn?" she asked sharply.

"Dixie's tied in her stall," I said slowly, giving her a look. "Like your neighbor Nicole's mare."

Kris took that in. "You mean you think . . ." She glanced down at Jo. "Like that morning?" she asked.

"I think so."

"Oh, no." Kris bent down so she could look into Jo's face. "Honey, are you sure you didn't see anybody?"

"Yes, I'm sure." Childish she might be, but Jo sounded definite.

"So," I said, "if you're feeling up to it, why don't you go on down to the emergency room and get Jo checked out while I call the cops."

"I guess we have to," Kris said slowly.

"Yes, we do have to," I told her firmly.

"All right," Kris stood up, holding Jo's hand. "Come on, sweetheart, let's go."

Two hours and a couple of phone calls later, it was midnight and Jeri Ward sat in Kris's living room. Kris and Jo had returned from the hospital; Jo was all right, they said. No concussion.

I'd achieved Jeri's presence here by a persistent refusal to speak to anyone else about "the nature of the problem," and a constant repetition of the statement that Detective Ward was already involved with the case. This wasn't, strictly speaking, true, but fortunately Jeri was on duty and eventually came on the phone line. I explained the situation briefly and got her assurance she'd be right out.

So here we all were—Kris still in her skimpy halter dress with a black sweater thrown over it, Jo in pajamas, and me in the faded sweats I'd pulled on to rush over here. Jeri Ward, in contrast, wore dark blue slacks with a clean line and a tweed jacket in shades of blue and cream. Very simple, very classy.

Kris said hesitantly, "Can we keep this out of the papers?"

"You can have my word that I won't say anything to them," Jeri said crisply. "I can't answer for more than that."

"I understand." Kris hesitated. "Can you get any fingerprints or anything—out at the barn?"

"My techs are working on it now," Jeri said. "Also, we'll do a semen analysis. Assuming it is semen, of course."

We all looked at Jo. "Semen?" she said.

Might as well get this over with. Jo was going to find out eventually.

"Sweetheart," I said, "we think some man was, well, sexually abusing Dixie. He must have seen the lights come on and hidden, then hit you over the head and run away."

"Oh." Jo thought about this. "You mean, like, you think he was having sex with a horse?"

"That's right," I confirmed.

"That is really weird," she said.

"Yeah, it is," I agreed. "And nasty."

"What sort of person would want to do that?" Jo asked.

"Good question." I looked over at Jeri.

She shrugged. "I haven't run into this particular problem before. But sexual crimes are relatively common. All the way from rape, sometimes including other violence, down through stuff as innocuous as flashers and public urinators. The common thread seems to be an inability to resist the inappropriate act. The perpetrator becomes compulsive; he just has to do this one specific thing in order to be satisfied."

"I suppose most of them don't have a happy sexual life at home," I ventured.

"You'd be surprised," Jeri said. "Sometimes they do. Sometimes, in fact, they're happily married. They just work their darker impulses out in these weird ways that their spouses often doesn't know about. But most of them are, in some sense, sexually frustrated."

Kris and Jo and I were all quiet. I knew that our minds were following the same trail. Who was the strangely twisted human being who had done this thing?

Jeri Ward looked at me. "Gail, you told me about this before. When you checked my horse. Was the other incident here?"

"No." I looked warningly at Kris. "I really can't tell you," I said to Jeri. "I promised I wouldn't."

"It's important, Gail." Jeri's voice was level.

"I know. But for the sake of keeping my word, I need to talk to this other person first."

A long silence. Then Jeri spoke in a gentler tone to Jo. "Can you tell me everything you remember?"

Once again Jo recounted the story, not varying at all as to details.

"You never saw anyone?" Jeri asked.

"No, no one."

"Did you see the horse?"

"No."

"She was about two-thirds of the way from the house to the barn where I found her," Kris interjected. "She couldn't have seen into the stall from there."

"But you heard the horse?" Jeri asked.

"Not when I was outside." Jo paused. "I heard neighing when I was in the house, and then it stopped and I went back to watching TV. Then I heard more neighing. That's when I decided to go outside and check."

"Did the horse sound upset?" Jeri asked.

"No." Jo hesitated. "No, not really." She thought a moment, looking confused. "It was weird, though. That's the reason I went to see. That neighing."

"What about it, honey?" Kris said gently.

Jo looked doubtful. "At first it just sounded like Dixie neighing. And then, later," she looked at Jeri Ward, "it didn't sound right."

"Why not?" Jeri asked.

"Well, it didn't sound like Dixie."

"You mean she sounded different?" I asked.

"No." Jo shook her head and looked at me, then back to Jeri. "I don't think it was Dixie. I think it was another horse."

"Another horse?" Jeri sounded confused. "How could you tell?"

"I wasn't really sure." Jo still looked doubtful. "It just didn't sound like Dixie's voice. I mean, at first it did, and then it didn't. I thought maybe another horse had gotten loose and was out there."

Jeri still looked as if she wasn't sure how to take this.

"I could tell if I heard a horse neighing in my barnyard that wasn't one of my two," I volunteered.

"For sure?" Jeri asked.

"No, not for sure. But if you've owned a horse for a long time, their voices become very distinct to you. I can tell Gunner's nicker from Plumber's quite easily. Still, once in a while, just like people, they won't sound like themselves."

Jo nodded at this. "That's what I mean," she said. "I wasn't sure, and I thought it just didn't sound like Dixie. At first, when I heard her neigh, it did sound like her. I wondered what she was neighing for; she doesn't do that very often. Then I heard this other neighing, and I thought maybe there was a horse out there and Dixie was neighing at it. That's when I went out to check."

We all took that in.

"Is there any likelihood that you would have a loose horse running around here?" Jeri asked Kris.

Kris shrugged. "It's possible. There are a lot of horses in Harkins Valley. But we're almost a mile from the closest place that has any."

"Did you see another horse?" Jeri asked Jo.

"No. I really didn't see anything."

Jeri looked at Kris. "How about you? Did you see another horse? Or hear one?"

"No. I didn't see or hear anything unusual. I just saw Jo, lying there between the barn and the house." Kris's voice was very carefully even, but I could hear the underlying strain. She must have thought, feared, for at least a few seconds, that Jo was dead. It wouldn't be something you would get over quickly.

We were all quiet for a minute. I tended to give credence to Jo's suspicions of an unknown horse. Dixie was unlikely to start neighing for no reason.

"When you heard Dixie neigh to begin with," I asked Jo, "what did it sound like? What kind of a neigh was it?"

Jeri Ward looked a question at me.

I half shrugged. "A horse gives a sort of friendly nicker when you come to feed him in the morning, or when he spots another horse he recognizes. He's more likely to snort than neigh if he sees another kind of animal, like a deer for instance. When you take one horse away from his companions, he neighs louder and shriller; he sort of squalls. It sounds a lot more frantic. And a horse might neigh loudly like that if a strange horse arrived in the middle of the night."

Jo nodded vigorously. "It was more like that. Not nickering, neighing. I thought Dixie had seen another horse and was neighing at it, and then I thought I heard the stranger horse neighing back. They sounded kind of excited, you know."

Jeri looked confused but game. I was glad that she'd recently acquired a horse of her own. The concepts might be unfamiliar to her, but at least she wasn't dismissing our horse talk as a bunch of foolishness, as a non-horseman might be inclined to do.

"So Dixie sounded like she heard or saw another horse and was neighing at it?" I asked Jo.

"Yes," she said definitely. "And then I thought I heard another horse answering back."

We were all quiet once more. I suspected that the others, like me, were trying to puzzle out what bearing the unknown horse, if real, might have on the situation. Was it a coincidence? A loose horse running around just when the horse rapist was in the barn? That seemed unlikely.

"Do you think he rode here?" I said out loud.

We stared at each other. Nobody said anything.

After a minute, Jeri stood up. "I'll go out and talk to the guys," she said.

After she left, I said to Kris, "Maybe you two should get some sleep."

"I think Jo should." Kris stood up, holding her daughter's hand. "Okay, sweetheart?"

"Sure." Jo looked at me. "Thank you, Gail."

I was surprised. "Of course. But for what?"

"For coming. You made us feel better."

I gave her a brief hug. "You're welcome. Go to bed and try and get some sleep."

Five minutes later Kris returned from Jo's bedroom and Jeri Ward came back in the door, both at the same time.

"What can you tell us?" I asked Jeri.

She lifted her eyebrows. "Doesn't look like there are any fingerprints; we think he wore gloves. We'll do the usual analysis on the semen. It appears that a horse was tied behind the barn, not too long ago." Jeri looked at Kris. "Do you tie your horse back there?"

"No, never. I tie her out in front, by the stall where you found her."

"Well, it could be that this unknown horse was tied there. We're going to wait until daylight to make a closer examination of the scene. Is there a trail behind your barn?"

"Yes," Kris said. "It runs up the bank behind the house and then follows the ridge in both directions."

"Where can you ride to from here?"

Kris and I looked at each other and shook our heads. "Just about anywhere," she said. "If you go one way, you'll end up in the Lushmeadows subdivision. If you go the other, you'll end up in a network of trails that will take you toward Corralitos, and a lot of other places."

"I could ride from my place to here. I did it, last weekend," I said. "Or, at least, I rode to Lushmeadows, and, as Kris says, a person could easily ride from there to here."

"All right," Jeri nodded. "I need to ask you to stay completely away from the barn for a day, while we pursue our investigation."

"I have to untie the horse and put her back in the corral, and I have to feed her," Kris pointed out.

"Let's go out and go over that right now," Jeri said. To me, she said, "We need to talk, Gail."

"Can it be tomorrow?" I asked. "I'm pretty tired."

"Tomorrow is fine. I'll be here in the morning. You can reach me on my cell phone." She handed me a card.

"Okay," I said. "I'll be in touch. Night, Kris."

"Night, Gail. And thanks again."

"You bet." I put my hand on the doorknob and turned to go. Jeri's voice stopped me.

A cold, quiet voice, not unpleasant, exactly, just detached. Her cop voice. "Don't forget, Gail. I'll need the name of the other party you spoke of. It's important."

"Right," I said. "See you."

And then I was gone.

FIFTEEN

Another foggy morning. Tired, depressed, and worried, I lay on my side in bed, looking out the window at solidly gray skies. Condensed fog dripped steadily off the roof and the porch was wet and dank. Not much to get up for. But I had to. The animals needed to be fed and I had one very important errand to run. I had to go see Nico.

I got up, pulled on jeans and a sweatshirt, worked my way through the morning chores, and climbed in the truck. I didn't know how early Nico got up; I hoped it was early.

Eight o'clock on a Saturday morning was not an appropriate time for a social visit, and I knew it. At least I wasn't on call this weekend; my pager wouldn't buzz in the midst of a tricky conversation.

Fortunately, Nico was up. There were lights on in the kitchen, and I could smell coffee through the top half of the Dutch door, which was open despite the fog.

"Nico," I called. "It's Gail."

A moment, and she appeared, wearing jeans and a sweater, looking as rumpled and just-woke-up as I assumed I did myself.

"Hello, Gail," she said, with that warm smile.

"I'm sorry to disturb you so early, but we've got a problem," I said.

"Would you like to tell me about it over some coffee?"

"That would be great." I accepted with alacrity; I'd skipped my coffee this morning.

Once the ritual of pouring coffee and offering cream and sugar had been accomplished and we sat at the table in the windowed breakfast nook, I told Nico what had happened last night at Kris's.

"So you see," I finished up, "we really need to tell Jeri Ward about what's been happening here."

Nico had listened to my story with a composed face and she answered me quietly. "But I cannot, Gail."

"It's important," I protested. "You could be in danger."

Nico shrugged, a very Gallic gesture.

I stared at her in consternation.

"I have work I wish to accomplish here," she said. "If the police find out I am here illegally they will deport me, and I do not want that to happen."

"But . . ." I started, then stopped, aware already that nothing I could say would convince her.

"Please do not speak about me to this detective," Nico said.

What could I say? "It's your choice," I told her at last, "but I am really concerned. Has it happened again?"

"No, I do not think so."

"Will you tell me if it does?"

"If you wish."

I looked at her across the table; her face struck me as incredibly simple and pure. As always, I found myself intrigued, wanting to know her better. And I was worried about her.

"Can you think of anything that's changed lately?" I asked her. "Did someone new move in next door? Has a stranger been by here to look at paintings or something and noticed your mare?"

Nico sat quietly, holding her coffee, thinking. "I do not know of anything like that." She paused. "Except for George, and it cannot be him."

"George?"

"George Corfios."

"The one who moved in at Warren's place. You know him?"

"Yes, I met him years ago, when I first moved to this area. We have

127

ridden our horses together on the beach. He rode over to visit me when he first moved here."

"So, how well do you know George?"

"Not well. But I have known him for many years now. He is an artist, too."

"He is? I thought he was a carpenter."

Nico smiled. "Both. He makes furniture. He made the bed and dresser that I have. Would you like to see them?"

"Sure," I said. Inwardly my mind was churning. George Corfios had ridden here on a social call; he had ridden to Kris's on a social call. In both places the mares had been "raped." Nothing of the sort had happened in this area until he moved into it, as far as I knew. Could it possibly be a coincidence?

I was following Nico through her studio, glancing at paintings as I went. Once again, my eyes went to the tawny, undulating landscape with the mysterious cobalt blue water-shape in the center. It had been the first painting I had looked at when I stepped into this room, what, only a week ago? It seemed much longer than that.

Then I was entering a short hall with an open door to my right that revealed a small bathroom. Nico was going through the door at the end of the hall; I followed her.

Once again I stopped, my eyes widening in pleasure. Nico's bedroom was as plain as my own. The bed and dresser were solid, simple oak pieces, both primitive and graceful. They suited the whitewashed adobe walls perfectly, as if they'd been made for the room. Which, in fact, they had.

"When I moved here, George was one of the friends who came to visit me. I asked him to make some furniture for my bedroom. I think he has, how do you say, captured the spirit of the place very well."

"Yes," I said. The bed and dresser were undeniably beautiful. But all I could think about was the uncanny coincidence of George knowing both Nico and Kris—the two owners of the "raped" mares. And both attractive single women, I added to myself.

After a minute I said, "George is someone you like?"

"Yes." Nico trailed an affectionate hand across the wood of the dresser. Her face looked reserved.

128

"The furniture is lovely," I said truthfully. "And I've decided which painting I want."

"That is good." Nico smiled.

I felt a little startled; the words had just come from my mouth. I wasn't aware that I'd chosen. But apparently I had.

Turning, I led the way back to the studio and up to the first painting that had caught my eye. "This one," I said definitely.

Nico smiled again. "I like that one also."

"How much is it?"

She seemed to be thinking. "For you, it is two thousand dollars."

I nodded, wondering how I could possibly justify such a sum for a painting.

"You may make payments if you wish," Nico said.

"Really? That would be great." The feeling of financial relief was accompanied by another buoyant thought. If I made payments to her, perhaps I could continue getting to know Nico.

"Would you like me to deliver the painting? I have a van that is good for transporting them."

"That would be great," I said again, with enthusiasm. "When could you come?"

Nico consulted some inner calendar and said, "Wednesday evening, I could come."

We made arrangements. I gave her directions, my phone number, and a deposit for the amount of five hundred dollars. Despite last night's stress, and my worry and suspicions, I felt remarkably light-hearted at the thought of owning the painting, as well as the idea of knowing Nico better.

Nico walked me out to my truck. I stopped by the driver's side door and stared at the black mare, peacefully eating hay in her corral.

"Nico, I'm really, really worried about that guy who comes to . . ." I struggled for a word and gave up and shrugged, "the horse. I wish you'd let me call the police. They aren't going to be concerned about your residence status."

Nico met my eyes steadily. "Gail, I cannot."

"Okay. But you will tell me if anything happens."

"If you wish."

I got into my truck slowly, wishing I knew what the right answers were here. Should I override Nico's wishes? She might never forgive me, and again, was it really my decision? I had the definite sense that Nico wasn't going to be receptive to my suspicions about George.

In the end I said nothing. Just, "I'll see you Wednesday, then." But I drove away wondering. Not least of all what to say to Jeri Ward.

Her dark green sheriff's sedan was parked in Kris's driveway when I got there; reluctantly, I pulled in.

As I expected, our encounter was less than positive. In front of a pale and quiet Kris, I told Jeri that I'd promised to keep the other "victim's" identity a secret, and I was going to keep my promise.

Jeri's lips tightened. "Why don't you think that decision over, Gail. You could be putting this person's life at risk."

"I know," I said wearily. "I'm not happy about it either. I'll call you if I change my mind."

Jeri said nothing, but all friendliness was gone from her expression. After ascertaining that Jo was still asleep but seemed fine, and Kris didn't need me for anything, I took my leave, feeling even more disheartened than I'd expected.

It just didn't take anything these days to knock my equilibrium astray. A little disapproval and I was instantly sunk in a mire of depression. All I wanted to do was go home and lie on the couch.

Once again, though, fate had other plans. Which initially took the form of my small, excited red dog barking pleadingly from her pen.

"All right," I said. Letting Roey out, I yielded to her entreaties to play Frisbee. Twenty or so tosses later, we started back toward the house. The cat emerged from his spot on the porch and walked to greet us.

Roey charged up to him and licked his face, knocking him down in the process. Bonner seemed undisturbed, absorbing the dog's noisy welcome without a quiver. But I noticed that when he got up and walked off, he limped a little.

This wasn't unusual. The cat was getting old. He had come to me as an adult stray, four years ago, and had survived the move from Soquel to Corralitos, as well as the replacement of my old, sedate dog with a rambunctious puppy. Bonner still seemed active and healthy,

130

but his arthritis was beginning to show and his muscles had started to atrophy a bit. I was pretty sure he must be in his teens.

Still, he was a pretty animal, a fluffy tabby with a lynxlike face and a white chest and paws, and he had such a peaceful demeanor I'd nicknamed him the Buddha cat. I wished I had a tenth of his serenity.

I stroked his head now and he purred. I smiled. The old cat was happy enough, at least. Somehow I found that cheering. I might not be doing so well, but the animals in my care were still fine.

Letting the dog and the cat in the house, I looked around in renewed discouragement. The place was a mess. Instead of lying on the couch, I needed to scrub floors. I had no idea where in the world I was going to find the motivation.

But you get what you need. I'd only been in the house ten minutes when the phone rang. Picking it up, I said, "Hello."

"Gail?"

"Yes?"

"This is Blue. Blue Winter." His voice sounded oddly deep; I realized I'd never spoken to him on the phone before.

"Hi, Blue."

"Are you busy?" Blue sounded as tongue-tied as I felt.

"No. Actually I just got home."

"I was wondering if you'd mind if I dropped by today. I have something I'd like to give you."

"Uh, no, I wouldn't mind." My eyes roved wildly over the gritty floor, piles of dishes on the counter, and general impression of rubble and disarray. "When would you be thinking of coming?"

"Whenever would be good for you."

"How about this afternoon? Say four o'clock," I said promptly.

"All right." He paused. "Maybe I could make you a margarita."

"Oh yeah. That's right. You're a tequila fan." Memories of last summer's pack trip rushed through me.

Blue laughed, sounding more relaxed than he had so far. "I could bring all the makings," he offered.

"Okay." I said. "Margaritas it is."

"See you at four," he said, and hung up.

For a second I stared at the receiver in my hand, surprised at the rush of anticipation I felt. Last night's drama and this morning's frustration receded abruptly. Blue had actually called, dammit. He was coming over.

Another minute of taking this in and I got to my feet and surveyed the room with some determination. Now I had a motive to clean the house.

SIXTEEN

Five hours later I peeled my dirty jeans and sweatshirt off and replaced them with clean jeans and a knit tank top in steel blue-gray. The house was as cleaned up as it had been in a long time—floors and sinks scrubbed, clothes and dishes clean and put away, all dog and cat hair vacuumed off the couch and carpet. I brushed my hair in front of the antique mirror and decided against putting on any makeup. I wanted this meeting to feel as simple and natural as possible.

Shoving my feet into comfortable clogs, I went out in the garden to cut some flowers for the house. The beds were lush with color, at the height of their June opulence. My choices seemed endless. Still, I knew where I would go. I had a rose grower coming over. The bouquet on the table was definitely going to be roses.

The question was which. In the end I went with my favorites—the Tea roses and Noisettes. Putting together a selection of rich apricot, peach, cream, and pale straw-gold, I added a few sprigs from my wild grapevine. The brilliant green and silver of the freshly unfurled grape leaves was the perfect foil for the warm, yet gentle colors of the roses. Arranging all this in a glass vase, I stood back. Unaffected and unfancy, the bouquet looked what it was, a loose gathering from a country garden. This was fine with me.

Blue was due to be here soon. For a second I dithered, wondering whether to put out the chips and salsa that I'd rushed to the store to buy, but then gave it up. Picking up my current book, the second in the Harry Potter series, I settled myself in the wicker couch on the porch. Time to relax, read, and drop my fussing. Things looked as good as they were getting, me included.

Still, I felt a rush of anticipatory nerves as a dark green pickup pulled up my driveway. The truck, liberally blotched with dried mud about the fenders, and well-coated with dust—a farmer's truck—parked itself near the house, and Blue Winter got out.

From my position on the porch, I could see the late afternoon sunlight brighten the already vivid red-gold curls visible under the brim of his gray fedora hat. He carried a brown paper grocery bag in one arm; reaching over the side of the truck bed with the other, he pulled out a potted plant.

A rose, I realized a second later. The rose grower, naturally enough, wasn't bringing me a bouquet of florist's flowers; he was bringing me a living plant for my garden.

I was pleased. Standing up, I said, "Hi, Blue."

"Hello, Stormy." Blue smiled, that slow, grave smile that had so intrigued me last summer.

"Let me guess." I smiled back. "You brought me a rose. That's great."

Blue was looking around my garden. "You've got quite a few," he remarked, "but I don't see this one. I remember you said you liked Tea roses and Noisettes; I took a chance you might not mind my favorite China rose."

Blue lugged the potted rose up on the porch; I smiled at the sight of it.

Blue's favorite China rose was a delicate creature, with silky single blooms spangled all over the plant, looking just like multicolored butterflies. And truly multicolored—the blossoms ranged from pale apricot to coppery red, with various shades of pink and coral in between.

"Mutabilus," Blue said. "So called, I suppose, because the blooms change color as they age. And don't be fooled by how dainty it looks; it's a very tough rose."

134

"I love it," I said truthfully.

Blue grinned. "I also brought the makings for margaritas." He lifted the brown paper grocery bag a few inches.

"Why don't you come inside," I said. "I can give you the tour, what there is of it, and you can make us a drink."

"Sounds good to me."

Blue followed me through the door and into the main room of the little house; I turned to catch a glimpse of his face as he entered. As I'd hoped and half expected, a wide smile broke out as he looked around. Many people greeted the house this way.

It was so small and craftsmanlike, so carefully detailed, and yet it was not in any way cute. There was a certain starkness to the wooden floor and walls, a sense of drama in the open ceiling and big windows. It was in no sense a "doll's house," and yet there was that aura of specialness that came with its surprisingly small size.

"This is great," Blue said.

"Isn't it? I'm very happy with it."

"Did you build it?" he asked.

"No. But I did build the barns and the fences that you see. Or really, I had someone build them for me." That someone being Clay Bishop. I felt a small glow of petty satisfaction at the thought of him. Clay wasn't the only one who could find another date.

Blue was unpacking his paper bag and assembling bottles, lemons and limes, a juice squeezer, and a pitcher on my kitchen counter. It looked as though the tour was going to wait until after we had a drink.

I watched his back, noting the red-gold curls, the broad shoulders under the green canvas fabric of his shirt, the long legs. Turning his head, he said over his shoulder, "How was your day?"

"Not so good," I said. And without thinking much about it, I began telling him the story of last night's adventure and the corresponding tricky involvement of Nico and her mare.

Blue listened, interrupting only to hand me my drink with a "Cheers, here's to you."

I took a long swallow, blinked, and told him, "Thank you; I needed that. You make a mean margarita."

"My favorite drink." Blue took a sip of his own drink and asked me, "What are you going to do?"

"I don't know," I said in frustration. "I'm really worried about Nico. Not to mention Kris. It's such a, well, creepy thought, that someone's coming to their barns at night to rape their mares."

"That does seem pretty weird," Blue agreed.

"Of course," I said, arguing with myself, "it's not like any real harm is being done. It doesn't do the mare any damage; it would really be much worse if this person were raping women." This, however, did not change my purely visceral reaction to the concept of the horse rapist, as I was well aware.

Blue stared at me with a characteristic level expression, one I had learned to know last summer. "Some harm was done to your friend's daughter."

"That's just it," I said. "Maybe this person had no intention of hurting anyone, but he bashed Jo over the head to keep her from seeing him. Or so I suppose. That could happen to Nico, or Kris, too."

"How's your friend Kris doing?"

"She's doing what there is to do. When I left her house this morning there were police all over the place. If the horse rapist has any brains, he'll stay away. But he's going to think Nico's is still safe." I looked at Blue. "And the worst thing is, I think I know who it is."

"You do?" Blue looked startled.

I explained how George Corfios had come upon the scene recently, how he had ridden to both women's houses in the past, how we thought that the horse rapist had ridden to Kris's house on a horse.

"So, you see, in a lot of ways he fits. But I didn't tell Jeri Ward, the detective, about him, because I'd have to bring up Nico, and I promised Nico I wouldn't. Damn, this is a mess." I took a long swallow of undeniably potent margarita.

"What's this George guy like?" Blue asked.

"Well, I've only met him once. Dark, handsome, physical-looking. He's a carpenter by trade. I have to admit, he doesn't look like the type to be raping horses; I'm sure he could find plenty of willing women. It's just hard to believe it's all a coincidence. He moves into the area, the horse rapes start happening, he just happens to know both

Nico and Kris, and just happens to have ridden his horse to both their houses?"

"How do you know these rapes, if you want to call them that, just started happening?"

I thought about that. Drank some more margarita. "Of course, I don't know."

"That's what I was thinking. This could have been going on for a while. Maybe from before George moved into the area. It's not something that most people would tell you about."

"You're so right."

I stared out the big windows at my vegetable garden and took another sip of my drink. "I really don't know what to do," I said. "Nico has a good reason for not wanting me to tell the police about her, and I don't want to betray her trust. But the whole thing seems so volatile."

Blue said nothing to this, just made steady inroads on his margarita. Aware that I was not being terribly hospitable, I went to the cupboard and produced tortilla chips and salsa. Placing these in bowls on the table, I offered, "Have a seat."

Blue was just starting to sit down when both our eyes were caught by a moving red shape coming up the driveway. It rounded the turn at the bottom of the hill and emerged in full view, revealing itself as a small, shiny, vividly red convertible sporting the dealer license plates characteristic of new cars.

"You have an upscale friend," Blue commented, watching the car with interest.

"I don't know who that is," I said. I didn't recognize the make of sports car either.

"The car's a Boxster," Blue said.

"What's that?"

"Porsche's newest model."

"Oh."

"They're nice cars."

I thought Blue's voice had a mildly wistful quality.

By this time the Boxster was close enough for me to ascertain that I did indeed know the man behind the steering wheel.

"That's Clay," I said out loud.

"A friend?"

"Yeah. He built this house and my barn, too." This was begging the issue of what exactly Clay was to me, but I didn't feel any obligation to tell Blue.

We both watched Clay park the sports car and unfold out of it, something he did gracefully, as he did everything. Stepping out, I waved him over. "Hi, Clay."

Blue followed me out on the porch, and Clay approached us with his usual easy smile, but I had the inner sense he was rapidly evaluating the situation. Once again I felt a perverse little glow of satisfaction and was conscious of hoping he was jealous.

I glanced at Blue. As I expected, his face showed nothing. He looked a little more remote, that was all.

"Blue, this is Clay Bishop. Clay, Blue Winter." The two men shook hands; I made no effort at further explanations.

"Would you like a margarita?" Blue asked.

I was sure he meant it in a friendly way, and no doubt about it, the margarita makings were his; it wasn't my place to offer them to Clay. Still, the question made it sound very much as though Blue were the host here, and Clay's eyes shot to mine.

"Blue very kindly offered to come over and make me a drink," I said. "A good drink, too."

"I'd be happy to pour you one." Blue addressed Clay politely.

"Thanks, that would be great."

Blue stepped into the kitchen, returned with the pitcher and a glass, poured Clay a drink, and freshened our glasses. I brought the chips and salsa out on the porch. We all sat down a little warily.

"Nice car," Blue said.

Clay smiled, a smile that went right to his eyes. "Yesterday was my fortieth birthday," he said simply. "I bought myself a present. I guess it's just your classic midlife crisis."

Blue laughed. "I bet it's fun to drive."

"It is that."

"It's pretty," I said idly. I was not a big sports car fan. Pickup trucks had always seemed sufficient to me.

Inwardly I was adding things up. Yesterday, when Kris and I had seen Clay having dinner with the unknown Sue, had been his birthday. This was something I hadn't even known. And Clay had certainly not invited me to have dinner with him. Still waters run deep, or something like that, I told myself. There was obviously a lot I didn't know about Clay Bishop.

"Well, happy birthday, belatedly," I said.

"Thanks." Once again there was awkward quiet, broken only by the clink of ice cubes in glasses.

"Would you like a tour?" I said to Blue. "The house isn't very big, but I'm happy to show it to you—and the garden and the barn, if you're interested."

I glanced over at Clay. "Clay built all this, so he can give informed commentary. That is, if you'd like." I added this diffidently to Clay.

Clay gave me his pleasant smile. "Of course."

"And I'd like to look at your car," Blue said.

"Sure." Clay smiled again, seeming completely self-possessed. Maybe he wasn't jealous.

The next hour passed in a reasonably comfortable way, though I was aware of a sense of strain. I would infinitely have preferred to be entertaining one or the other of these men rather than both. However, given the circumstances, things went smoothly.

Blue admired my house and property, we both admired Clay's car, Blue made another round of margaritas. I was just wondering if I ought to offer to cook everybody dinner when Blue stood up.

"I need to be going," he said simply. "It was nice to see you, Gail. Nice to meet you, too." He shook Clay's hand. Collecting his margarita makings, he turned to leave.

I didn't know what to say. Should I go after him, invite him to come back, what? In the end I remained on the porch and said merely, "Thanks for coming over. I enjoyed it."

"You make a great margarita," Clay added.

I watched Blue get into his truck, thinking that he must assume that Clay was, at the very least, my steady date. Which was, in a sense, true. And yet, I wanted to explain, it isn't like that. I'm still free.

Once the green truck disappeared down the driveway, Clay looked at me questioningly. I said nothing. I didn't feel the need to explain Blue's presence.

Taking this silence as it was meant—Clay was nothing if not quick—he asked me, "Would you like to go for a ride in my new car? That's actually why I brought it over."

"Sure," I said without enthusiasm. Going fast in a sports car was not my favorite thing, as I frequently pointed out to Kris. "Just don't scare me," I added.

"I promise," Clay said.

Five minutes later we were zipping along the back roads, Clay maintaining a reasonable pace. I had to admit, the Porsche felt solid and reassuring; it went around the corners as though it were on rails. Clay had a wide and excited grin on his face; I could see how much he was enjoying this new toy.

We ended up in Harkins Valley; Clay slowed as he approached the Bishop Ranch. "Would you like some dinner?" he asked. "I was going to make risotto."

It took me a minute to assimilate this. Clay was offering to cook me dinner. I was intrigued. Not just about what sort of cook he might be, but also about the opportunity to see his home. I'd never been inside it before. And I had an endless curiosity about houses and gardens and the various ways that people approach their dwelling space. Not to mention, I was hungry.

"All right," I said. "Thanks."

And Clay turned in at the Bishop Ranch entrance.

SEVENTEEN

I'd seen Clay's house many times; I'd even had a beer on the porch once. It sat at the other end of the property from the main ranch house, where brother Bart lived with his mother. Clay's house was much smaller, and had obviously been the foreman's house at one time.

Clay confirmed this opinion as we walked toward the front door. "The ranch was built around the turn of the century," he said. "This was originally the foreman's house, and that little building over there," he pointed, "was the bunkhouse."

Clay's house, like every building on the place, was painted barn-red with white trim. The exterior was tidy enough, but he didn't seem to be a gardener. A small patch of lawn and several large old shrubs—lilac and philadelphus, it looked like, one red rose—no doubt dating from the ranch's early days were the only plants to be seen.

Clay held the front door open and I stepped inside. My first impression was pure surprise. Somehow I had expected something different from the craftsman who had built my house. But this little boxlike room was very traditional, almost conventional, and looked as though it had been remodeled only slightly, if at all.

The short beige carpet was a non-statement, as were the cream-colored walls and low ceilings. The old-fashioned molding around doors and windows had been painted a contrasting warm brown—attractive, if a bit Victorian for my taste. There were a few well-worn pieces of furniture, a wood stove in the corner, and an open doorway leading into what appeared to be the kitchen.

Clay saw my glance and answered my unspoken comment.

"I'm just a tenant," he said. "I haven't done much in the way of remodeling. Some day I hope to build a place of my own. Of course, the Porsche will set those plans back a year or two."

"You're just a tenant?" I asked curiously. "I thought it was your family's place."

"Not exactly." Clay looked noncommittal, as if uncertain what to say.

Not wanting to be rude, I didn't probe.

In the end, he volunteered, "Bart's my half brother. The ranch belonged to his father. Our mom married my dad when Dave Bishop died. But my dad died a year later. Mom kept living here; she changed my name to Bishop because it seemed simpler. But this ranch goes to Bart, not me, when she dies."

"Oh." This seemed to explain a few things, including the strong physical differences between the brothers, Clay's lack of involvement in the "family" business, and the fact that Bart lived in the main ranch house.

"Bart and I get along real well," Clay said. "I pay my rent here by doing handyman work. That way I can save almost all the money I make building houses. It's a good deal for me."

"I see," I said. It made sense that under the circumstances he wouldn't want to spend a lot of time and money on the house.

"Can I get you something to drink?" Clay asked.

Bearing in mind the margaritas I'd consumed, I said, "How about a glass of wine?"

"Do you like Merlot?"

"Yes, that would be perfect."

In a minute Clay emerged from the kitchen with two glasses of the deep red wine. Handing one to me, he asked, "How about keeping me company in the kitchen while I cook?"

"Of course."

Stepping through the open archway, I surveyed a plain, old-fashioned kitchen, painted white with brown trim and very similar in tone to the room I'd just left. There was a round table in the corner. I seated myself there and watched Clay pour olive oil in a large cast-iron skillet. I didn't offer to help. One of the rules of life I'd evolved as I neared forty was that I preferred to do all the cooking and cleaning in my own house, and to let other people do the same. I no more liked to fumble around someone else's kitchen searching for the correct implement than I enjoyed watching my guests bustle through the process of washing my dishes and putting them in places where I didn't want them put.

I sipped my wine and asked Clay, "Do you like living here?"

"Well, enough," he said easily.

"Do you remember the place before all the land was sold off to the subdivision?"

"Barely. My mom sold it when Bart and I were just kids."

"Warren White must have been a young man then," I said idly.

"Yeah, Warren's about ten years older than I am. He told me Lushmeadows was his first big project; he was twenty. It made his fortune."

"Uh-huh." I nodded, not much interested in Warren and his fortune.

"How about Bart? Does he like living here and running the boarding stable?" I was mildly curious about brother Bart.

Clay shrugged. "It's hard to tell. Bart's life hasn't been exactly happy."

I waited.

Eventually Clay went on, talking as he chopped vegetables. "Bart got married young, nineteen, I think, and he and his wife had a couple of kids. Then she left him, and somehow she got full custody of the kids. He only gets to see them once in a while. It made him pretty unhappy. He quit his job and was sort of a bum for a while. He moved back here eventually and took over the boarding stable.

"Of course, it was a good thing in some ways. Mom used to run it, but she came down with cancer and she's been in poor health ever since. I don't know what she'd do without Bart living there helping her." Clay sounded distinctly relieved; I thought I could imagine that the burden of taking care of his mother full-time wasn't one he wanted.

Well, this explained why I'd never seen Mrs. Bishop. And it might explain some of Bart's animosity as well.

I reflected for a moment how intricate and revealing people's backgrounds were. Suddenly Clay and his family seemed to have some substance beyond their facade.

Blue Winter jumped into my mind. I knew nothing about his family or his background. At the thought, I looked at Clay, who was gently ladling chopped onions into the skillet. He was handsome and personable and I liked his company, no doubt about it. But that intense flare along the nerves that I felt when I looked at Blue was missing here. I didn't watch Clay's hands and think about how it would feel if they were to caress me.

Sipping some more Merlot, I wondered about this. Clay's hands, now chopping bell peppers, were every bit as attractively shaped as Blue's; his long forearms were as well muscled. I had a hard time fathoming what created that simple but intense physical connection, that sexual draw.

Did the horse rapist feel that toward mares?

The thought startled me in its incongruity. I almost laughed out loud. For God's sake, Gail, I remonstrated mentally. This whole train of thought was getting a little too weird.

Clay glanced at me curiously and I smiled. "It looks good," I said, indicating the simmering skillet.

He smiled back. I resolved to concentrate on the present circumstances and forget the damned horse rapist.

But I couldn't. Last night's alarming scenario was imprinted firmly on my mind, along with all the questions that arose from it. Looming larger, I found, was this strange curiosity about the mind and motivation of the pervert—for surely his behavior could or should be described as perverted?

I made conversation with Clay and sipped my Merlot and wondered: What was it Jeri Ward had said? "This sort of thing can become compulsive; the perpetrator has to continue it."

Shit. If that was the case, it was just a matter of time till the guy returned to Nico's or Kris's. And was it George? Try as I might, I had a hard time picturing that dark, handsome face above a body engaged in the literally bestial act.

Clay was serving the food; I made yet another effort to detach from my train of thought and keep my mind on appropriate dinner-table conversation.

The risotto was excellent; Clay had used red bell peppers and smoked chicken to enliven it. Remembering, not for the first time, that I'd barely eaten anything all day, I enjoyed as much of the elegant dish as I could. Sadly, the lack of regular meals seemed to have shrunk my stomach; I could only absorb small portions these days.

Clay and I chatted desultorily but pleasantly; I was aware that my attention was wavering. Still, an idea that had been in the back of my mind jumped to the front and I asked him, "Would it be convenient for you to give me and my horse another ride home with the stock trailer tomorrow? Say in the late afternoon."

"Sure. If you want, I'll even go on a ride with you," Clay offered.

"That's okay," I said quickly, and then amended what sounded like rudeness with "I sometimes like just to cruise the horse around by myself. You know what I mean?"

"Yeah, I do." Clay smiled quietly.

What he didn't know was that I had a notion to explore the trails behind Kris's place on horseback—see if I could discover for myself how the horse rapist might have arrived.

"That was a great dinner, Clay," I said. "And I hate to be a spoil-sport, but I'm really tired. I was out late last night." No doubt he was, too, I thought, remembering Sue.

Clay made no comment, merely offered to drive me home. Once back in my own driveway, I leaned toward him quickly for the obligatory good-night kiss, conscious of the impulse to get it over with.

Clay, however, kissed me lingeringly and with warmth; I had to admit it felt good. As I unfolded myself out of the Porsche, I realized I was no closer to understanding my feelings toward this man. They were, in a word, mixed. I felt safe and comfortable with him; at the same time I was aware that I really had no idea what he felt toward me. Clay was in many ways an enigma; I didn't know whether I found that disconcerting or interesting.

Clay smiled at me from the driver's seat.

"Good night," I said.

"See you tomorrow," he replied.

With a brief, assenting wave, I turned and let myself in the house, conscious of more conflicting feelings. I wanted to be alone . . . and I was curious about Clay. I wondered what it would feel like if I let the kisses escalate.

Maybe some day.

EIGHTEEN

I awoke the next morning to the familiar despondency. Getting up required a major effort of will. I made the coffee and fed the animals, feeling as if I was dragging a large anchor every step of the way.

Then I sat on the couch, sipping coffee and staring out through the big windows at the foggy landscape. I should call Kris; the thought was there but the energy wasn't. Still, I picked up the phone and dialed.

Kris sounded as down as I felt. "I couldn't sleep last night, Gail. I kept thinking I heard someone out at the barn."

"Are the cops still there?"

"No, they're gone. That detective was apologetic, but she said they didn't have the 'resources' to mount a guard on us. I sent Jo to stay with her father. But I'm a basket case."

"Jeez, Kris." My problems suddenly seemed insignificant. "Do you want to come and stay here?"

"I don't know." Kris sounded a little perkier. "Thanks for offering."

"Do you want me to come over?" I asked.

"No, I'm leaving. First to go see Jo, and then I'm going over to the school to work on my grading. I just want to get out of here."

"You'll be all right?"

"Sure." Kris didn't sound entirely convinced. "I'll be fine."

"Call me if you need me," I told her.

"I'll do that."

I hung up the phone. Stared out the windows some more. Now what?

The solitary ride through the hills that I'd been planning seemed like too much work. But I'd told Clay I was coming; he'd be waiting for me.

Why, I wondered, not for the first time, wasn't I cheered by Clay's obvious interest in me? Not to mention that Blue Winter had actually called and come over. This was the man I'd been thinking about since last summer. Surely I ought to be feeling good about that?

Lethargy was like a lid; it wouldn't let any light in. I felt mildly pleased by the men's attention—a feeling that was barely skin-deep. Inside, where the sadness lived, an empty wind blew through me, leaving me desolate. I couldn't imagine where to go from here. A happy life seemed impossible.

I put my coffee cup down, frightened by my thoughts. Summoning up the will power that had taken me through so many struggles, I forced myself up and away from the couch. I was not, I was damned well not, going to lie around all day thinking hopeless thoughts. Instead, I flogged my body out to the tool shed, got the weed whacker, and mowed the grass along the drive.

When I was done, the place looked a lot neater, and to my surprise, my heart felt considerably lighter. The sun was breaking through the fog; I saddled Plumber and rode down the driveway to the sound of Gunner's plaintive neighs.

Once again I took the trail through the hills, this time purposefully. I was going to ride to Kris's.

Plumber plodded steadily along, his ears working forward and back, forward and back, his eyes bright. I ascended the first ridge and dropped down the other side, picked my way through the abandoned apple orchard.

Then it was up again, through the dusty scrub. Quail scuttled for cover in the greasewood; a jay squawked noisily. I jumped when something rustled in the brush—all my senses on ultra-alert. I hadn't forgotten the cougar.

I wasn't sure whether Plumber had either; he seemed calm, but unusually watchful.

The creepy feeling along my nerves grew stronger as we descended into the steep redwood-filled canyon. The dark solitude seemed positively eerie. I thought of the cougar; I thought of the horse rapist. At the moment it seemed entirely plausible that both were hanging out here.

Giving myself a mental shake, I clucked to my horse as we crossed the creek. This was just a redwood forest, it wasn't the haunted forest. I almost expected to see a sign: I'D TURN BACK IF I WERE YOU.

Still, we made it up the other side intact, though puffing, at least on Plumber's part. I let him breathe for a minute, then sent him toward the trail that forked downhill, the trail I'd meant to take last time. By my reckoning, this trail led in the direction of Kris's place.

Now we were passing the cougar's bush. The odds of him being there again were absolutely zero, I told myself. I looked steadily into the bush; Plumber looked, too. Nothing happened. The cougar was long gone.

On we went, pursuing what looked to me to be an easterly direction. We were in scrub country now; a mix of greasewood, manzanita, ceanothus, and Scotch broom lined the trail. We topped another rise, descended into a swale, and were in the redwoods again. The trail climbed a ridge, winding up in gentle switchbacks.

When we reached the top I stopped to let Plumber breathe and to reconnoiter. Plumber was tired. He stood still; the only sound I could hear was his breathing and the note of an unknown bird. And then, suddenly, another sound. Muted rustling, like the wind.

Not the wind, though. The trees were still. I listened. A long silence. Then, abruptly, the noise again. This time I could pinpoint it—straight ahead, down the trail. I went in that direction.

When the noise came again, I both saw and heard it—the distant flash of a red car as it passed through the trees. I had come to a road.

To Harkins Valley Road, it turned out. One look around, and I knew exactly where I was. Less than a quarter mile from Kris's place. I followed the trail in that direction.

Back up the ridge we went and soon, just as Kris had said, I saw a branch trail leading back in the direction of her house. We picked our way down it; in a minute Kris's barn was visible through the trees.

I sat and stared. No one seemed to be about. Kris's car was not in the driveway, neither were any cop cars. The last thing I needed was to run into Jeri Ward. But everybody appeared to be gone.

Slowly I approached the barn. This is what the horse rapist did, perhaps. Rode down this hill in the dark, watching and listening. That argued that he had some familiarity with this trail.

I tried to remember what sort of a moon was out last night. Couldn't. But it would have been pretty dark under these trees, even with a full moon.

We were at the back of Kris's barn now; I could see the trampled spot next to the fence where the stranger's horse had apparently been tied. I tried to picture this man, whoever he was, tying his horse to the railing, sneaking into the dark barn. My shoulders twitched uncontrollably.

The only thought that came to mind was that it must be someone who knew Kris, knew she owned a mare. I tried to picture George Corfios in this role; it was difficult.

Approaching the tie-up spot, I noticed a pile of relatively fresh droppings, which must have come from the stranger's horse. They were green, the droppings of a horse who was on a diet of primarily alfalfa hay. Of course, most horses in this part of California were fed alfalfa. Still, a horse who ate oat hay or forage-mix hay would have yellowish droppings; a pastured horse would have brownish droppings. I wondered what George Corfios's horse ate.

Whatever Warren White was feeding his horses, no doubt. And that, I thought, I could find out. Any horse who did not eat alfalfa hay was not the horse rapist's horse. This was potentially very useful information.

Fired up by my new idea, I turned Plumber back up the hill. The sweat had dried on his neck and he was no longer breathing hard. "Come on, boy," I told him. "Just a little bit further."

NINETEEN

It took about twenty minutes to ride to Lushmeadows. I ambled through the subdivision, glancing at horse barns as I went. Plenty of stacks of alfalfa hay were prominently visible. As I'd feared, eliminating suspects on the basis of what they fed their horses wasn't going to be easy. Alfalfa hay was just too common.

Mike O'Hara was in his barnyard grooming Sonny as I rode by. I waved, and he came over to the fence to greet me.

"Hello, Gail."

"Hi, Mike," I responded. "Sonny looks good."

"Yes, he's fine."

"No more bellyaches?"

"Nope." Mike regarded me steadily. "That was a terrible thing that happened to Kris's daughter."

"How did you find out?" I asked, surprised. "Was it in the papers?"

"Kris told me," Mike said simply. "She came over, told me what happened, and asked if she could call me at night if she heard anything suspicious. I'm more or less her closest neighbor."

No closer than George or Warren White, I thought. It was interesting that Kris had asked Mike instead. I wondered if I should discuss my suspicions of George with Kris.

151

"So what did Kris say?" I asked Mike curiously.

"Just that Jo had apparently surprised a burglar when Kris was out, and he hit her over the head and knocked her out."

"Oh," I said. No mention of the horse-raping aspect, I noticed.

Mike glanced at me. "I offered to come over, have a look around, but Kris said it wasn't necessary."

"That's right, you used to be a cop, didn't you?"

"Thirty years," Mike nodded. "Up near San Francisco," he added.

I nodded slowly in return, thinking that Mike was probably a good choice for backup. He would know what to do in an emergency.

Glancing at the angle of the sun, I smiled and said, "I'd better keep moving."

"You be careful, Gail. Especially when you're out by yourself."

"I'll do that," I said. "See you later."

Looking into Mike's barn as I rode by, I noticed that it, like the others I'd passed, contained a stack of alfalfa hay. As did Warren White's, I found out when I reached his driveway. Neither Warren nor George was out in the yard; I turned Plumber and rode back down the road toward the Bishop Ranch.

This whole idea about the hay was proving to be a big waste of time. Everybody fed alfalfa hay, it seemed.

Crossing Harkins Valley Road, I rode up the Bishop Ranch drive, Plumber plodding wearily now. He was tired. I was, too. I was very glad I'd asked Clay to give us a ride back home.

Locating Clay proved to be easy. He stood in a group of four men outside the big barn. The other three were brother Bart, Warren White, and George Corfios. The men were talking and laughing together; I approached the group unnoticed.

Clay was the first to see me; he gave me that warm smile and a "Hi, Gail. You made it."

"Sure I did," I said to Clay. The other men greeted me briefly. I dismounted and Plumber bumped me with his nose, then rubbed his head against my arm. He was itchy under his bridle, I knew. I scratched his ears and the back of his neck, and he bobbed his head up and down and twitched his upper lip with pleasure.

I saw Bart's look and could imagine the negative comment that was probably coming. Meeting his eyes, I continued to rub Plumber's face.

My unspoken "Shut up you asshole" must have registered loud and clear, because Bart looked away and kept quiet. His face had a hostile expression, though.

Ostentatiously he resumed his conversation with Warren White, which appeared to be about some airheaded female boarder with a horse she couldn't control. Bart's posture, with his back almost turned to me, effectively shut me out of the talk.

This was just fine with me. I rubbed Plumber's neck, watched the men, and thought my thoughts.

Bart made a comment to Warren that was inaudible to me; both men laughed. I recognized the tone. That old we're-all-assholes-together laugh, I called it to myself. That excluding, completely male, inevitably derogatory laugh, usually in a certain type of man, accompanied by some sort of comment heavily embroidered with the word "fucking." I had heard this laugh and this tone many, many times; I had come to believe that it signified a deep insecurity and was a sure tip-off that the guy would be difficult to deal with. Men who favored this particular mannerism could be just about counted on to be neither confident, intelligent, nor mature.

Resisting the urge to give Bart yet another glance that would certainly have revealed the intense distaste I felt, I kept my eyes firmly fixed on Clay. Neither he nor George was taking part in whatever adolescent bandying the other two were playing out. Both just smiled from time to time and kept quiet.

Shifting my gaze to George, I tried to decide if I was facing the horse rapist. I felt no intuitive twinges one way or the other. George's dark face was relaxed, reserved, nonthreatening. I could not imagine him assaulting a horse.

That was just the trouble. For that matter, I couldn't imagine any of these men assaulting a horse. Or any other man I knew. The only picture I could come up with was giggling seventeen-year-old boys. But that somehow didn't equate with the solitary stranger who had ridden a horse to Kris's and bashed Jo over the head.

There was a gap in the conversation; just for the heck of it I asked Bart, "What do you feed all these horses? Alfalfa?"

For a moment I thought he wouldn't answer, but eventually came a grudging, "Yep. Unless the customer wants something different."

As I had supposed. Any of these hundred or so boarded horses could be the horse rapist's mount. At the thought, I felt intensely discouraged with my amateur sleuthing and an equally intense desire to go home.

I looked plaintively at Clay; he caught the glance as quickly and accurately as if we were longtime lovers.

"Ready to go?" he asked quietly.

"Yes, if you don't mind."

"No problem."

And in another minute he was efficiently hitching his truck to the stock trailer, every move displaying the deft competence I had come to think of as his trademark.

I loaded Plumber, waved a casual good-bye to the other men, and climbed in the cab. Clay drove out onto Harkins Valley Road without a word.

We passed Nico's house and then Kris's; all I could think of was the strange threat that seemed to hang over both. Was it just the two of them, I wondered.

I glanced at Clay's quiet profile and a jarring buzz went through me, as if I'd been stuck with an electric cattle prod. What had Clay said, driving me to town a week ago? That a neighbor woman had been murdered?

My mouth seemed to open without volition. "Clay, that woman you knew who was murdered, did the police ever figure out who did it?"

Clay looked at me a little oddly, but he answered easily enough. "Not that I know of."

"She was just found dead out at her barn?"

"That's right," he said quietly. "Someone hit her over the head."

"I take it she had horses, if she had a barn."

"Yeah. Two Morgans."

"Mares?" I asked.

Once again, Clay shot me a curious glance. "One mare, one gelding."

A mare. Damn. I was quiet. For some reason, I just didn't want to talk to Clay about this. It wasn't that I didn't trust him, I assured myself. It was just . . . I just didn't, that was all.

Clay was looking at me very curiously now; I felt impelled to give some sort of explanation for my questions.

"I was wondering if I knew the woman. As a client," I said lamely. "I couldn't place her name, but I thought I might remember her horses."

This unlikely statement actually contained a grain of truth. I did frequently remember people's horses and problems—that bay mare with a stone bruise—when I had no recollection of their names.

"Did you know her?" Clay asked. "Her name was Marianne, Marianne Moore."

"No, I don't think so."

We were quiet, the somber subject of the murdered woman seeming to hover over us. Inwardly my thoughts were racing noisily. Had this other person been a victim of the horse rapist, too? Surely this was something I should bring up with Jeri Ward.

The thought of Jeri Ward brought another wave of discouragement rolling over me. I just didn't feel up to being grilled by the woman.

Clay was pulling into my driveway now. In another minute I was unloading Plumber. Putting the horse in the corral, I fed him and Gunner and Daisy. When I was done Clay glanced at me inquiringly.

Politeness dictated I ask him in for a beer, but I just couldn't do it. I was too tired, and I had too much on my mind.

"Thanks, Clay," was all I could come up with. "I appreciate it."

"No problem." Clay heard the farewell note and responded with his usual grace. "Anytime."

He climbed back into the pickup. "I'll call you," he said. And waved good-bye.

I trudged up the hill to the house, wondering what to do. Call Jeri Ward? Call Kris? It all seemed like too much.

In the end I did nothing. Poured myself a glass of wine and curled up on the couch with the dog by my feet.

I didn't want to deal with this weird situation anymore. For once in my life I was going to take the advice I'd been given so often. This time I was going to mind my own business.

TWENTY

Monday morning did not begin auspiciously. I arrived at work to find that a call from the woman with the mysteriously recumbent gray gelding had arrived there before me.

"She's pretty unhappy with you, Gail," Jim said.

"She is?" I was quite honestly surprised. "Why?"

"Well, she hauled that horse up to the veterinary hospital at Davis, and after three days of very expensive care, they told her that the only thing wrong with him was an HYPP attack, and she could just as well have left him at home and given him rest and fluids."

"You're kidding." I shook my head. "Damn. It sure didn't look like that was the problem."

"No," Jim agreed. "And believe me, I'm not blaming you. One thing about this business. You'll go through weeks, months even, where everything you touch turns to gold. And then you'll have times when everything you touch turns to shit. It's just the way it is. It's happened to me, plenty of times."

"Right," I said. And headed out for the first call of the day—yet another colic—with an outwardly detached demeanor. Or so I hoped. Inwardly I was reeling.

I'd felt pretty good about the way I'd handled that case. I'd spent

157

an ungodly amount of time and done my best to help the woman with a difficult and puzzling problem. To be told she was angry with me was a real blindside.

This seemed to be my season for dissatisfied clients. The timing couldn't have been worse. Despite Jim's words my heart just kept sinking farther and farther. My job, often a source of comfort and distraction, was loading more bad feelings on my already overburdened shoulders. Sooner or later, I thought, would come the proverbial straw.

But there was nothing for it but to keep plugging away. Life currently felt like a long, blank corridor with no doors, no escape. Perhaps it was taking me somewhere; I was no longer sure. All I knew was that I felt trapped. I couldn't quit. I had to keep going.

I made it through a day of more or less routine calls and arrived home in the evening hungry and tired. Not a thing in the refrigerator but some half-limp lettuce, a little cheese, and the obligatory bottle of Sauvignon Blanc. Oh well. That and a tomato out of the garden would make a dinner of sorts.

First of course, I had to feed the animals. And then, I told myself, before the glass of wine I had some phone calls to make.

Sitting down on the couch, I dialed Kris's number. Her "hello" was so subdued I barely recognized her voice.

"How's it going?" I asked cautiously.

"Not so good, Gail. I can't seem to get over being afraid."

"Are you sure you don't want to come stay with me?"

"I don't know." Kris sounded confused. "What I think I really want is to get away from here. School's out next week; I'm thinking about going down to visit my sister for a while."

"Oh."

"She lives in San Diego," Kris went on. "It would be a real change for me. And that's what I feel like I need. A complete change."

"What about Jo? And—Dixie?"

"Jo's all right with her dad. And I could board Dixie for a while. Maybe turn her out where I have Rebby. I just really want to get away."

"All right." I could understand why she might feel that way. "Let me know if I can help."

"I will, Gail. And don't worry, I'll be okay. Your life's tough enough right now, you don't need to add me to your problems."

To this I had no ready answer. In a sense it was true, as no doubt Kris knew.

"I just wish I could be a little more help," I said.

"I know you do. And I appreciate your offer. But I don't want to be driven out of my own house. What I want is a vacation."

"I understand," I told her.

"Thanks," she said. "I'll let you know what happens."

We said good-bye, both of us a little regretfully. I would miss her if she was gone, I knew; she was the one person I currently counted as a close friend.

Staring at the receiver in my hand, I tried to make up my mind about the next call. It ought to be to Jeri Ward. But every time I tried to picture myself talking to the woman, my brain froze up. How could I refuse to talk about Nico and mention the suspicious circumstances surrounding George Corfios? Should I bring up the issue of the murdered woman—what had Clay said her name was? Marianne? The police knew a lot more about that than I did, anyway.

I vacillated, torn between what seemed at times to be my civic duty and the notion that the police neither needed nor wanted the help of a meddling amateur sleuth.

"Mind your own business, Gail," I said out loud.

The dog cocked an ear at me and I picked up the phone book. Sure enough, the number was there. I dialed—not Jeri Ward, but Blue Winter.

He answered on the first ring. "Hello?"

"Hi. It's Gail. Gail McCarthy." Already I felt stupid. Completely tongue-tied.

"Hi, Gail. How are you?" Blue sounded cordial; I could read nothing more into his tone. That was the trouble with the damn phone.

"I'm fine. I wanted to thank you for coming by, and for bringing me that rose."

"My pleasure."

Now what, I wondered. Should I launch off into a speech about how Clay wasn't my boyfriend? That would really make me look stupid.

Instead I went with, "I'd like to invite you over to dinner; the trouble is, I'm on call this week and the coming weekend. How would next week be?"

"Fine," Blue said quietly. "I'd like that."

"Would next Saturday work for you? The problem with week nights is that I never know when I'll get home."

"I understand. Saturday's fine. It's a long way away, though." This time I could hear the smile in his voice.

I smiled back. Maybe this phone call wasn't going so badly. "It is that. Give me a call in the interim if you'd like."

"I might do that. Thanks for calling, Stormy."

"You're welcome. See you later."

This time I hung up the phone with the last vestige of a smile still lingering on my face. No doubt about it, I was really attracted to this man. That was a good sign, anyway. Surely I couldn't be as depressed as I sometimes feared if I still felt even a little of the old sexual draw?

I made my salad and poured myself a glass of wine, still thinking about Blue. When the phone rang, I jumped.

Picking the receiver up off the table, I said, "Hello?"

"Gail?" the voice was female. "It's Jeri Ward."

"Oh, hi." Now I was in trouble.

"Have you given any thought to telling me about the other victim?" Jeri was nothing if not direct.

"Lots," I said honestly.

"Well?"

"I can't talk about her. I promised I wouldn't, and I feel I need to keep my word."

Silence greeted this statement. Then, "I understand why you might feel this way, Gail, but I think you're making a mistake."

"I know you do. I have plenty of doubts about it myself. I do have a couple of things I'd like to tell you."

"All right."

I took a deep breath and explained as briefly as I could that George Corfios had recently moved into the area and ridden his horse to Kris's, and I wondered if this wasn't a little too much of a coincidence. "I have absolutely no other reason to suspect the guy," I finished up. "I just thought I ought to mention it."

"All right. What else?"

"Well, you know there was a woman murdered in Harkins Valley not too long ago? Marianne something?"

"Umm." Jeri Ward sounded noncommittal.

"She had horses. A mare. And she was found out at her barn, hit over the head with something. I was just wondering . . ."

"I'm not in charge of that case," Jeri said briefly. "However, we'll look into it. Anything else?"

"No, not really." I thought about telling her that the horse rapist's horse undoubtedly ate alfalfa hay and gave up the idea. She probably wouldn't think it was useful.

"Give some more thought to telling me about the other victim, okay?"

"I'll do that. And I'll try to convince her to tell you herself. Have you learned anything helpful in your investigation?" I asked tentatively.

A moment's pause. "He definitely wore gloves," Jeri said crisply. "The semen, and it was semen, shows him to be O negative. And we have his DNA profile. We think he hit the girl with a shovel. That's about it." Her tone seemed to rebuff any more questions.

"Thanks," I said.

"We'll be in touch," Jeri replied, and hung up.

Once again I was left staring at a quiet receiver. This time without a smile. It was true, then. Some strangely warped man was having sex with horses. Despite the fact that it had been on my mind for over a week, I was still shocked at hearing the incontrovertible evidence. Once again I tried ineffectually to imagine what sort of man would do such a thing. Or would even have the faintest desire to do such a thing.

Nothing came to mind except the notion that, if it wasn't kids, it must be someone with deep psychological problems. What, after all, was the typical psychological profile of a sex offender?

I hadn't a clue. But there was someone I could ask. An absolutely appropriate authority. I had an appointment with a shrink tomorrow.

TWENTY-ONE

I presented myself at Dr. Alan Todd's office punctually at five o'clock. All was as it had been the last time—the empty waiting room, the switch on the wall, the stack of *New Yorker* magazines on the end table. I flipped the switch and sat down on the couch to wait, ignoring the *New Yorkers*.

What should I say today, I wondered. Various thoughts chased in and out of my brain—no consensus.

Then a step outside the door and the click of the doorknob turning.

"Greetings," said Dr. Alan Todd with a cheerful smile.

"Hello," I more or less muttered, somewhat disconcerted by his perky form of address. Once again I preceded him down the hall to his office.

We seated ourselves in the same chairs as last time; Dr. Todd picked up a manila folder from his desk, opened it, and placed it in his lap. Folding his hands on top of it, he looked at me.

"How are you today?" he asked.

"All right, I guess." The words echoed untruthfully in my head. "The same as I was," I amended. "I'm still depressed. Sometimes I feel like I'm dealing with it all right, but a lot of the time I feel overwhelmed."

The doctor nodded encouragingly.

"Any criticism bowls me over," I went on. "I feel devastated. And I feel lonely all the time, like I need some support I'm not getting."

I looked at him. "And that's not me. I've always been comfortable being solitary; I *liked* feeling that I didn't need anyone."

"Have you ever felt close, connected, as if you were getting the support you're currently missing?" he asked.

I thought about it. "Yes and no," I said at last. "I had a boyfriend when I was in college who I think I felt close to. And I felt very safe with Lonny, the man I was in a relationship with for the last five years. But no, not really connected. I think I wouldn't let myself feel *too* connected."

"Why?" he asked.

"It didn't feel right, I guess." I thought about it some more. "I suppose it felt too scary. After my parents died, I was very conscious of wanting to create a security for myself that rested on no one but me. I definitely did not want to be emotionally dependent on anyone else, ever again." This last came out more vehemently than I intended, and I stopped, surprised at the depth of emotion in my voice.

"So you felt dependent on your parents for security and closeness?" he asked.

"I suppose. I mean, doesn't every child feel dependent on his or her parents?"

"Of course. Was it a comfortably close feeling?"

"I don't know," I said slowly. "I can barely remember, to tell you the truth. I have images in my mind of myself as a little girl playing on our family apple farm, and I can remember my parents quite clearly, but I don't have any memories of feeling close to them. Or of being cuddled. No warm fuzzies," I said flippantly, and a little defiantly.

The shrink watched me quietly. We both let the silence grow.

"Are you telling me," I said at last, "that what's wrong with me is just that my parents weren't nurturing enough? Isn't that the standard diagnosis?"

"Perhaps. What happens to us when we're children does tend to shape our emotional makeup."

"So I'm to blame my mom and dad for my current depression?" I knew I sounded cynical; the truth was that this whole conversation was making me uncomfortable.

"I don't know that blame is the right word," Dr. Todd said. "Most parents try to be as loving to their children as they can be. Usually, if they are unable to be very nurturing, it's because their own parents weren't able to be very nurturing with them."

I shrugged. "All right. So what happens now? I can understand that I was a lonely child and my parents were probably unable to be very nurturing, so I never felt close to anyone. Where does that get me?"

The shrink regarded me steadily. "An intellectual understanding is only so useful," he said at last. "Generally speaking, your problem is about feeling, not thinking. As we discussed last week, I tend to think that you need to be able to get in touch with those feelings of sadness and anger and fear, be able to feel them, rather than just intellectually acknowledging that they might be there."

I took this in. "And how do I do that?" I asked.

"The awareness that you want to do it is helpful. Often it takes some time, but will happen on its own, as long as the awareness and the willingness to feel are there. Therapy can help. And sometimes it can happen suddenly, in a kind of catharsis, usually linked to some sort of traumatic event."

This didn't make a whole lot of sense to me. Still, I thought about it. "Are most emotional problems in adults caused by what happened to them in their childhood?" I asked carefully.

"I suppose you could say that. The emotional wounds we receive in our childhood go very deep. A young child has no defenses. He or she is completely dependent on the parent."

"So can sexual problems, perversions, usually be traced to a person's childhood?"

The shrink kept his eyes on my face and said nothing.

After a minute I realized he thought that I was talking about myself, and was waiting for me to say more.

"I'm sorry," I said. "I've shifted subjects. There's an ongoing problem in my life right now that doesn't have to do with me; my question's related to that. I don't think I have any sexual aberrations. Not that I've noticed, anyway."

The shrink looked at me with his hands folded; I wondered whether he believed me.

"What's the nature of the problem?" he said at last.

I sighed. "There's this guy who's been sneaking into people's barns at night, having sex with their mares. Have you had any experience with, um, bestiality?"

Dr. Todd looked startled. "No," he said.

That was the thing. This particular problem was so weird it surprised even psychiatrists. It was just so far outside the normal run of human behavior.

Or was it really?

As if he could read my mind, the doctor said, "Of course, it's not that uncommon historically, or in literature. I haven't come across it in my practice, though. I would think it might be more common in, um, isolated rural areas."

Well, that made sense.

"But you have had experience with people who have other sexual problems? Flashers, maybe? Or rapists? Child molestors?"

"Occasionally," he said.

"Are there any common denominators?"

He thought about this a minute. "Well, sexual crimes tend to be committed by people who were in some sense abused when they were young. Sometimes physically, sometimes emotionally. Such people are usually very frustrated and angry inside, and find release in the inappropriate act."

"Anything specific you can think of regarding this particular act?"

"No, not really. Except that it seems as though there may be some inherent potential for violence there."

"This person has already hit a little girl over the head and knocked her out," I said.

"Then I would say that there is definitely potential for violent behavior. In all probability the act with a horse reflects some sort of rage and frustration with women."

"That makes sense," I said.

We looked at each other. "Just how are you involved with this?" Dr. Alan Todd asked me.

165

"Two of my friends have horses that have been, uh, abused," I said, meeting his eyes briefly.

Even knowing the man as slightly as I did, I could read the concern on his face.

"I'd be very careful if I were you," he said. "Very careful. I think this person could be dangerous."

TWENTY-TWO

I couldn't get Dr. Todd's words out of my mind. They stuck there, providing an edginess that needled me throughout the following day as I dealt with an ongoing roster of equine problems.

And the edginess was still present when I finally sat down on my porch to wait for Nico.

I'd taken a couple of hours off, to Jim's consternation, in order to ready my house for Nico's visit. Once again it was polished and tidy, with a vase of roses on the table, a plate of fruit and cheese and a bottle of my favorite Sauvignon Blanc in the refrigerator; I'd even made some bread.

Now I sat on the porch with a book in my lap, looking out over the garden and thinking.

It was a fine fog-free evening for once, the air soft and warm, the sun slanting gently in from the west to light the blues and apricot shades in the perennial border and the Tea roses nodding along the grape stake fence. Nearer at hand, the rambling rose, Paul's Himalayan Musk, twined dainty blue-green tendrils around the pillars of the porch; the blush-pink blossoms released a sweet and yet spicy fragrance into the air. A pair of house finches had nested in the vine; the vividly red male sat nearby, watching me and singing his territorial song.

The garden was at its best. I looked forward to having Nico see it and the house. I just wished I could shake the omnipresent sense of sadness and worry.

Still, the air was soft on my skin and full of the scent of roses. A family of quail—the babies no bigger than walnuts—trooped through the vegetable garden, the parents clucking protectively. A dove perched quietly on the birdbath, looking like a plaster decoration. Life went on all around me, full of sweetness.

I stared at the rambling rose blossoms silhouetted against the evening sky. This young vine sang a song of joy, unclouded by my sorrow. In a sense, this could be a comfort, this knowledge that beauty went on, despite my grief and cares. But at other times, what seemed like the profound indifference of the natural world to my particular troubles was yet another source of despondency.

Who knew? I had no answers, only questions. Would I some day feel all right again? How to survive in the interim? And what, if anything, should I say to Nico?

The sight of a white van coming slowly up the hill told me that I'd better figure out the answer to that last question pretty damn soon.

I waited for Nico to park the van and get out, surprised at the eager expectancy arising in me. I was glad to be getting the painting, but it was more than that. It was Nico herself I was looking forward to.

I waved to her from the porch and she waved back, then came toward me. She was dressed much as usual—jeans, a linen blouse, her dark hair twined in a knot on the back of her neck. She smiled as she greeted me, that fine-boned face as purely and simply radiant as I remembered it.

"Hi, Nico," I said.

"Hello."

"Would you like a tour first, or shall we hang the painting?" I asked.

"Whichever you would like. I would love a tour," she said.

"Let's do the tour first, then, and then hang the painting and have a glass of wine."

Nico smiled an assent; I led her out to the garden, and then down to the barn. We stopped many times along the way for her to ask me about plants she didn't know and the names of roses that she liked. She came to a halt in the barnyard with a delighted smile at the sight of Jack and Red.

"You have chickens!"

"Yes. Just barely. What with all the varmints that live out here, I have a hard time keeping them."

"I had chickens when I lived in France," she said wistfully.

She greeted the horses and the cow and admired my vegetable plot; I offered her cuttings of any plant that took her fancy. Like me, I could tell that she was chiefly drawn to the roses, admiring each in turn and finally requesting a cutting from the classic Tea rose Jaune Desprez—a soft peachy-pink blend with a creamy gold tint.

"Doesn't 'jaune' mean yellow in French?" I asked her.

"Yes, that is right."

"This rose is hardly yellow," I said, holding a blossom up to smell it. "But I guess when it came into commerce, over a hundred years ago, there weren't any yellow roses to speak of in the trade."

"I think that is so." Nico smiled again. "Roses are interesting, are they not?"

"Yes," I said, "they're so romantic. Such a long history with humans who have been passionate about them."

I clipped some cuttings from a long cane and we proceeded back up the hill to the house, Nico stopping at her van to unload the painting.

It was carefully wrapped in a sleeve of brown paper; I felt a keen sense of anticipation as she carried it through the doorway.

To my pleasure, Nico stopped when she stepped into the house and gazed around.

"But this is beautiful."

"Thank you," I said.

After a careful look, she carried the painting to my empty wall. "And this will go here?"

"That's right." I had a hammer and nail ready.

Nico gently removed the paper sleeve and held the painting up in the center of the wall. We both sighed. The golden tones in the painting echoed the tawny gold of the pine walls; the cobalt blue pool stood out intensely. The painting looked dramatic, harmonious, right. It gave the room focus.

With some fiddling, I drove a nail into the essential spot and Nico set the painting in place. We both stepped back to admire it.

"It is perfect here," Nico said at last.

"Shall we toast it?" I asked.

"Of course." Her smile was as wide as my own.

I produced the wine, fruit, cheese, and bread and set them on the table. We both seated ourselves where we could watch the painting as I poured the wine.

"To life," Nico said.

"And to you, and your art," I added.

We both sipped; I was torn between looking at my new possession and looking at Nico.

This surprised me. I simply wasn't used to feeling this degree of attraction to a woman. Of course, it wasn't sexual, I reassured myself.

Or was it?

This thought was even more startling. Was I perhaps going through a change of sexual orientation? About to become a lesbian at forty? I'd known other women who went this way.

I took another swallow of wine and asked Nico how her work was going. Seeming to sense my preoccupation, she talked easily of her painting. I watched her in relative silence, trying to gauge my own reactions.

The beauty and clarity of her face and words, the grace in her slim hands, the light in her eyes—these all appealed to me mightily, and yet the appeal wasn't sexual, I didn't think. I had no urge to reach out and caress her, no curiosity as to what it would feel like if she caressed me. That intense physical awareness that I felt when I was with Blue Winter was missing here.

What was here was a deep attraction of another kind. I delighted in her, in her way of being, in her appearance and her personality. I wanted to know her better. Though I felt no need to touch her, the thought of touching her was not unappealing. It was intimacy with her that drew me, a wish to feel close and connected, as the shrink had said.

I had no idea what she felt about me. As in all new relationships,

I was uncertain where I was permitted to tread; I didn't know whether my attraction to her as a person was welcome or unwelcome.

"Do you enjoy being a veterinarian?" Nico asked me.

"A lot of the time I do. Not so much lately. To tell you the truth, I've been depressed, so I haven't been enjoying anything much lately." I found I had the impulse to be absolutely honest with Nico.

"I have been depressed once," she said. "I know how this can be."

"What happened with you?" I asked her.

"The depression came many years ago, when I lived in Spain. I do not know why it came. I could not eat, or read; I cried all the time. Nothing anyone said was any help."

"And what happened?"

"It passed, eventually. It took about a year. It left as it came; I did not know why. But I did come to believe it had a purpose."

"What was that?" I asked.

"It changed me. It softened me. I became more grounded in myself; I needed to struggle less." Nico spread her hands eloquently. "I cannot really explain it, but in the end, for me, it was a gift."

Now this was a different point of view.

"A gift?" I asked.

"Yes, a gift. It taught me to see things differently; I feel I am more aware. For me, it was like, how do they call it, the saint's dark night of the soul."

"Oh," I said.

"It is a common theme in spiritual writing," Nico went on. "This dark time routinely comes to those who are ready to grow. It is the, what is the word, prelude to a time of great growth and fulfillment. The dark night before the dawn. Or so I have found."

Well, this was a new way of seeing things. Though at the moment I felt unable to regard my depression as anything other than a curse. Still, Nico's words were having a curious effect on me. I could feel myself opening up—a little—to the notion that depression might lead somewhere, that is might be something other than a complete negative.

"Did you do anything to help it go away?" I asked.

"Not really." She smiled. "Except that I accepted it. I accepted myself, and how I felt. I quit resisting the sadness. I allowed myself to be sad and to think that feeling sad was okay. And then it left of its own accord. Not all at once. Slowly. But it left."

An echo here of what the shrink had said. Accepting one's feelings seemed to be key. I simply had no idea how to accept feeling shitty as the status quo. It went against all my instincts.

Nico seemed to read my thoughts. "It sounds wrong, but it is true. It goes away much quicker when you stop fighting it."

I nodded, not knowing what to say.

She smiled understandingly. "And how do you like it?" she asked, indicating the painting. "Does it look as you had hoped?"

"Yes, it's perfect."

And the conversation drifted on to painting and houses, gardens and horses. I poured more wine; between us we polished off the food. I felt a deep sense of peace.

When she rose to leave I realized that I'd never brought up the subject of the horse rapist; it had never even come into my mind. And I couldn't bring myself to say anything about it now.

Instead I said, "Would you like to go out for a drink sometime? You said once that you missed going out to the cafés in the evening."

"Yes, I would like that," Nico said.

"How about Friday?" I asked, eager to see her again.

She seemed to consult an inner calendar. "That would be fine," she said.

"I have to work," I told her, "so perhaps we'd better meet there." I gave her directions to Clouds, thinking she might enjoy Caroline, and we agreed to meet there at seven for drinks and dinner. I was being surprised by how elated I felt about it.

"I will see you then," Nico said, turning to say good-bye.

"Yes," I said. "And thank you." Impulsively I reached out to hug her.

She hugged me back with good grace; I had no sense of resistance or resentment. Her smile was as clear and pure as water, with something of its translucency, when she turned away.

As for me, I was surprised at myself. Everything about the way I related to Nico was unlike the Gail McCarthy I was used to. Maybe Nico was right. Maybe depression was a path to change.

TWENTY-THREE

Friday evening I had an emergency. I got the call just as I was leaving the office.

"My mare foaled while I was gone," the unknown female voice said. "The foal's down and I think it's dying. Can you come?"

"Of course." I took directions and hung up, feeling frustrated. So much for my evening out.

I called Nico and told her what was going on.

"Shall we meet later?" she asked.

"If you want, I'd love to."

"Let us say nine o'clock then," she said. "Will that be late enough?"

"Almost for sure," I said. "I'll call you if I can be earlier. See you then."

Hanging up the phone with a renewed sense of expectancy, I headed out of the clinic and climbed in my truck.

This call was up in Zayante—an odd little hollow in the coastal mountains. Thick with redwoods, Zayante had been a major hangout for acid-dropping hippies in the wild old days of the sixties and early seventies. A legacy of shacklike houses (known to no building inspector or tax collector) and many long-haired and bearded denizens had resulted—a legacy that persisted, despite the steady urbanization of the county. These days Zayante was a somewhat unsettled mixture of old hippies and young yuppies, the latter drawn by the low housing prices in the area.

Driving up into the mountains, I followed winding narrow roads toward Lompico, the backwoods heart of steep, shadowy Zayante. My client lived near Lompico.

The place, when I found it, was disheartening. Unadulterated redwood forest, by the look of it, it had been cluttered up by a collection of junk. The classic rusting car bodies were augmented by several sagging shacks—roofs patched with plastic tarps—and piles of rotting lumber and other debris. Nowhere could I see anything that looked like a barn or a horse.

A woman emerged from the largest building, a somewhat derelict cabin, and walked to meet me. She wore a dress of some faded material and had long graying hair and oddly serene eyes.

I introduced myself as Dr. McCarthy; she gave me her name and assured me I was in the right place.

"Where's the horse?" I asked.

She gestured toward the tree-covered slope in front of us. "Up there."

I could see nothing but forest.

"Have you caught her?" I asked.

"I can't catch her," the woman said simply. "And she tries to attack me if I go near the foal."

Great.

"I can take you to where she is," the woman said. "One of the boys is up there with her."

"All right," I said.

I collected the things I thought I'd need, including a tranquilizer for the attack-prone mare, and requested that the woman bring a halter and a bucket of grain. These objects assembled, we moved off into the forest, the woman in the lead, and two shaggy ponytailed and bearded men, who had emerged from the cabin in the meantime, in our wake.

We walked perhaps a quarter of a mile; on the way I elicited the information that the woman had no idea when the mare was due to foal, thus no idea if the foal was premature or not. The mare, it seemed,

174

ran loose in this piece of forest in the company of two other mares and a stallion, all doing just as they saw fit.

"She usually has a foal about this time of the year," the woman said.

It was rapidly dawning on me that I was—not for the first time—in the less than desirable situation of dealing with non-horsemen who had horses. Horses that were in all probability never caught or handled, thus never taught any respect for or confidence in humans. Such horses could be almost as difficult and dangerous to work on as their undomesticated brethren.

"She's down there," the woman pointed down into a gully; at the bottom I could see the red back of a sorrel mare, standing near the bank of a small creek. About fifty feet from the mare, a man with a long gray ponytail and black cowboy hat rose from a crouch to stand and waved us over.

I made my way down the slope, keeping an eye on the mare, my companions trailing behind me.

"Where's the foal?" I asked.

"He's down in the creek bed," the black-hatted man said.

I looked, but could still see no sign of the foal. The mare, however, stood over the creek—a series of potholes connected by trickles, this time of year—her ears pointed sharply forward, nickering anxiously from time to time.

"Can you catch and handle the mare normally, when she doesn't have a foal?" I asked the company at large.

"Yes," the woman said doubtfully. "She's friendly. She likes to be petted. I don't catch her very often though."

"Is she broke?"

"Broke?"

"Broke to ride," I said.

"Oh, no." The woman sounded sincerely shocked. "She lives free."

Great. Just great. I had no doubt that the "free" mare never had her feet trimmed, either. Or got her shots. Or got wormed. Probably this woman meant well, but it was not doing her horse a favor to neglect those services that a civilized society can provide for its creatures, including its animals. More or less like raising your child without

175

benefit of a balanced diet or health or dental care, in the interests of having him or her grow up naturally.

However, this wasn't the time or place for a lecture. Not that it would have helped, anyway. It's been my experience that people do what they want and/or need to do; telling them they ought to do otherwise rarely has any effect.

"I need to examine the foal," I said. "You say the mare attacks anyone who goes near it?"

"She runs at us," the woman said. "She acts like she'd bite, or strike out at you with a front foot."

"Hmmm. We'd better try and catch her first," I said. "Does she know you the best?" I asked the woman.

"Yes."

"Why don't you try offering her some grain and we'll see if we can get the halter on her. We'll approach her from the far side, so she's between us and the foal, that way she won't feel threatened."

"I don't think she'll let me catch her," the woman said simply.

"Well, see if you can get her to eat grain," I said. "If she has her nose down in the bucket I can probably get this tranquilizer in her neck. Then we should be all right."

"Okay."

The woman approached the mare slowly from the uphill side. I followed a few paces behind, palming the shot in my hand. From her spot by the creek, the mare regarded us with some degree of agitation, tossing her head and stomping her front feet, but didn't appear unduly frantic. We both talked soothingly; the woman proffered the bucket, shaking it gently so the mare could hear the grain inside.

I could see the foal now, down on its side, his hindquarters submerged in one of the potholes. The bank was quite steep here; I had no doubt the baby had been unable to climb out. He looked ominously still.

The mare's ears came forward at the rattle of grain: I noticed she was very thin, every rib showing. She stuck her nose in the bucket willingly enough and I slipped the shot into her neck with no trouble. In a few minutes she was swaying slightly, a glazed look in her eyes. The woman put the halter on her. I made my way down to the foal.

Once I managed to drag him out of the water and up on the bank, I examined him carefully. He appeared normal and undamaged, looked as if he were full-term. But his skin was cold to the touch, his gums very pale, his pulse almost undetectable. During the five minutes or so it took me to check him over, he took only one breath.

At a guess, this baby was almost dead of exposure; I was pretty sure he had slipped into the creek bed shortly after he was born and been unable to get out. The combination of cold water, too much struggle, and the inability to get to his mother and the life-giving milk had killed him. Or almost killed him.

"Is he alive?" the woman asked.

"Barely," I said. "I'm afraid we're too late. But we can still try. We need to take him to the house where we can get him warm."

"All right," she said. "I can have one of the boys carry him."

At her gesture, the black-hatted man picked up the foal and started up the hill with him.

"Maybe someone else could lead the mare," I suggested. "She'll need to go slow; she'll be unsteady."

One of the bearded men nodded and took hold of the mare's lead rope. We trooped up the hill in the gathering dusk—a sad little cavalcade.

The cabin, derelict as it appeared on the outside, was surprisingly high-tech once we were inside. In fact it was crammed with computers and odd-looking screens that I couldn't readily identify. The woman produced warm towels out of a dryer, and we dried the little horse and tried to stimulate him by rubbing and massage. To no avail.

Despite our efforts, the foal never took another breath, and the faint pulse faded and disappeared.

"I'm sorry," I said, twenty minutes later. "He was just too far gone. He's dead now."

The woman seemed resigned, her expression no more or less tranquil than when I'd arrived. She sighed, and looking around quietly, said, "I knew he was doomed as soon as I saw that cowboy in the black hat standing over him."

This made no sense to me. But then, I had no idea who the various "boys" might be or why the black-hatted one might be an omen of death. I wasn't sure I wanted to know, nor was I sure I was interested in what was starting to look like a lot of remarkably sophisticated surveillance equipment.

Much pot was grown in these hills. It was big and highly illegal business. If I had stumbled on the modern-day equivalent of a boot-legger's still, I wanted to know nothing about it.

I took my leave as quickly and gracefully as possible. The truck clock said eight o'clock. Enough time to get to Clouds by nine, but not enough to go home and change. Fortunately I'd prepared for this eventuality by wearing a pair of newer jeans and boots and my nicest chambray shirt, as well as stuffing my turquoise beads and black silk blazer in the truck. With these two additions and a quick hair and face touch-up in the parking lot, I'd look presentable enough. There was mud on my jeans from dragging the foal out of the creek—but what the heck, the light would be dim.

I walked into Clouds at ten to nine. The place was crowded and lively, but I didn't see Nico anywhere. I found a seat at the bar and greeted Caroline.

"What'll you have?" Her smile was as wide as ever, but she looked rushed.

"One of those," I said on impulse, pointing at an elegant pale pink drink in a martini glass that sat on the bar near me.

"A cosmopolitan." Caroline grinned and put the drink together al-most more quickly than I could follow the steps. Very pretty it looked, too, in a frosted glass on the mahogany bar.

I took a sip; the drink was perfect. Not too sweet, smooth, not harsh. Just what I wanted.

Taking my time, I sipped and watched the crowd, waiting for Nico. As usual, I found that watching people in a bar entertained me quite nicely. Slowly the sad, uncomfortable feeling from the last call began to melt away.

Such was the lot of a vet. There was no reason that poor foal had to die. It was ignorance that killed him, the same ignorance the head groom rails about in *Black Beauty*. Ignorance that does more harm than malice ever thought of doing.

Ignorance had created a situation where a perfectly healthy foal had died of exposure in the middle of summer.

I took a long swallow of my drink. I ran into this sort of thing all the time. I couldn't change it; I could only do my best to help. It was important not to take it too much to heart.

Still, the unnecessarily dead baby was undeniably sad. I finished my drink, looked carefully through the crowd at the bar.

Caroline approached me and glanced a question at my glass. I shook my head.

"Have you by any chance noticed a slim, dark woman in here, about my age, looking around for somebody?"

"Nope. But I might not have. We haven't had a slow moment. My stalker was in, though." She grinned and rolled her eyes. "He's a real creep. Left me a note on a cocktail napkin. It said, 'I can feel you want me and I want you.' Then he left. Can you believe it?"

I shook my head. "That's weird." Once again I wandered if Caroline's stalker was really Warren White. I'd never liked Warren, but I wouldn't have said he was that strange.

"I'll have a glass of Sauvignon Blanc," I told Caroline.

It was now nine-twenty; surely Nico would be here soon.

But she wasn't. I finished the wine fifteen minutes later and went out to the truck to call her home. No answer. Not even a machine.

I stared at the car phone in my hand. From what little I knew of Nico, I couldn't believe she would simply fail to show up. It didn't seem right.

Starting the truck, I rolled out of the parking lot and down the highway toward home. Minutes later the Corralitos exit took me inland.

I pulled in my driveway at ten o'clock, by the truck clock. I fed my hungry animals and went in the house. No message from Nico on the answering machine. I dialed her number. Once again, no response.

Without thinking about it, I climbed back in the truck. I was worried about Nico. I would go and see.

TWENTY-FOUR

Lights were on in Nico's house when I got there, and the white van was in the driveway. I climbed out of my truck after cracking the windows for Roey. I'd taken the little dog with me; I often felt happier when she was by my side during night calls.

Flashlight in hand, I approached the house through the kitchen garden. The Dutch door stood open.

"Nico," I called.

No answer.

I walked into the kitchen.

"Nico. Are you there?"

Still no answer. No one in the main room, either, though the lights were on. Only the silent paintings, brilliant on the white walls.

Now what?

"Nico!" I called again, louder.

No response.

Should I look in the bedroom? It seemed like an unwarranted invasion of her privacy. And yet.

That open door . . .

I turned and walked back through the house, out into the garden, back toward the barn. No lights on there. A gibbous moon illuminated the night as I walked toward the barn, showing me the dark shape of the building, throwing shadows under the apple tree.

I walked toward the stall. All was quiet and yet, what?

Motion, something, disturbed the night. I stopped. Turned my flashlight on. It showed only the dark blank of an open stall doorway.

Some rustling, some branch breaking behind the barn. A horse neighed. I thought I could hear the muffled thud of hoofbeats. Roey barked excitedly from the pickup.

I swung the flashlight wildly around. I could see nothing. Dark trees, corral fence, that gaping black stall door.

My heart pounded. I wished I'd thought to bring my gun.

"Nico!" I yelled.

Nothing. No answer. No movement. And then a rustling noise from the stall.

"Nico!" I called again.

Roey barked louder, no doubt hearing the fear in my voice. Another soft rustle from the stall.

"Nico, are you there?"

I played the flashlight on the stall doorway. It caught a gleam—the phosphorescent blue sheen of an eye. And then, a nicker. There was a horse in the stall.

I stepped closer. Now the flashlight showed me the black mare's shape. I took another step, and another, until I was standing one pace away from the doorway.

The mare watched me, ears forward. She was cross-tied in her stall.

"Nico," I said again.

Nothing.

Taking a deep breath, I stepped to one side, where I could see through the doorway at an angle. Still nothing—only the mare.

I moved to the other side. Shone the flashlight in. And saw a leg.

A leg clad in black fabric, a sandaled foot. One by one the details registered, as if in slow motion. I stepped forward; the flashlight revealed a human form lying face down. A white blouse, dark hair—Nico. On the floor in the corner of the box stall. Her pants were pulled down.

I ran the flashlight rapidly around the stall; it was empty except for the mare. Reaching Nico's side even as I looked, I dropped to my knees and turned her over.

Her face was bluish, tongue protruding slightly, eyes wide open. I knew before I tried to get a pulse that she was dead.

For a long moment everything blurred. I heard a rushing in my ears and squatted to a sitting position, putting my head down between my knees. I still held Nico's hand, not yet cold, in my own.

I sat there, perfectly still, fighting dizziness. Slowly the rushing noise receded. I lifted my head.

Nico's frozen face caught me unprepared; I closed my eyes, not knowing if I was praying or merely babbling.

Please, please, please. Don't let this be.

Another voice answered.

Hold it together. You have to hold it together.

After a minute I stood up, keeping my eyes carefully averted from Nico. Giving her hand a final pat, I laid it down. Then I turned and left the building.

The moonlit night remained. Shadows of branches laid bars across the gravel drive. I walked to my truck and climbed in. Roey licked my face.

I locked the doors and turned on the phone. Dialed 911. My voice was steady as I requested police assistance at the scene of a murder and gave directions. Then I hung up the phone.

A huge blankness. Not fear, not grief—just an enormous emptiness. This could not be. This was not. And yet it was.

I stared through the window at the quiet night, closing my mind to any feeling. Hold it together. Just hold it together.

Roey sat next to me. I put my arm around her and rubbed her chest and she licked my cheek. I waited.

Eventually came the sound of sirens. In a minute, a sheriff's car pulled into the driveway. I climbed out of my truck, explained to a male sheriff's deputy who I was, and led him to the barn, feeling as though I were in a trance.

Indicating the stall door, I stepped back and let him enter. Still the same moonlit night—the blue silver light, the dark shadows. Nothing had changed; nothing was the same.

The deputy emerged from the stall; before he could say anything, I asked if I could wait in my truck. He assented, already dialing on his cell phone.

I went back to the pickup and sat down next to the dog. Stared out my window at a patch of night sky obscured by tree branches. Tried not to think about anything.

Time passed. Emergency vehicles arrived, sirens blaring, lights flashing. More sheriff's cars, an ambulance, a fire truck. I stayed where I was, seeing and hearing the activity but not really paying attention to it. My mind seemed to have shut off. Nothing seemed real.

Some time later, another man approached my truck. A man in a suit. I opened the door.

"Yes?" I said.

"I understand you found the body, Ms. McCarthy?"

"That's right. Dr. McCarthy."

He said nothing. He was a big, thick man with a solid look to him and a wide jaw.

"Can you explain how you happened to arrive here?" he said.

I explained. I explained everything to the best of my abilities without mentioning the horse rapist at all. When I was done I gave him my address and phone number and said that I would like to speak to Detective Jeri Ward.

He looked at me. "She's not on tonight."

I met his eyes and read hostility. Toward who or what I wasn't sure.

I shrugged. "May I go home now?"

He consulted his notes and gave me another look. "Will you be available to give us a statement tomorrow?"

"Yes," I said.

"You can go."

I shut the truck door as he turned, and started the engine with my other hand. It was midnight. Backing out of the driveway, now a crime scene, took a few minutes. I did not look at the barn, or Nico's house. I kept my mind on maneuvering the truck between sheriff's cars and fire trucks without denting anything or anyone. Finally, I was on the road.

The dog still sat next to me; I could feel the warm weight of her body leaning into my side. The road was fairly empty this late at night; my headlights made a path through the darkness.

I did not think about Nico; I merely drove. Drove until I was home, and climbed in bed with my clothes on and shut my eyes. Finis.

TWENTY-FIVE

Jeri Ward woke me up at eight o'clock the next morning. I stumbled to the door in last night's jeans and shirt to find her on the porch, hand raised to knock again.

"Come in," I said.

I saw what looked like a brief flick of concern in her eyes as she glanced at my face—gone as soon as it came. No doubt, I looked a wreck. The contrast with Jeri's pristine appearance might have amused an observer, had there been one.

Roey sniffed Jeri's pants leg and wagged a friendly greeting. Jeri patted the dog and followed me into the main room. I sat down on the couch and waited.

I saw Jeri's eyes go around the room, saw the appreciative widening. I kept my own eyes on the window. I did not look at Nico's painting.

Jeri looked back at me—once again, that flicker of concern. "Can I make some coffee?" she asked.

"If you want." I didn't move. Perhaps, I should have offered to make the coffee myself, but I just sat.

Jeri found the coffee-making accoutrements on the counter, made a pot of French roast, and brought me a cup. Pulling one of my two chairs up to the couch, she sat down next to me, coffee in hand.

"Can you tell me about it?" she asked.

"I don't want to talk about it," I said without thinking.

Now Jeri looked very concerned. "Gail, you're going to have to talk about it. Why don't you drink a little coffee?"

Obediently, I took a sip.

Jeri waited for several minutes while I absorbed coffee, then said gently, "I take it Nicole Devereaux was the other victim you wouldn't tell me about."

"Yes," I said. I drank some more coffee.

"Why did she demand the secrecy?"

"She wasn't a citizen and was here illegally. She didn't want to be deported."

"I see."

We were quiet.

"He killed her," I said finally.

"Yes." Jeri sighed. "She was strangled. We think she must have come on him just as he was, uh, about to begin." She winced. "There was no semen on the mare, but the woman had been raped—after she was strangled, we think."

I said nothing.

"Gail, it's not your fault," Jeri said.

"Yes. It is. Partly, anyway."

"This might have happened whether you told us or not."

"Might," I said.

"We wouldn't have been able to mount a guard on her," she said.

"But he might have realized you knew. It might have scared him off."

"Maybe," Jeri said. "Maybe not. This sort of sexual crime becomes compulsive. The perpetrator has to repeat the act. At a certain point in the process, he'll take any kind of risk. We run into this all the time with rapists."

"That's what he is now—a rapist," I said.

"And a murderer. And it is the same person," Jeri said. "The semen we found on the woman matched the semen we found on Kristin Griffith's horse. It's the same man."

"What about the other murder?" I asked.

186

"There's nothing conclusive there," she said. "No fingerprints any-where, and since no one was interested in the horse angle at the time, nobody knows if a horse was abused. The woman wasn't raped."

For a second Jeri was quiet. Then she said, "I've been taken off the case."

"You have?" I said blankly.

"The detective who went to the crime scene last night, the one who talked to you. Do you remember?"

"Vaguely," I said.

"His name's Matt Johnson," Jeri said. Once again she was quiet. Then she said, "He's an ass."

I looked at her.

"He was hired about the same time I was, and he's been steadily promoted ahead of me, due, in my opinion, to the fact that he's a man and I'm a woman. In any case, he technically outranks me, and he doesn't like me. Once again, in my opinion, because I'm a woman. He's in charge of the Nicole Devereaux murder investigation, and when we both discovered the overlap between my investigation and his, he asked that I be removed from the investigation. And that's what the lieutenant did."

I still stared at her blankly.

"Gender issues are very much alive in the sheriff's department," she said, answering the question I hadn't asked. "Don't you find that in your line of work?"

"Sometimes," I said.

"It becomes more obvious when you're dealing with a hierarchy. My current boss is not keen on female detectives. He pretty much sides with Matt Johnson against me, every time."

I could hear the anger in Jeri's voice. But I had no comment, no thought.

"Anyway," she said, "I just wanted you to know why I won't be involved from here on in. I'm sorry."

I nodded.

"You'll need to go down and give them a statement today," she said. "And you'll have to tell them what you know about the previous occasions at Nicole Devereaux's."

I nodded again. I found I did not feel much like speaking. I couldn't imagine giving a statement to anyone.

"Do you want me to drive you down there?" Jeri Ward asked.

To my own surprise, I nodded again.

"Go ahead and get changed then," she said quietly. "I'll make you some toast."

"I need to feed the animals," I said and got up.

"Can I help?" she asked.

"No, I can do it. It will just take a few minutes."

I plodded out the door and down to the barn, wondering vaguely what was going on with me. My reactions seemed to be those of a withdrawn child. I didn't understand myself, couldn't explain myself to myself. But then, I didn't try much. I didn't want to think.

Once in clean clothes, with my hair brushed and my face washed, I accepted another cup of coffee and a couple of pieces of toast from Jeri and followed her obediently out to the green sheriff's sedan.

As we settled ourselves in the seats Jeri looked over at me. "Are you all right, Gail?"

I met her eyes and shrugged. I didn't know what to say.

Jeri kept looking at me.

"I feel numb," I said at last.

"Can you handle this?" she asked me.

I shrugged again. "I guess so," I said.

After a pause, she shrugged back and started the engine. "Then let's go."

TWENTY-SIX

The whole statement process took about two hours. I survived. Somehow I managed to answer questions while keeping my mind blank. I didn't think; I didn't feel. I stayed numb.

Jeri drove me home with the concerned look in her eyes more pronounced than ever. As I climbed out of her car she made me promise to call a friend when I went in the house. I agreed that I would.

Once inside and with the door safely shut against the world, I ignored the phone. Instead, I settled myself at one end of the couch and stared out the windows. I had no idea if I'd ever move again.

All I wanted to do was sit and be quiet. Not think, not talk. Most particularly, not feel. I had the sense that a huge weight was poised above me, ready to crush me if I made the slightest wrong move. The safest thing was to hold still and be numb.

But the phone rang.

It was Kris. "Gail, I read about it in the paper," she said. "Are you all right?"

"I don't know," I said.

"I'm coming over," Kris said, and hung up the phone.

In another fifteen minutes she was sitting next to me on the couch, wearing the same concerned look Jeri Ward had worn. Somehow one glance at me seemed sufficient to provoke this instant worry.

"How are you doing?" Kris asked me.

"I'm still alive," I said.

"What does that mean?"

"I don't know, Kris. It seems like all I can do is just keep being." Weird as this sounded, it felt true.

Kris shook her head. "You'd better call the shrink," she said.

"No," I said. "I'm not going anywhere. I don't want to talk to him. I just want to stay here."

"Oh, Gail," Kris sounded genuinely distressed. "I wish I could help you."

"I'm not sure anyone can help," I said.

"And I'm going away, too." Kris grimaced. "I'm afraid every night now, staying in my own house, and Jo doesn't even want to come there any more. She's afraid, too. And after this . . . well, I just need to get out of here. It was the same guy, wasn't it?"

"Yeah," I said.

"Gail, that's terrible. I don't even want to think about it."

"Me either."

Kris shot me another concerned look. "I was going to ask if you could feed Dixie; the woman who boards Rebby doesn't want any mares in that field. She thinks they'll make the geldings fight. But I'll try to find someone else."

"I can do it," I said.

"Gail, you've got enough to deal with."

"I can feed your horse," I said. "I have to go to work. I have to live my life, Kris. Feeding your horse is no big deal. You know I have to keep going."

Kris was quiet. "That's true," she said at last. "All right, if you want to. The key's where it always was."

"In the big flower pot on the front porch?"

"Right. And I feed her a fat flake of alfalfa, night and morning. Starting Monday night, for two weeks."

"No problem," I said.

Kris stayed for another hour, carefully not talking about Nico or the murder, until she finally ran out of innocuous conversation and I ran out of monosyllabic replies. When she left, Kris looked even more worried. Nothing I said seemed to reassure her.

"Gail, I wish you'd call the shrink," she said.

"Maybe I will."

"Please." Kris took her leave and I went back to my spot on the couch.

Roey jumped up next to me and curled herself next to my thigh. I sat in the corner and stared out the windows. The fog was clearing. Faint sunlight lit the low hills.

Four hours later the fog crawled back in, long white fingers creeping over the pines and eucalyptus.

Still I sat. I wasn't hungry; I wasn't thirsty. I could not fathom my strange state.

Three more hours and dusk darkened the foggy sky. My back ached from sitting. I could hear Plumber nicker. Reluctantly and stiffly, I pushed myself up off the couch. The animals needed to be fed, even if I didn't.

I made my way through the evening chores, doing what was necessary by rote. Nothing seemed real, nothing had any meaning. Not Plumber's bright, inquiring eye nor Gunner's out-thrust muzzle. Not the red-red tail hawk watching me from the pine snag on the ridge nor the apricot-colored rose Francesca, in full and glorious bloom along the grape stake fence. Nothing touched me, nothing moved me. I felt nothing.

Only the sense of an immense weight hovering above me, ready to cut loose. I kept my mind still; even my movements were slow and cautious. I did not want to tip the balance.

Chores done, I made my sluggish way up the hill to the house, Roey frisking alongside of me. Even her exuberance was unsettling. I shut her in the pen and fed her and went back to sit on the couch.

Some hours later I was still sitting there in the darkness when my pager buzzed.

It took me a minute to comprehend the noise. I'd more or less forgotten that I was a vet, that I was, in fact, on call. With infinite slowness, or so it seemed, the thoughts sorted themselves out. I turned the pager off and called the answering service.

"A John Jay has a colicked horse out at the Bishop Ranch," the woman said.

"All right. Tell him I'll meet him there."

"The horse is in a stall in the main barn," came back the reply. "He said he'd be waiting for you."

I hung up the phone and tried to gather myself together. I had to get up and go be a vet. A competent professional on whom lives depended. It seemed impossible, but I had to.

Getting up off the couch itself seemed beyond me. I needed a mental whip to scourge my unwilling body, but my mind was limp as cooked pasta. There was simply nothing there to drive with. Reaching deeper, I found the still, small core of will.

You must, I told myself, and I got up. My legs felt as shaky as my brain, but I walked out to the truck. It wasn't until I was rolling down the driveway that I remembered I hadn't eaten anything since the two pieces of toast Jeri had made for me this morning. No wonder I felt weak. Oh well. Nothing for it now.

I drove the short stretch to the Bishop Ranch resolutely not thinking about how I would deal with a difficult case. I did not think about anything, just kept the truck on the dark road and my mind blank. It seemed the only possible way to exist.

All was quiet at the Bishop Ranch. The three-quarter moon had risen above the ridgeline and its gray-silver light mingled with the orangey glow from the low pressure lights that were scattered about the barnyard, showing me the old buildings and corrals. A few vehicles were parked here and there, but I didn't see any people. The horses visible in a shed row off to my right all had their heads down, munching hay.

Automatically, I looked toward Clay's house. Both his truck and the new sports car were visible in the driveway, and lights were on in the windows. The big white truck with BISHOP RANCH painted on the doors—the truck Bart usually drove—was parked near the main ranch house. Lights were on in the windows there, too. But still, no people apparent.

I shrugged and got my flashlight out of the truck. The big barn was to my left, and this was where the client was supposed to meet me. I headed in that direction.

No doubt the barn had lights, but I didn't know where they were. Using my flashlight, I searched for a switch near the door, but found nothing. I shone the beam down the barn aisle but could see nothing— no human beings, anyway, just the occasional horse face looking over a stall door. Perhaps the colicked horse was at the other end. I started walking.

The flashlight beam showed me quiet horses in their stalls; the shadowy cavern of the big barn stretched away around and above me. An owl hooted softly somewhere up in the beams; I could hear the rustles and thuds of horses moving, the steady *chomp, chomp* of horses eating. That was it. No one hailed me, there were no lights, no sound of a disturbance.

About halfway down the aisle I stopped. Something was wrong. The client hadn't arrived yet, maybe. I felt the quiet darkness and it did not feel right.

Some tension, some intensity, something palpable—was it footsteps? I took a step backward, swung the flashlight in an arcing sweep.

All my instincts screamed a warning, fear rushed into the blank hole of my mind. The flashlight swept wildly down the aisle; I saw a figure and turned without thinking to run.

In the turn the light caught someone just behind me; I screamed, startled out of any wits I had left.

"Why, Dr. McCarthy." Bart Bishop bared his teeth at me. "Did I scare you?"

I said nothing, just gripped the flashlight and looked at him. I saw something in Bart's eyes, something I could not place, and then a voice spoke from behind me.

"Gail, what are you doing here?" Clay's voice.

I turned to find Clay approaching from the other end of the barn; his was the figure I'd seen, then.

I took a deep breath. Gathering my wits, I spoke to both brothers. "Someone called me out here for an emergency colic. Someone named John Jay. He was supposed to meet me here in the big barn."

Bart and Clay looked at each other. After a minute, Bart stepped over to what appeared to be a big supporting post and reached behind it. With an audible click, overhead lights switched on, illuminating the barn.

We all looked around. No one was visible but the three of us.

"I don't have any boarders named John Jay." Bart said. He made it sound like an accusation.

I could feel fear seeping out of my bloodstream and anger pumping up. "Why didn't you turn those lights on earlier," I demanded of Bart. "You nearly scared me to death, sneaking up behind me like that." At the same time, I noted there was a flashlight in Clay's hand, a flashlight that had certainly not been on as he walked down the barn aisle toward me.

"How the hell am I supposed to know there's no boarder named John Jay?" I demanded again, my voice rising.

Bart looked at me and narrowed his eyes. "I didn't know what you were up to, sneaking into my barn in the middle of the night. I thought I'd better see."

"For God's sake, what did you suppose I was up to? You could see my truck parked out in the driveway in plain sight. Why the hell didn't you just turn the lights on and say, 'Hey.' And for that matter, what were you doing sneaking around the place at night yourself?"

"I always check the horses before I go to bed. It's a good practice." Bart watched me steadily.

I said nothing; I could feel my hands shaking.

Clay looked concerned. "I'm sorry we scared you, Gail. I saw someone pull in when I was looking out my window, saw the flashlight go into the barn. I didn't know it was you. I was just checking."

I nodded. The shakes were growing stronger; I wasn't sure I could trust myself to speak steadily.

Tightening my jaw muscles, I said, "It must have been a prank. I'll be going."

I started walking. Out of the corner of my eye, I could see Bart shrug and continue strolling down the barn aisle, looking casually into the stalls as he passed. Clay fell in beside me. His eyes were worried.

"I'm really sorry, Gail. I know you found that other woman down the road last night. I was going to call you, but I didn't know if I should. We're all a little paranoid around here since we heard."

"Right," I said. I did not feel up for conversation. I knew Clay was going to think I was angry, but I didn't care. All I wanted was to get in my truck and get out of here. I could feel that I was about to start crying.

Clay stayed by my side until we reached the truck. I started to climb in, but his hand on my arm detained me. I didn't look at him. I knew there were tears on my cheeks. "Gail, I'm really sorry," he said again.

"Right," I said. "It's okay. I've got to go."

Still not looking at him, I climbed in the pickup, waved a quick good-bye, and started the engine.

Something was shifting, something was changing. I knew Clay was looking after me, but I did not look back. The tears were flowing faster now; my breath was coming in gulps.

I sobbed all the way home.

TWENTY-SEVEN

The weight had shifted. I could not stop crying. Overwhelming waves of grief rushed over me, too painful to bear. I sat on the couch and sobbed and sobbed, gasping for air.

I thought of Nico as I had seen her last; I thought of her bright, pure face in life. I thought of my parents; of Lonny, who wasn't here to hold me; of Blue, my old dog; of all loss, all grief.

Like lava, searing pain poured out of me, streaming down my face. I cried, feeling I would never stop, sobbing noisily and messily in the empty darkness, staring at the blank windows, knowing that balance had gone and I was falling.

It was like tumbling into an abyss, in free fall, going down and down, with no bottom in sight. I was lost. It seemed as if Gail was no more. Only endless grief.

I don't know how long I cried. It seemed like hours. It seemed like forever. Eventually the tears slowed to a trickle and the gasping sobs eased. The pain became a quiet river, rather than a raging torrent. It flowed steadily through my limp body and exhausted mind, running out of my eyes gently.

I still sat on the couch, facing the dark windows. I found I was waiting for dawn. I had no idea how far away it was; I did not turn to look at the clock. I merely watched.

Swirls of anxiety and grief went through me, tears flowed sporadically now. I watched the night sky from a desolation of loneliness and waited.

I am in the abyss, I thought. I am in the dark night of the soul. The words came unbidden; I remembered that Nico had said them to me.

My mind seemed to be working again. I found myself wondering what happened now, now that I was here at the bottom. I had never cried like this in my entire life, that I could remember. My whole body ached from crying.

And yet, there was relief in it. I could feel, I was feeling, the terrible sadness. No doubt this was what the shrink had meant when he talked about feelings of grief that I'd repressed for so long. Feelings about myself as a lonely child, feelings about my parents' death. Every time I thought of my parents, a few more tears leaked out of my eyes.

And then there was Nico. I found I could think of Nico now, in fact, I couldn't stop thinking of her. Of her grace and beauty, of the horror of her death. Mixed with grief was a steadily growing rage, every time I saw her dead body in my mind.

He had done this, the evil man who came at night to the horses. I remembered the fear I'd felt in the Bishop Ranch barn and wondered if he had been there. Had I felt his presence? Had the call been a pretext to get me out there where he could kill me?

I felt strangely detached from fear now. Grief and anger were taking up all the emotional space I had. There was no room for fear.

But I remembered the fear—intense, visceral—and I wondered if the horse rapist had been there. Had he been scared off by Bart and Clay's arrival? Or, my mind blinked, was he Bart? Had Bart got me out there to try and kill me? Why would he, my brain rebutted. I never suspected him.

Because, came the answer, he thinks you might have seen him at Nico's. I had seen nothing, but I remembered the confused sense I'd had of horses and motion, I remembered how I'd swung my flashlight around. If the horse rapist had ridden to Nico's, perhaps he had been riding away and was afraid I'd seen him.

And was he Bart? Or, even more unwelcome, could it be Clay? Clay had come out to the barn, too.

I could not believe it was Clay. Despite the fact that I found him hard to read, I felt I had a sense of his essential goodness. I could not believe I would find myself attracted to a man who was capable of murder.

But Bart now, Bart was different. I very much disliked Bart. Had Bart set me up to be murdered and been disturbed by his brother?

No ready, instinctual answer came to mind. But I had a conviction that someone had been stalking me in that barn. And it was certainly at least odd that Bart, recognizing me, had chosen to sneak up behind me in the dark, rather than turning the lights on and calling out. At the very least he'd meant to scare me.

There was a lot of hostility in Bart, that much was clear. How he was working it out, what he was actually capable of, was much less clear.

But someone, some man, was capable of raping horses, of bashing a little girl over the head, of strangling a woman and raping her after she was dead. Some very twisted man was capable of a lot of violence.

With the thought, anger rose in me. He had killed Nico; I believed he meant to kill me. This stupid, warped, evil man who cared nothing for the destruction he wrought. This despicable creature so absorbed in his own desire to fulfill his strange sexual needs. He had killed Nico, ended all that beauty and talent, as a means to his own disgusting, paltry end.

The thought made my blood boil. Anger felt good, much more comfortable and empowering than grief. The tears were gone now.

I spoke out loud to the night. "Supposing I kill you, you son of a bitch. Suppose I put an end to you."

After that I was quiet. I watched the windows, watched the night, and thought.

It seemed to take forever. What felt like hours went by and nothing happened. Just thoughts chasing themselves through my brain and starting to make a pattern. The sky outside the windows stayed dark. I began to think it was still the middle of the night.

But I kept on waiting and watching. And it finally happened. Subtly but unmistakably, the sky began to lighten. First light, almost indistinguishable from darkness. The very faintest graying of the sky above the eastern ridge.

Dawn had come.

TWENTY-EIGHT

Two hours later I was pouring French roast in the filter when the dark green sheriff's sedan pulled up the driveway. A woman got out of the car—Jeri Ward.

Stifling the urge to look in the mirror, I walked to the door and opened it. "Come on in," I said. "I'm just making coffee."

A few minutes later I was seated at the table with Jeri, coffee cups in hand, once again providing my usual disheveled contrast to her neat and put-together appearance.

"I just came by to check on you," she said. "You didn't look like you were doing so good yesterday."

"I know," I said. "No doubt, I don't look a whole lot better today."

"Well, you sound better," Jeri said.

I smiled, surprised I was able to do it. "I am better," I said. I regarded her carefully. "You say you're no longer on this horse rapist case."

"That's right," Jeri said, "This is a social call. I'm on my way back from a domestic violence problem."

"Then can I tell you something in confidence?"

"It depends," she said. "I'm a cop, remember."

"All right," I said. "I'm going to tell you this and assume it's in

200

confidence. I will not tell it to any member of your department, and if you tell them, I will deny it."

Jeri shrugged one shoulder and waited.

I recounted the story of last night's experience at the Bishop Ranch.

When I was done, I told her, "So you see, nothing happened. There's nothing to report. It's just a feeling I had. I'm not obligated to tell anyone."

Jeri nodded slowly.

"The thing is, it gave me an idea. An idea I think I'm going to follow through with. I could use some help. And you would be my first choice, if you were willing."

"What's your idea?

"My friend Kris Griffith is going away tomorrow for two weeks, and I'm going to take care of her place. Feed her horse, water her plants, you know how it goes.

"Anyway, after last night I was thinking about this horse rapist person and how you said the act becomes compulsive. So, of course, he'll probably need to do it again pretty soon. And if he's true to his pattern, he'll return to one of his former spots. Like Kris's."

Jeri looked at me. "No, Gail," she said.

"You can't stop me," I said "I have every right to go over there, feed the horse, and sleep in the barn if I want. It's nobody's business but mine. If you tell that Matt Johnson," I said, "I will say you made it up and are trying to make trouble for me."

"Gail, that's crazy. Do you want to get killed?"

"No, I don't want to get killed. I want to—" I stopped myself in time. "Catch him," I continued, "before he hurts or kills someone else. Like me, for instance." I looked at her. "You could help me."

"Just what do you have in mind?"

"I've taken care of Kris's place before when she went away," I said. "She leaves her car in the driveway to make it look like she's home, takes a taxi to the airport. I usually turn different lights on every time I'm there, turn the TV or radio off and on. So we always make it seem as if she's there.

"What I'm thinking is that this time I'll do the same, but park my truck in a cul-de-sac down the road where it's hidden and walk to the

201

house every evening. I'll feed the horse and wait in the barn. Until he comes."

"And you want me to do this with you?"

"If you want," I said. "Two would be better than one."

Jeri was quiet, considering.

"You have a gun?" she asked.

"Yes. A .357 pistol," I said.

"Can you shoot at all?"

"Reasonably," I said.

She was quiet some more. "I'd get in a lot of trouble," she said at last.

"Not necessarily," I said. "Are you on call this week?"

"No," she said.

"I'm not either. What if it's just a social thing, two of us spending an evening together. We happen to be over at Kris's, to feed her horse, and this guy shows up and goes after the horse. Naturally, you nab him. Where's the problem?"

Jeri thought and slowly smiled. "I could put it that way. Matt would be pissed as hell."

I got the definite impression this pleased her. "No one will hear otherwise from me," I said.

Jeri looked straight at me. "Gail, if I consider, for even a minute, going along with this crazy scheme, you have to promise me one thing."

"What?"

"You leave me in charge. If this guy comes, you do what I say. Period."

I thought about it. "I get to be there," I said at last. "I want to be there when we catch him. I won't budge on that. But other than that you're in charge."

We regarded each other for another moment and Jeri nodded very slightly. "All right," she said. "Does Kris Griffith know about this?"

"Not exactly," I said. "She knows I'm taking care of the place, that's all. I don't want to worry her. The same story can apply if we catch him."

"All right," Jeri said again. And then, more to herself, "I really want to catch this bastard."

"Me, too," I said.

We confirmed a few more details, and Jeri took her leave. As she started toward the door I asked her, "How's ET?"

"Oh, he's doing fine," she said. "He's gaining a little, and he seems to feel fine. I rode him yesterday," she added. "Just in the arena." She looked back at me. "That guy Bart is sure an ass," she said. "I had him come out and pick up Nicole Devereaux's mare—the one thing old Matt didn't want to deal with. Bart said he'd take care of her, but he was a little prick about the whole deal."

"Uh-huh." I nodded and said nothing more. Best to keep my suspicions of Bart to myself.

Jeri let herself out and I made eggs and toast for breakfast. By my reckoning, it had been twenty-four hours since I'd eaten.

Two hours later I'd fed the animals and fielded a call from Kris. I'd assured her I was fine and that the horse and her place would get taken care of. She was relieved, I could tell. She'd been stressed enough herself and was in no shape to deal with my problems.

I was just about to step out the door when the phone rang again. It was Blue.

The sound of his voice triggered an odd mix of emotions. Part pleasure, part apprehension, and part reluctance to deal with anything else now.

Still, his "Hi, this is Blue," was far from unwelcome. "Just thought I'd call and touch bases with you," he said.

"Oh . . . yeah." Damn. I'd completely forgotten I'd asked him over to dinner. "Look," I said, "there's a lot going on with me right now."

"Oh?"

Realizing that he hadn't already heard about it—perhaps he didn't read the paper—I said, "Remember that situation I told you about, the woman whose horse was being abused?"

"Right."

"I found her murdered on Friday night."

"Oh no," Blue said.

"It looks as though the same man did it."

"That must have been terrible for you."

"It wasn't easy," I said. "And I'm afraid I need to ask you to put our dinner date on hold for a while. I'm just not sure how things are going to go."

"Whatever you'd like."

I heard the instant retreat in his voice, and as was my habit with this man, felt myself softening toward him. For whatever reason, perhaps our suddenly intimate proximity on last summer's trip, I always read his seemingly aloof reserve as shyness, felt that he was vulnerable under his apparent detachment.

"It's not that I don't want to see you," I told him bluntly. "I'd love to have dinner with you. But there's some stuff arising out of this woman's death that I have to deal with."

"Are you doing all right?" Blue asked.

"More or less. I promise I'll let you know when things get resolved and I'll cook you that dinner."

"I'm looking forward to it," he said quietly. And then, "Take care of yourself, Stormy."

"I will," I said.

But as I hung up, I sincerely doubted that Blue would consider my current plan to be taking care of myself.

TWENTY-NINE

Jeri met me at eight o'clock the following evening. We took her car, a small gray sedan, less conspicuous than my truck, and parked it in the cul-de-sac, as planned. Side by side we walked to Kris's house, not speaking.

I fed the horse while Jeri reconnoitered. After a few minutes, she came back with a report.

"It's like I remembered. If he does it the same way as before, he'll come in the main door of the barn." She glanced around. "If you stay behind the haystack and I wait in the tack room, we'll have him covered from two angles. And I should be able to see into the stall."

"See into the stall?"

"Yeah. He'll take the mare into the stall, we assume, and do you-know-what."

"You're going to watch him?"

"More or less." Jeri looked at me. "The semen will give us definite proof that we've got the right man."

"I see," I said. Somehow I hadn't pictured waiting in the shadows while the horse rapist actually did the deed. But what Jeri was saying made sense.

"When he's done," she said, "I'll arrest him. You stay put and be quiet."

"What if he, uh, resists arrest?"

"Keep on staying put and being quiet. I don't want him to know you're there."

"Even if he tries to kill you? Even if he's getting away?"

"That's right," Jeri said crisply.

I gave her a look. Even in the dim light of summer dusk she read it perfectly.

"Look, Gail. That's my job. To catch the bad guys and protect the citizens from harm. It's my responsibility to make sure you don't get hurt. If you do get hurt, I'll be in all kinds of trouble."

"Uh-huh," I said.

We looked at each other.

"I know it sounds bossy and dictatorial," Jeri said. "But it is my job and we agreed I was in charge. I don't want him to know you're here."

"Right," I said. "I'll hide and wait."

Jeri gave me a doubtful glance, but after a minute she shrugged. We both settled into our respective places. I rearranged a few hay bales so that they shielded me completely, while at the same time providing me with a handy crevice to peer through. Jeri took a stance behind the tack room door. We waited.

We'd agreed earlier to wait silently from nine until midnight. As far as we knew, the horse rapist had always come during these hours. After midnight we'd go home and get some rest, be ready to watch again the following night.

I rested my pistol on a hay bale, shifted my weight from time to time, careful always to take a position that I could hold if need be. I could not see Jeri from where I stood, but I could see the open barn doorway. I waited.

A barn, even a little barn like Kris's, has a life of its own at night. I could hear the soothing rustle and munch of Dixie, out in her corral, eating hay. Smaller, closer rustles were probably mice. The gentle sounds of a summer night drifted in through the open doorway—

crickets chirping, an owl hooting, the occasional swish of tires on pavement as a car passed by on Harkins Valley Road. All was peaceful.

And here we were, waiting for a murderer. It seemed bizarre. And yet, with my whole being, I wanted to catch this man. More than that, I wanted to kill him—something I didn't plan on telling Jeri.

Every time I thought about him killing Nico, red-hot rage bubbled up inside. That something so fine should be destroyed by such a bestial creature—that her life had been taken by such a thing . . . I'll kill you, you bastard, I chanted softly to myself. I'll make an end to you. I'll make sure you never walk this earth again.

The focused hatred that coursed through my veins was completely foreign to me; I would never have imagined I could feel this way. All parts of me seemed to rise up in a fierce instinctual protest against this defiler of innocent creatures, this rapist, this murderer. I hated him. He was unfit to live.

I shifted my weight, rearranged the position of my gun. He would come. If not tonight, then some night. And we would see.

Thinking, watching, waiting passed the hours. The barn grew colder. I was glad I had thought to wear several layers of sweatshirts. No jackets, nothing that would rustle. All dark colors. I endured the chill and waited.

Eventually came Jeri's soft voice. "It's twelve-thirty."

"All right." Slowly and stiffly I worked my way out from behind the haystack.

Jeri emerged from the tack room, just visible as a human shape in the moonlight that filtered through the doorway. "Not tonight," she said.

"I guess not. Maybe tomorrow."

After a final glance around, we headed out of the barn and back down to the car, Jeri's flashlight illuminating our way. Once back at my place, she left quickly with only a brief, "See you tomorrow."

I fell into bed and to sleep almost at once, tomorrow echoing in my head.

But it wasn't tomorrow. Or the next night either. By Thursday night, the endless watching and waiting were getting to me. I was starting to feel sleep deprived, what with getting up every morning at six and never going to bed before one. It was hard to focus on my job. And it was becoming more and more difficult to stay awake as I huddled in the barn. I wondered how long I could do this.

The intense desire for revenge that drove me was still there, but fatigue was eating away at it. I had no idea how Jeri felt. We didn't speak about our enterprise much, just went through the necessary motions. No doubt Jeri had participated in such stakeouts before and was familiar with the problems.

But for me this endless, patient stalking was an entirely new experience. Hide and wait, with life itself on the line. Adrenaline crashed through me at the slightest noise; when a deer rustled through the trees outside the barn, my heart pounded erratically and I gripped the pistol with suddenly sweaty hands.

Like a hunter waiting for a tiger to come to a goat, waiting for a man-eating predator to appear out of the forest. With a mix of fear and keen anticipation, I waited on Thursday night, as I had waited every night, with the hunter's instinct alternately fighting sleep and the sudden rush of nerves.

Leaning my head against the haystack, I listened to the familiar little noises of the night—nothing new there. The wet, foggy chill in the air wasn't new either. My eyelids drooped over my eyes. I gave it a minute, then pushed them back open. All was quiet. And then Dixie neighed.

Sparks shot along my nerves. I shifted my weight carefully and placed myself where I could see well through the crevice in the hay. Taking a deep breath, I let it out slowly and did my best to relax my tired but suddenly tense muscles. Still, be still.

Dixie neighed again. And then another neigh, lower-pitched. Not Dixie. A different horse.

His horse, I thought, his horse. I shot a glance toward the tack room, where I knew Jeri waited, though I couldn't see her. Surely she had heard it, too.

Another neigh from Dixie, another answering nicker. The confused sound of muffled hoof beats—perhaps Dixie trotting around her corral. I waited, my eyes fixed on the barn doorway.

I could hear the clang of the metal corral gate. Dixie's halter, I knew, was hanging on the post next to the gate. Small, soft sounds that could have been footsteps, could have been anything, came from the direction of the corral.

Then a creak, as of hinges, as though the corral gate was being opened. I took another deep breath. Tried to relax my muscles and steady my nerves. Pressed my face to the crack in the hay wall and gripped the gun.

Now I could see a light. A faint, bobbing golden glow, the erratic illumination of a hand-held flashlight, growing steadily brighter. The open rectangular shape of the barn doorway became distinct. My eyes strained out into the darkness.

In a moment I could discern an approaching horse, the tawny color showing even in the dim light. Dixie. Being led by a man. I narrowed my eyes.

A dark man, dark hair, dark-skinned. Unrecognizable. Jeans and a denim jacket, a ball cap. No one I knew.

I stared. No. A man with a dark ski mask pulled down over his face. Holes for eyes. He was in the barn now. His way of moving was somehow familiar, and yet I didn't know. I saw that he was wearing rubber surgical gloves on his hands, carrying the flashlight in one and leading the mare with the other.

In a moment he led the mare in the stall, out of my sight. But not, presumably, out of Jeri's.

Who the hell was it? I felt I knew him; there was something familiar in his stance, his carriage. But the dark mask was disconcerting, throwing off my perceptions. In the dim light, I had not gotten any definite impression.

My heart thudded steadily. I could hear motion from the stall. Small, soft, shuffling sounds. I knew what he was doing but I didn't want to think about it. I did, quite desperately, want to know who he was.

I shifted my weight softly, gripped the gun, and peered through the crack in the hay. Held my breath and heard a definite sound from the tack room. A creak, as of weight coming down on a board. Jeri must have moved. I heard it. Had he heard it?

I froze. He was coming out of the stall, quickly, moving fast into the tack room. Too fast.

I heard Jeri shout, "Police," trailing off into a yell.

A loud thud. I could see nothing. I started to move and froze again. He was coming back out, running out of the barn, out of the doorway.

I pushed out from behind the stack, ran to the tack room. Jeri was down on the floor, just visible in the moonlight that leaked into the barn. She was moaning, half mumbling. I felt the pulse in her neck— strong and fast.

Even as I bent over her, she started to raise herself up.

"I'm going after him," I said.

In another minute I was outside the barn. I could see him mounting a horse, plain in the light of the high half moon, his leg swinging over the rump of a horse that was turned away. He looked back as he drove the horse toward the hill behind the barn, seeing me there by the corral. I saw only his dark, masked face and the horse's rump. I would never catch him on foot.

I didn't think. I ran for Dixie. She was haltered; the upside-down bucket handy by her side. I untied her and climbed on her in one motion, guided her by the lead rope, holding the pistol with my free hand.

I could hear Jeri's voice, talking to me, as I kicked Dixie forward. "I'm going after him!" I yelled again, and ducked my head as we trotted through the barn doorway.

Then we were out in the night and I kicked Dixie harder, clinging to her mane with the hand that held the gun. She broke into a lope and we headed for the trail up the hill.

I gripped hard with my thighs and knees and twined my two free fingers tightly in her mane. Kris had told me once that Dixie was a great bareback horse, with a flat back and smooth gaits—thank God for that. I couldn't ride Gunner bareback—his spine cut me in two.

Dixie was easy, but I hadn't ridden bareback in years. She was lunging up the hill now; I clung with every atom of strength I possessed, trying to steer with the lead rope.

But Dixie knew the trail, knew there was a horse ahead of her. She wanted to catch him as much as I did—the herd instinct driving her. All I had to do was hang on.

I could hear him, hear the thudding hooves, hear branches breaking ahead, but I couldn't see him. I couldn't see much. A half moon was up, but its light didn't penetrate down into the forest we were scrambling through.

Up and up, I clung to the mare with my thighs and knees and calves as she lunged through the darkness, both of us hearing the horse ahead.

At least I knew where we were going. Up to the ridge, and then, unless I missed my guess, to Lushmeadows.

I gave no thought to what I would do if I caught him. I gripped my gun and the mare's mane and hung on.

You will not get away. You will not. My mind chanted steadily. Branches lashed my face and I ducked low over Dixie's neck to shield myself. I could feel her muscles bunch and strain through my jeans, hear her grunt as she plunged upward. Every fiber of strength I possessed went into staying on.

Limpetlike, I stuck to her back as she stumbled, hung on as she drove upward. No room for fear, no room for thought. Nothing but the violent lurching motion, both rhythmic and erratic. The dark forest was a blur of barely discernible tree shapes. I could smell the mare's warm, sweet horsey odor over the earthy tanbark smell of redwoods, feel her sweat starting to soak through my jeans. And I could hear the horse ahead.

A few more lunging strides and we were up on the ridgeline. The ground leveled out; moonlight filtered through the trees in pale gray splotches. I urged Dixie and felt her respond with more speed even as I sensed her beginning to tire.

Down the trail we galloped, through patches of faint light and deeper shadows.

Dixie swerved suddenly to miss a sapling; I barely clung on, my weight lurching precariously over her left shoulder, my legs clutching for all they were worth. In another stride I pulled myself upright again, and drummed my heels on her ribs.

Thank God I had spent hours riding bareback as a teenager. Even though it was years later, that particular skill, so different from balancing in stirrups, came back to me now. I could stay on; I was catching him.

The ground was more open now, the moon threw sharp shadows. I looked down the trail and thought I could see the moving shape of a horse and rider in the distance. I kicked Dixie again and clucked.

He was ahead of me, but I was staying with him. I tried to remember just where this trail went. Back down to the road, I thought.

Sure enough, the level ground was starting to slope downward. Damn, damn, damn. Riding downhill bareback at the gallop was going to be nearly impossible.

But I could see him. I wanted to catch him; I needed to catch him. I dug my knees into Dixie's shoulders, leaned back a little, trying to keep my weight balanced and in the middle of her. I could hear and feel her grunting breaths as she strained forward, wanting to catch the horse ahead.

And then in an instant everything was changing. The horse in front of us stumbled, just visible in the moonlight. The slope threw him forward and he crashed onto his knees, scrambled a stride, and went all the way down onto his right shoulder and rolled, as if in slow motion, in a big somersault. I heard a startled yell from the rider, saw him fall to one side, saw the horse's body come down right next to him with a heavy *whump.*

In another few strides, we were upon him. I pulled back on the halter rope with all my strength and yelled, "Whoa." Obediently Dixie shortened her stride and lunched to a halt. I half jumped, half fell off awkwardly, clutching my gun in one hand and the halter rope in the other. In the periphery of my vision, I could see the other horse scramble to his feet and trot away, down the hill, no doubt headed home. Dixie nickered and tugged to go after him.

I hung onto the lead rope tightly and pointed my gun at the figure lying on the ground. He was gasping in loud audible grunts; he'd had the wind knocked out of him. Good.

212

I stared at his helpless form and pointed my pistol right at the center of his body. I'd be sure to hit something vital that way. Given the .357's power, it would be almost certain to kill him. He gasped and wheezed and struggled to get up.

"Don't move," I said, "or I'll kill you."

He turned his face toward me. In the moonlight, I could see the faint sheen of his eyeballs. The dark mask still hid his features, but I knew who I was speaking to. I'd seen his horse.

Once again he tried to rise. I spoke louder. "Stay sitting on the ground and put your hands above your head or I will shoot you."

For a second he hesitated and then continued to flounder to his feet.

Something broke inside me. I raised the gun, sighted down the barrel at his chest, and tightened my finger on the trigger.

"You listen, you bastard," I said clearly. "I *want* to kill you. Move one more time and I will. Gladly."

I meant it and he must have heard it. Slowly he subsided to a sitting position and raised his hands above his head, his face turned to mine. The eyes inside the ski mask looked past the barrel of the gun to my face. I stared back at him.

"Well, Mike," I said.

THIRTY

Mike O'Hara stared at me from behind his mask and said nothing. But I had no doubt whom I was looking at. I'd seen Sonny's crooked blaze too clearly in the moonlight; I knew his size and shape and bay coat. Like many horsemen, I recognized horses I knew at least as easily as I did people.

Mike's stance, his way of moving and holding himself; it all fit together, though he was still unrecognizable behind the dark mask.

"But why?" I said out loud. "Why?"

Mike's breathing was coming a little more easily now; to my surprise he tried to speak between gasps.

"You don't . . . under . . . stand." He was having a hard time getting the words out.

"You're damn right I don't understand."

Anger rose in me. Here was Nico's killer; here was the murderer. I had caught him.

I raised the gun a little. "Why?" I demanded.

"I can't . . . talk," he gasped.

"You can," I said. "Take your time. If you don't talk, I'm going to kill you. And I may kill you, anyway."

I could feel the desire that came over me with the words. End his miserable, despicable, worthless life; I could hear the voice in my brain. Rid the world of this evil thing.

"Talk," I said.

"I never meant . . . to hurt anyone," was what he got out.

"You managed to kill and rape at least one woman and hit a little girl over the head. I never would have believed it of you."

The man groaned, whether because he was winded or because of what I'd said, I didn't know.

"I never meant to," he said.

Something cold seemed to be solidifying in me. "You tell me, Mike," I said. "I want to know."

He was quiet, except for his breathing.

"I'll tell you what, Mike," I said conversationally. "I'll just let you know where I'm coming from. I would really like to kill you, shoot you right now in the gut and watch you die. Don't think I couldn't do it. I could. Easily. For what you did. You deserve to die. You and I both know it. Your one chance is to talk to me. So tell me, Mike, how did a good solid citizen like you, an ex-cop, church-goer, the whole nine yards, start wanting to fuck horses?"

I could feel him cringe. Strange as it was, there in the dark redwoods in the moonlight, me holding a gun on him, the ski mask hiding his face completely, yet I could still feel the wince.

And then he spoke, more in his normal voice—quasi-dignified, slow, a little didactic, still breathless. "Gail, you really don't understand."

"So explain."

There was a long pause. Then Mike's voice, sounding hesitant. "My wife is a good woman, but she didn't like sex—never did. She didn't understand how I felt."

"Right, Mike. You feel women don't understand you. No doubt you felt your mother didn't understand you. Let's cut to the chase here. Lots of men are in your position. They get a divorce, or a girlfriend, or they beat off. Why not you?"

Once again, I felt the wince. Then, "I love Hannah." The words seemed to burst out of him. "I didn't want to hurt her. And being unfaithful to her was wrong. I knew that. For a while I did that, what

215

you said last, but I hated it. I couldn't stand myself, the way I felt. And then one weekend, we were visiting a woman friend who had a mare. I went for a walk out in the pasture. I was thinking about, well, sex. And this mare must have been in heat. There was a gelding in the field with her, and he was climbing on top of her, trying to breed her. And I just started thinking."

I could picture it. Many geldings have the impulse to hump mares; some could actually get an erection and penetrate the mare. I'd seen it. I saw it now through the eyes of this frustrated, sex-starved man.

"I caught the mare," he said, "and tied her to a tree." He was quiet again. "It was better," he said at last. "I hadn't hurt Hannah; I hadn't hurt anyone. And I felt better."

"What was better about the mare as opposed to your hand?" I said crudely, and saw him turn his face away.

"She was willing," he said. "She didn't mind. Hannah always hated sex; it always hurt her. She never wanted me to do it. I know it sounds stupid, but my mother was always unhappy with my dad and angry with us kids. What I wanted was a woman to be willing, to accept me."

"This was a horse, not a woman," I said. "She wasn't accepting you in any real sense. What did you do, make up some kind of pretty fantasy?"

"I guess that's right," he said heavily. "Ever since the first time, when I watched the gelding climb on the mare and she just stood there willingly, I've always sort of seen myself as another horse, coming to a mare. And she accepts me."

"Is that why you always rode your horse to these rendezvous? So you could get in the role?"

"I guess. I know you're making fun of me, Gail, but it was terrible for me. It got to where I absolutely had to do it to feel any peace at all."

"Why didn't you just buy a mare of your own?"

"It wouldn't have worked. It had to be a woman's horse. After the first time, I waited a long time to try it again. And then I rode to a neighbor woman's house. I knew she was single, knew she had a mare. In one part of my mind I was always a man going to a woman; I

216

thought about the woman who owned the mare. But I never wanted to hurt them. I never even took my gun. And then there was this other part of me that was a horse going to another horse."

"So how'd you progress to murder, you bastard?" I was not feeling any sympathy for poor, trapped, frustrated Mike. But I wanted to know. "Did you kill Marianne Moore?"

"How did you know?" he sounded shocked.

"I guessed," I said.

"She came out to the barn one night. She saw me. I hit her over the head with my flashlight. I only meant to knock her out, but I caught her too near the temple."

"But you couldn't quit. Not even after you'd killed another human being."

"Gail, I really couldn't. I was almost afraid to. Afraid of how much desire would build up in me. Afraid of what I'd do to Hannah."

This last made me see red. "You lousy fucker," I virtually shouted at him. "I don't care if you screwed your wife till you made her bleed. That was between you and her to work out. But you wouldn't work on it. Instead you had to take out your stupid testosterone-driven needs on other innocent people. You killed Nico, damn you."

I leveled the gun at him. "How could you do that? You go to church; I suppose you believe in God; you spent your life enforcing the law. What could have twisted you enough to make you kill? Tell me."

"I didn't mean to!" His voice rose to match mine. "I just wanted to come to the horse. She caught me. I grabbed her. I had my hands around her throat before I even knew what I was doing. And then, afterward, she was so quiet, so willing."

"You bastard. You absolute, unmitigated bastard. I don't care about your stupid pathetic needs. I don't care about you. I don't feel the slightest sympathy for your desire to protect your goddamn naïve frigid wife. You killed one of the finest human beings I've ever met, and now you're going to pay for it."

Rage was bubbling through me, cathartic as tears had been the night I'd watched for dawn.

"You went after me at the Bishop Ranch, didn't you," I said. "Admit it."

"I was afraid you'd seen me," he said. "I was afraid you knew. I had to protect myself, protect Hannah."

"But Clay and Bart came along," I said grimly. "Otherwise I'd be dead."

"I didn't want to hurt you," he said.

"Right. Just like you didn't want to hurt Nico. Well, you know what, Mike, I don't feel any fucking sympathy for you, not one little bit. I think you're a completely despicable creature, lower than any animal I've ever known. I think that killing you is putting you out of your misery."

"No, Gail. What about Hannah?"

"Fuck Hannah," I said savagely. "All you can think about is you and what's yours. Your wife, your life. You couldn't spare a thought for those other women, who had lives they loved, too. You didn't give a damn. You killed Nico and now I'm going to kill you."

I leveled the gun barrel at him. "I'm going to kill you, Mike, like you killed Nico, without a thought for your precious life, your wife, all the things you value. I'm going to murder you the way you murdered her."

"You can't," he said, his voice suddenly crafty. "You'll go to jail. It wouldn't be worth it."

"No, Mike," I said, "I won't. No jury on earth would convict me. Out here in the forest like this, I'll say you came after me and I had to shoot you in self-defense. It will fly."

He stared at me. The mask hid his features, but I could feel the intensity of his concentration. I knew the dark forest was all around us; I could feel Dixie at my elbow, hear her soft breath, and yet there was only the one reality of our locked eyes.

And then he began to get to his feet.

"I'm getting up, Gail," he said conversationally. "And you're not going to shoot me. You're not a killer. I'm getting up now," he said again.

"Stop," I told him. "I will kill you. Don't think I won't."

"I think you won't," he said heavily, raising himself up on one knee.

I leveled the gun, sighted down it again. Tightened my finger on the trigger. My heart pounded steadily. Suddenly I didn't know if I could kill him. I waited, trying to find the will.

If he moves toward me, I told myself, I will shoot.

He was on his feet now, looking at me.

"You won't shoot me, Gail," he said, and took a step in my direction.

I squeezed. Even as Dixie's muzzle bumped my elbow, even as the gun went off with a deep, echoing *ka-boom*, even as my arm flew back with the recoil, I saw Mike go down on the ground and come back up, start toward me. I pointed the gun at him again.

And I heard another voice yell, "Freeze!"

I froze. Mike froze. Jeri Ward said calmly, "Put your hands up in the air, now." I could see her in the moonlight, her gun pointed right at Mike. I had mine aimed at him, too.

For a moment he hesitated, but the balance of the situation had changed. I felt calm and centered, in charge once again. Slowly Mike raised his hands in the air.

Jeri stepped forward. "Keep him covered, Gail, while I cuff him."

"Will do," I said, and did.

THIRTY-ONE

Ten days later I was recounting my story to Kris, sitting in her living room. Dixie had survived the adventure unscathed; Kris was incredulous to hear that the marauder had been Mike O'Hara.

"I don't believe it," she said over and over again. "Not Mike."

I could understand her feeling. Conservative, upright, right-wing Mike O'Hara seemed on the surface an unlikely candidate for such a role. But I'd had over a week to assimilate the knowledge, and it made sense to me now.

"Well, think about it," I said. "He is obviously a very repressed personality; what's he going to do with all that bottled-up lust? Turns out he's an ex-Marine as well as an ex-cop; there's a lot of potential for violence there. I honestly believe he didn't intend to harm anyone, but things just escalated."

What I didn't say to Kris was how much I'd wanted to kill Mike. I still didn't know for sure whether I could have or would have if Jeri hadn't managed to stumble up the hill after us, or if Dixie hadn't sent my first shot off track. But I felt in my heart that I could have killed him.

Oddly enough, this gave me a sense of relief. Somehow I had come full cycle, through depression and grief and fear and anger to action. And action seemed to be the remedy I needed.

"How are you feeling?" I asked Kris.

"Better. A lot better. Between my vacation and knowing no one's out there stalking me, I feel okay. How about you?"

"I'm better," I said. "A lot better. But I went to see Hannah yesterday."

"Oh my God, Gail. How was she?"

"Devastated. It was really hard to see. She wasn't even angry at me for my part. Just broken. It made me hate Mike even more. She would have been so much better off if he'd just dealt openly with her, instead of hiding his problem from her. He could have told her how much he wanted and needed sex, given her a chance to be there for him."

"Do you hate Mike?" Kris asked.

"Sometimes," I said. "I hate what he did. I hate that particular version of hypocrisy and cowardice, that refusal to deal with what is. Mike didn't want to deal realistically with his sexual desires, which weren't bad in themselves—and all this horror came of his hiding from the truth."

"It's his church that says 'the truth shall set you free,'" Kris said quietly.

"I don't think he ever heard," I said. "Like a lot of people, his mind was closed to any ideas other than his preconceived notions. His wife was a 'good' woman; her lack of interest in sex wasn't something he saw as a mutual problem to be solved. It was something he had to deal with himself. He convinced himself his sexual urges were virtually unnatural, and contrived an unnatural way to deal with them. And he was very, very angry about it inside.

"It was such a weird conversation," I told Kris, thinking about that strange scene. "I think now that he never would have told me what he did except that we were in the dark and he was wearing a mask the whole time. It made him feel hidden and safe."

"That is weird," she said, and shook her head.

I said nothing, but I was sure that it was true.

After a minute I asked her, "Are you going to be around for the next month?"

"Sure," she said, "as far as I know."

221

"Would you want to do me a favor?"

"Of course."

"It's a big one."

"That's okay."

"I need someone to take care of my animals and my place for the month," I said. "I'm going to go to Europe."

EPILOGUE

I write this sitting on a balcony overlooking the Mediterranean Sea. I am in the town of Cadaqués, on the Costa Brava, in Spain. The Costa Brava, the brave coast, or so I think of it. Rugged Coast, however, is the way it is usually translated.

Rugged it is, pure and rocky and vibrant with color. The Mediterranean truly is a different color. Ulysses' "wine dark sea" is full of shades of purple and turquoise, impossibly clear and vivid (and warm)—a complete contrast to the misnamed Pacific of my home. I can see why a painter would choose this spot. And here, where Nico lived for many years, I have come to terms with her death.

Sitting on this third-floor balcony, I look out over a little fishing harbor called Port Lligat. Next door to me is the whitewashed cottage where Salvador Dali lived and painted. The terra-cotta tiles are warm beneath my feet; the wrought-iron railing and the cobalt blue wicker furniture are all of a piece with the white walls and deep blue water in front of me.

I have been in Europe almost a month; I will go home next week. My pilgrimage took me to Amsterdam and Brussels, through France to Spain. I visited the places where Nico lived, seeking . . . I'm not sure what I was seeking. But somehow, here in Spain, in these bleak hills with their dry stone walls, olive groves, and blue water coves, I have found something.

Peace, I guess. I am at peace with Nico's death, with my grief and my guilt, with myself. Depression has lifted; I can feel again.

I think of my little house with longing and pleasure; I imagine rubbing Roey's red, wedge-shaped head; I plan the roses I will plant on the grape stake fence to remind me of Europe. Enthusiasm leaps in my heart once more. I am ready to go home.

Home to my life, whatever it will be. I have received three letters since I've been here. One from Kris, one from Clay, and one from Blue. I can't predict what the future will hold. The only thing I know is that I do not know. But I am comfortable with not knowing.

If I am to be alone, there in my little house with my animals and my garden, so be it. I will be that simple, solitary figure—the Madonna with the dog at her feet, the good witch. Or if my fate is otherwise, if I will be a partner and a lover, I accept that also. For now, I hold an open mind.